MURDER-DE-SAC

JIM BENNETT

For Amy

CHAPTER ONE

'I'm telling you, he's doing something unnatural to it.'

'It's a junction box, Mrs. McGrath.'

'What does that have to do with anything? It doesn't mean that he can't be putting it to a wicked end.' Mrs. McGrath's stick remained firmly planted in the gap between Julie's front door and the jamb.

While some people acquire the art of being a nuisance, Julie was sure that Mrs. McGrath had been born a master. She never referred to Julie by name, nor was there any preamble of pleasantries. Each time she knocked on the door, she would launch into her newest request, as if they were continuing their previous conversation.

'What is it that you think he's doing?' Julie glanced at her watch for the seventh or eighth time. She really should have known by now that her neighbour wasn't one for subtleties. If Julie wanted to impress that she was in a hurry, she'd need to write it on her hand and slap it across the old dear's face.

'Do I look like Alexander Graham Bell to you? I haven't the foggiest what he's doing, but I know wrong when I see it.' She turned on the spot to face the supposed villain and near shouted, 'And that man is wrong.'

It may have been Julie's imagination, but the man, who had been working at the junction box on the other side of the road for about thirty minutes now, appeared to tense his back. Perhaps he could feel the glare of an increasingly agitated septuagenarian bearing through his cheap, grey-knit jumper. As she turned to face Julie again, Mrs. McGrath's eyes lingered on the recycling box full of empty bottles of the cheap supermarket plonk. Julie wasn't sure if it was the scene that was unfolding on her doorstep or the shame of her overindulgence, but she began to blush.

'Okay, Mrs. McGrath, there's no need to shout.'

'That's the problem with your generation. You never want to shout about anything. If good folk stand idle, then we're only a hop, skip and a jump from Hitler being in Number Ten again.'

'I don't think that's how it happened.'

'It's all the bloody same to me. I'm Scottish.'

Julie thought about explaining that Scotland had, in fact, played as much of a role in the Second World War as England. But seeing as Mrs. McGrath had apparently lived in an alternate history where the Führer and the British Prime Minister were one and the same person, it didn't feel entirely relevant.

As ever, Mrs. McGrath's appearance was slightly disheveled. In the style of Her Majesty during her visits at Balmoral, her hair was entombed by a red patterned neckerchief. The covering had been donned with such haste that mad wisps of grey-blonde hair escaped from its front. Her eyes had the haunted quality of a soldier who had spent a night on watch, waiting for some inevitable hammer of doom to drop.

'I don't understand what you want me to do about it.'

'What could a stubby thing like you do about it? I want to use your phone.'

'My phone?'

'Yes, your phone. Hurry up, will you, woman?' She bustled forward. Julie only relented when the pair had been standing nose to nose for several seconds, and it had become clear that the interloper wasn't going to relent. With the rubber grip at the end nearly entirely worn away, the bottom of Mrs. McGrath's stick made a nasty scratching noise against the tiles with every other step.

'Why can't you use your own phone?' Julie remained standing next to the open door hoping that her guest would take the hint that this wasn't an open ended visit.

'It's not been working.'

'It's not been working? Have you let anyone know?'

'How would I do that when I don't have a phone?' Mrs. McGrath asked, becoming exasperated. 'I bet you would have sent them a letter. Playing right into their hands.'

Her eyes darted around the hall, looking for a handset. After several seconds of not succeeding, she gave Julie a pointed look. When this didn't work, she gestured with her hands, hoping to reiterate the pressing nature of the situation that they found themselves in.

Julie pointed to the cordless device on the small table near the door, and Mrs. McGrath snatched it up. 'For the love of Christ, what's this abomination?' She put it to her ear and took it away again twice in quick succession. 'How do you get a tone?'

Frustrated with herself for again giving up ground so easily, Julie took a step towards Mrs. McGrath and took the phone from her. She fought the urge to close the door to the living room, hiding the general chaos that lay beyond. However, the look of disapproval on the old woman's face was so complete anyway, a messy living room probably wasn't going to make much difference. The few guests that Julie did receive always gave plenty of notice, providing plenty of time to tidy the place up. The times of unexpected visitors popping in for a glass of wine were long since passed. She hadn't fallen out with anyone or made a conscious decision to stop making plans with people. At a certain point in the last few years, a social life became something that happened to other people.

'You're not calling 999,' Julie said, handing the phone back.

'I bloody am,' said Mrs. McGrath, holding the phone to her ear again before she dialed.

'It's not an emergency.'

'It won't be if someone pulls their finger out.'

As she waited to be connected, she errantly began to pick the paint that was peeling off the wall. 'This has seen better days, hasn't it?' Her hand movement suggested she was referencing the entire property, not the hall alone. 'Lovely woman used to live here. Mrs. Jenkins.'

'Quite friendly, were you?' Julie asked, feeling increasingly agitated.

'Never saw her. Riddled with arthritis. Twice a day you would hear the stair lift going, and that was your lot. What's that husband of yours doing with himself?' she said, eyeing the now shabby skirting boards. 'Too high and mighty for a bit of DIY?'

There was a silence for a few moments.

'He died,' said Julie in a small voice. Mrs. McGrath didn't respond, so Julie pressed on.

'Don't you remember? You were putting your bins out when the funeral procession left the house.'

Mrs. McGrath made a noise of acquiescence that most would reserve for offhand comments about the weather. Julie remembered it well. The clattering sound of the lid hitting the bin was so incongruous against the eerie silence of the street that Greg's mum had let out a shocked little laugh. Mrs. McGrath had taken no notice of the slow line of black cars exiting the lane. Clearly, she had more important things to be concerning herself with, such as rogue agents dabbling in junction boxes. The day had passed by like a haze, much like the rest of that period, although punctuated with odd little moments of normality or absurdity.

The old woman started muttering, 'Come on,' over and over again and tapping her cane against the floor with increasing rapidity. It didn't look as if Mrs. McGrath was going anywhere soon. Julie left her in the hallway and started to collect her belongings, ready to leave. She placed her handbag in the hall. Each time she put an item inside, it gave her an excuse to ensure that no mischief was being done. Well, no mischief aside from the nuisance phone calls and the denuding of the wall behind the telephone table. Julie moved with more flourish than normal, clattering as she went with the hope of impressing on the impassive old goat that she was, in fact, in a hurry.

Julie would ordinarily do her make up in the hall mirror. It was at just the right angle and had the best light. But seeing as Mrs. McGrath was currently billeted in front of it, she had to make do with the mirror in Harry's room. Even in his formative years, her son had been tall, so Julie found herself stretching to see her face to apply the obligatory lick of lipstick. This small exertion made the muscles at the back of her legs groan, and she felt herself going faint. She perched on the side of her son's bed and put her hand to her brow.

It was still made, despite the fact that Harry hadn't been home for months now. She thought about the last time he had called several weeks ago. Julie was always careful not to impress herself on her son, and as usual, the conversation had only lasted a short time. Still, she could feel the urgency with which he wanted to return to his friends, how much re-entering her sad life even for a few moments was drawing him away from the better things in the world. At least he hadn't attempted to read her one of his god awful short stories, all of which centred around a young man who hadn't known anything of the world until he went on a fantastic journey and found himself. Julie thought that Harry should really start branching away from the autobiographical and try to use his imagination now. Otherwise, when he turned forty, he'd be writing tales about some pillock working in an office who writes painfully pedestrian fiction in his spare time.

Her forehead had a clammy heat to it, and she felt giddy. The morning after, it always seemed like a good idea to drink less; that was probably the point of a hangover. What was a bit more difficult was holding on to that feeling when you got home from another pointless day of work and were gasping for some small respite.

She stood again and considered her reflection. There was no avoiding it; she looked middle aged. At some point without realising it, she had opted for the haircut favoured by every other woman who had given up on life a little bit. Bobbed and feathered with some token highlights applied to the crown, it was easy enough to spritz with some dry shampoo and make it appear that she had made an effort. Sitting on the bed, she could feel the way her weight distributed itself, bunching around the middle and crowding her. When her thickening thighs had begun to press against the seams of her work trousers a few years ago, she hadn't felt the need to replace them.

Her eye was drawn to one of the photos on the shelves that surrounded the room. All three faces beamed at her from the frame: Greg with an arm around Julie and Harry a piece. Losing your husband of 20 years would be to most people one of the most upsetting things to ever happen to you. Julie had been distraught, and she missed Greg and the life they had together so palpably that sometimes she thought she might choke on it. But behind all that, she knew that there was a more general discontent to her that she would struggle to define, not that anyone would be interested. Her work wasn't satisfying, but that wasn't a recent development. She now had an empty nest, and if she was honest, she and Harry had never been that close. Greg's death had been the stone that dislodged some other sadness in her life, and ever since then, she hadn't quite managed to rally herself.

'I don't care which one of them I speak to,' Julie could hear her guest saying from downstairs. After a few seconds, this was followed by, 'Fine, which one has the best response times?' and finally, 'Oh, for goodness sake, the police then; let me talk to the police.'

She made her way back down into the hall, pinning her name badge to her shirt as she did. Her hope was that this would remove any semblance of doubt from Mrs. McGrath's mind that she was planning to leave the house imminently. What Julie failed to appreciate was that her visitor was well aware of the contrast between the two women's priorities, and yet still felt no compulsion to leave. Mrs. McGrath had now managed to remove a square foot of the paint from the wall. Greg had applied it in his usual slapdash fashion. At least it had covered the brick underneath, which Mrs. McGrath had now managed to expose. When this had failed to hold her attention, she had started to use her stick to remove the grout from between the floor tiles.

Julie steeled herself to make the situation plain to the old woman but was interrupted by a voice coming from outside.

'Excuse me, love,' said the telephone engineer, sticking his head through the open door, 'I need to check the line at your neighbours.' He was addressing himself to Mrs. McGrath. 'I can't get an answer. Do you know whether anyone's home?'

Before Julie could intervene, Mrs. McGrath was slamming the phone on the table and marching towards him. 'No one is home, sonny,' she said, pointing at him threateningly, 'because I am making sure that you don't succeed in your ill deeds.'

He looked confused. The man must have been something of an optimist. Instead of fleeing the scene like anyone with any common sense would do in the face of an armed and clearly unhinged geriatric, he stood steadfast and attempted to explain himself.

'Someone reported a fault on the line?' he asked more than said.

'Who did?' the old lady asked.

'I don't know. I don't work on the phones.'

'Oh!' Mrs. McGrath exclaimed, becoming excited. 'He's changing his story already. I thought you were supposed to be from the phone company.' She turned and gave Julie a smug smile, as if this one piece of information proved her hypothesis entirely.

'No, I mean I don't answer the phones. You know, when people call with the problems they're having.'

'You're very clever. Got an answer for everything, haven't you?'

He didn't seem so sure of himself now but persevered anyway. 'I think I've got it sorted. If I could just look at the port in your house...,' but before he could finish, Mrs. McGrath had lunged towards him.

'That's your game then, is it?' she said, brandishing her stick at him. 'Trying to get into a defenceless old woman's house on some nonsense pretext before you rob her blind.'

Cowed, the man took a step backwards and fell down the two steps which led to the garden. It took him a moment to regain his composure, at which point he scarpered away from the house with some speed.

'I've got your number, sonny,' she shouted from the door, 'just you wait.' She stormed back into the hall and picked the phone up again.

'Was that really necessary?' Julie asked as the startled man clambered back to his vehicle.

'He had a bit of Shipman about him. You could see it in his eyes.'

'The concern was that the telephone engineer was going to prescribe you a lethal dose of something?' Julie said, admonishing herself for buying into this backward narrative.

'I didn't mean it literally,' Mrs. McGrath said with genuine condescension in her voice. 'And he's not a telephone engineer.'

'How do you know he isn't a telephone engineer?'

'He had ladies' hands.'

'Mrs. McGrath, I need to go to work,' Julie said, recognising the impasse that they had reached. 'Are you almost done?'

'Leave me the keys. I'll bring them round later.'

Julie didn't want to leave this woman in her house. Then she thought about it for a moment longer and spending any more time with Mrs. McGrath was definitely the greater of the two evils.

'Post them through when you've locked up,' Julie said, placing the keys on the table next to the phone and leaving the house. She didn't think she could face seeing Mrs. McGrath again today.

The telephone engineer was now talking to Brian across the road. When he saw Julie walking towards him, he bolted back to his van and locked the door behind him. Julie thought this was slightly unfair, given that at worst she had been an engaged spectator.

'Hello, sweetheart,' Brian said before Julie could get into the car and pretend she hadn't heard him.

'Morning,' Julie said, hastily searching for her keys.

'How's the most beautiful girl in the world?' His voice was lurid, positively dripping with sleaze.

'Yes, fine, thank you. How's the leg?' She didn't really care but wanted to fill the conversational void before Brian could wheel out any more of his cringey terms of endearment.

'Oh, I'm battling on, my lovely,' he said, putting more weight on his good limb. Brian had that body type unique to middle aged men. A great, rotund belly sat atop two spindly little spider legs. He looked as if he had been drawn by a toddler who didn't yet fully understand the human anatomy.

One leg was currently housed in a support boot, with a pair of NHS crutches propped up against the wall next to him. For reasons beyond comprehension, he had chosen to wear a pair of khaki shorts that far from flattered him. The tight cap which sat on his melon sized head and the polo shirt open to the bottom button around his trunk sized neck were, in Julie's opinion, also ill advised. His high blood pressure gave him the ruddy complexion of one who spent their time wandering through the moors, rather than leaning on his front gate and making his female neighbours uncomfortable.

'Lovely shirt that, love,' Brian said. 'What colour is that, red?'

'It is, yes.'

'And your hair's looking nice. Bit blonder than normal, is it?'

'Maybe,' Julie said, when the answer was definitely no. She really should feel flattered that someone was trying to complement her, even if what they were saying wasn't flattering in the slightest.

The conversation stalled, and they stood looking at each other for a beat too long for Julie to just get in the car and leave.

'It's been a while, hasn't it? The leg, I mean?' Julie asked, hoping for a brief response, although now thinking about it, Brian really had been in that boot for a very long time.

'You have to be thankful though, darling. Some have it much worse.' He nodded to the accessible vehicle that was parked outside the house next door, number 32. Faces with differing levels of animation were peering at them out of the vehicle's windows. Some had fixed expressions, staring at some random point in the background. Others demonstrated a level of excitement that would only have been appropriate if they were on their way to Disneyland Paris.

Two men dressed in hospital scrubs were wheeling a man about Julie's age down the garden path. His head lolled to one side. A proper looking woman stood on the doorstep without a hint of emotion present in her features. After they loaded the man into the vehicle, she shot Julie and Brian a disapproving look, as if they were loitering teens.

'I don't get what the point is when he's a vegetable. What's he got waiting for him at the day centre? Shitting himself in a different chair?'

'She probably needs a break.'

'Wouldn't want her for a nurse. Cruel woman. I've got communal access through their back garden, right. To bring my bins in and what have you. Although it's a bit more difficult when you're on crutches. Anyway, I knocked over a plant pot, and it smashed. Nothing I could do about it. Within seconds, and I mean seconds, she was outside screaming her head off at me. There's no need!' This wasn't much of a surprise to Julie. She hadn't had much to do with Mrs. Sinclair, but during their limited interactions, her neighbour had always been cool with her. Almost like she was trying to rush through the exchange so she could return to something more important.

'What's the story there, anyway?' Brian asked, bringing Julie back from her reflections.

'He was in an accident, I think. Mrs. Sinclair keeps to herself really. Besides, it's not the kind of thing you can ask people about.' Julie fiddled with her keys and tried to decide whether she was jealous of Mrs. Sinclair. The husband that she had known may be lost to her, but at least there was still a semblance of him still there.

As she returned her attention to Brian, she realised he too had stopped listening. Instead of taking a few moments to ponder the sad fate of Mr. Sinclair, he was staring at Julie's chest. She crossed her arms over herself. However, with her work shirt being as tight as it was, it only exacerbated the problem. Brian's eyes were almost exploding from their sockets as he unashamedly continued to gaze on.

'Listen, love,' he said, finally looking at her in the eyes again. 'Why don't you let me take you for an Indian tonight? Two lonely hearts finding love again, eh? It would be like a fairy tale, wunnt it?'

'Brian,' Julie said, but stopped herself. Detailing the many reasons why their exchange wasn't going to lead to a date for the old fellow felt like a civil duty. But Julie wasn't much of a one for public service. Instead, she answered with a curt, 'I'm busy tonight. Maybe next week.' Hopefully, Brian would stumble across a passably attractive post woman and lose interest.

She climbed into the car and gave Brian a small wave as she pulled away. The telephone engineer continued to eye her suspiciously as she drove towards the exit of the cul-de-sac. The accessible vehicle that was transporting Mr. Sinclair and his comrades was struggling to pull out onto the main road. Julie sat contentedly behind them and thought idly that she was probably going to be late for work after all.

CHAPTER TWO

As she approached the layby, Julie pulled into the left hand lane and began to slow down. She indicated much earlier than necessary to allow the especially belligerent to go around her as early as possible. Even this measure didn't entirely work, the odd few important looking men giving her pointed looks and exaggerated flurries of hand gestures as they overtook her. After five years, it really didn't bother her that much anymore.

The recess at the side of the road was unremarkable in every way. If you were looking for it, and only if you were looking especially hard, there was a small, wooden sign on the far hedge with some faded writing scribbled on it. In its near dilapidated state, it was just possible to discern that it had the rough shape of an arrow pointing to a gap in the foliage. Julie got out of the car and removed the thin chain which hung across the space between the two bushes. After she had driven through, she reversed the process before driving the remainder of the way up the gravel path.

They wouldn't open for another hour. Julie and Mr. Peg had discussed this a few times. Mr. Peg was under the impression that by not opening the shop until 10 o'clock that they would instill such a sense of anticipation in their customers that, when they were finally allowed into the store, their commercial frenzy would be all the more fierce.

Julie was of the opinion that they were unnecessarily keeping the handful of pensioners who relied on them for some daily human contact out in the cold for another hour.

Mr. Peg was standing outside the main building with both hands clutched to his head. Julie took a few moments to compose herself before leaving the car.

There was always an agitated quality to Mr. Peg's eyes that was entirely disproportionate to the situation that he found himself in.

'Good morning, Mr. Peg,' Julie said, fixing her smile as she walked towards him.

'Julie, thank the heavens you're here. We're in the throes of a disaster.'

Previous experience made Julie sceptical that they were, in fact, in any real peril. She also thought that if someone was truly in any real trouble, they wouldn't take the time to use the phrase 'throes of disaster.'

'I don't understand what you mean, Mr. Peg?'

He looked at her startled.

'Did you not hear the deluge last night?' he asked, his voice already squeakier than it needed to be.

'I didn't, no.' Julie had been dead to the world by about half past nine but had noticed that the paving stones outside were a bit damp. 'Has it ruined some of the stock?'

'Worse,' he said, the pantomime in his voice growing. 'Even worse than that.'

He took her by the arm and led her to the rear of the shoddy structure that they laughingly called the shop. 'There,' he said, pointing at the roof. 'Look at that.'

Julie's eyes panned back and forth, but she couldn't find the slightest indication of jeopardy or even moderate inconvenience. She considered pretending she could see what it was that he was referring to, but the effort involved seemed too great.

'I'm sorry Mr. Peg; you're going to have to help me out. What am I looking at?'

'That!' he almost shrieked. 'That,' he repeated, jabbing at the sky.

'The tree?'

'The roof! Can you not see that slack water?'

Julie looked again and could, with a bit of effort, see what Mr. Peg was referring to.

'It's just a puddle. I'm sure the sun will dry it up in a few hours.'

'In a few hours is too late, my dear! The enemy is already inside the walls. What if it breaks through the roof before then and causes an electrical fire? What if it takes out Mrs. Jenkins, or even Mrs. Stevens? You know she isn't very quick on her feet.'

'Can you show me where it's leaking inside?'

They walked back towards the main entrance of the shop, Julie flicking the lights on as they made their way through the double doors.

Julie often found Mr. Peg in this sort of state. The issue was that the source of his anxieties ran from the mundane and easier to ignore to the genuinely troubling. As Mr. Peg was always crying wolf, it was very difficult to know when to take him seriously. Julie lived in constant fear that the call for help she finally ignored would be their first genuine emergency, and not like their most recent crisis, when Mr. Peg had rung Julie at home to inform her that they had run out of jam jars.

Mr. Peg had walked Julie to the middle of the first of the three rooms that made up the shop's inside space. To be fair to Mr. Peg, there was a fairly large amount of stagnant water spread across the tiles. The smell of damp, which was normally more of a background odour, was also now very prominent, pushing its way into your nose and lungs with each breath. However, for anyone who owned a mop and some semblance of common sense, it would take maybe no more than 20 minutes to clean in its entirety. Yet, if you were to go by the look on Mr. Peg's face, you could be forgiven for thinking that it was the first water that had made its way through the hull of the Titanic.

'Oh, that's not too bad at all!' Julie said, much too enthusiastically.

Mr. Peg gave her a condescending look, as if she hadn't grasped the gravity of the situation.

'Why don't you go and see how the perennials are getting on, and I'll have a think about how to fix it?'

Mr. Peg shook his head sadly but walked in the direction of the garden plant section regardless. He kept one hand on top of his crown.

Julie waited until he was out of sight before fetching the mop from the utility cupboard at the side of the shop. After she had collected the dirty water, she placed the bucket just inside the front door and sat on the high stool behind the till for a few minutes. After a suitable interval had passed, she picked up the bucket and poured it into one of the outside drains. She left the doors open as she went to try and air out the boggy smell.

Julie was about to go back inside when she saw a tall figure walking up the gravel path from the main road.

'We're not open yet,' Julie said in a slightly raised voice as she walked toward the man. The crunching of her wellies on the gravel made his response inaudible.

'We're not open yet,' Julie repeated slightly more loudly. The man continued to walk towards her, now with his hand cupped to his ear.

Julie felt a wave of exhaustion come over her and considered just letting the customer come in. Even this, the most minor of confrontations, was more than her willpower could take today after the onslaught of Mrs. McGrath. She wondered how long she would be able to go to sleep for in the back seat of her car before Mr. Peg would notice that she was missing.

Lost in her musings, Julie misjudged how close she was to the approaching figure, and therefore shouted, 'We're not open yet,' into his face from about three feet away. The man had been saying something at the same time that was entirely drowned out by Julie's shouting.

She could feel herself going a bit pink. He was about a foot taller than her five foot four. He had a strong jawline, but not in the way that you would notice one on a Hollywood star. Rather, his face was slightly too wide, and the jawbone looked like it was the necessary foundation to keep the rest of his features in place. The scruffy brown hair fixed atop his head reminded her of an old broom.

'Sorry, didn't mean to shout. We're not open yet.'

He smiled at her nervously. 'Sorry, I'm not a customer,' he said, offering her his left hand. 'Michael. No, sorry, I mean, Mike. No one calls me Michael except my Aunty Jean.'

'Hello,' Julie said, trying to sound chipper. 'Nice to meet you.' They continued shaking hands for much longer than was necessary or comfortable. When this most recent awkward interaction had ended, they continued to look at each other for a few more beats.

'I'm sorry to be rude,' Julie said, finally breaking the stalemate. 'But who are you?'

'Oh, right. Yes. Sorry. I'm the new pot man. Sorry, I should have said that.'

'That's good,' Julie nodded enthusiastically. 'I'm sorry, but I don't know what a pot man is.'

The smile on Mike's face became fixed. 'Ah, I was hoping you could tell me. Mr. Peg wasn't very clear in the interview.'

'You had an interview?'

'Last Thursday,' Mike said, pleased to be asked something he knew the answer to.

Julie inwardly sighed. 'My day off,' she said. 'He's always doing stuff like this. The month before when I left him alone, he ordered a metric ton of sand for god knows what.'

Mike's bark of a laugh startled Julie. This great lummox of a man had so much of the quality of a shaggy dog or a house plant that it had been easy to forget she was actually talking to another human being. 'Maybe don't tell Mr. Peg I said that though.'

'Sorry, yes,' Mike said, looking abashed. Julie tried to remember whether Mike had made it through a sentence without apologising to her yet.

'I'll take you up to Mr. Peg. Do you want to move your car first?'

'I don't have a car.'

'What do you mean, you don't have a car?'

'I don't have a car?' For some reason, Mike now phrased his response as a question. 'It's in for its MOT.'

'We're miles from anything. How did you get here?'

'Lovely morning for a walk,' Mike said. He still didn't sound very sure of himself.

Julie smiled and nodded before starting to walk back towards the shop.

'Is there somewhere I can put my lunch?' Mike held up the carrier bag he was holding in one hand.

'There's a fridge in the …,' Julie began to say, before taking a second look at the bag, which appeared to be holding some sort of congealed liquid. What Julie wanted to ask was, 'What the bloody hell is that?' but didn't think it was appropriate, given they had only met about four minutes ago. Instead, she asked, 'Is your lunch alright?'

'Right, yes. Bit of chilli.' He had been a bit pink through their whole conversation but had now become positively crimson. 'Couldn't find any Tupperware this morning.'

'And you didn't fancy any rice?' Julie asked as they began to walk towards the garden centre.

'Couldn't find any of that either. I probably looked a bit dodgy walking in now that you mention it. Looks like a bag of body parts.' Mike lifted his arm to give Julie a better look, guffawing as he did it. Unfortunately, as he held up his sack of terrors, he continued to look at Julie instead of the uneven path in front of him. He lost his footing and fell to the floor, the right hand side of his body crushing the bag as he fell against it.

'Christ, are you alright?' Julie said.

Mike lay on the floor looking shellshocked. The sauce had oozed out of the flimsy carrier bag and was plastered down the white t-shirt he was wearing. Julie did consider helping him to his feet, but he really was caked in the stuff.

After he was once again upright, he began trying to wipe the sauce off with his bare hands. This only served to spread the stain to the further reaches of his clothing, making what had previously looked like a minor mishap now resemble a fatal wound. It was at this moment that Mr. Peg emerged out of the rear yard and started to walk towards them.

'Hello again,' Mr. Peg said brightly, already having forgotten this morning's drama. He was carrying a pile of long stem flowers with him. When he got a bit closer, he began to eye Mike's messy top. He looked to Mike for an explanation, but the new employee just continued to smile.

'Everything alright?' Mr. Peg coaxed.

'Very good, thank you. Excited to get started.'

'You've got something on your t-shirt,' Mr. Peg tried.

'Right, yes,' Mike looked down at himself as if he hadn't already been aware. 'I've soiled myself.'

'Oh dear,' Mr. Peg now looked at Julie. 'Julie, do we have a shirt and trousers in the lost and found?'

'I'm sure we can find something,' Julie answered, wondering if they even had a lost and found box.

'Thank you, sorry,' Mike interjected. 'I don't need any trousers. I only got it on my top half.'

Mr. Peg looked increasingly more uncomfortable as the situation progressed. 'But you said you had messed yourself.'

'No, right, sorry. I meant I had soiled my top.' He looked to Julie for reassurance. 'I haven't shit myself or anything.' He continued to look from one to the other of them, trying to convey that this was a good thing.

Mr. Peg took a few seconds to think of an appropriate response but came up short. 'Julie, could you take these please?' He awkwardly handed her the long stem flowers. 'Bit past their prime, I'm afraid. Can you put them out to pasture?'

As Julie had left them standing there, she heard Mr. Peg launching into the speech he had given her on her first day here. 'Plants!' he had shouted theatrically. 'We serve as their humble custodians and are privileged to have the right.'

It was entirely by chance that she had discovered the job at all. She had been driving down the A-road when one of the tires had started making an alarming rattling noise. She had pulled into the layby to wait for breakdown assistance. It was only then that she had noticed the help wanted sign. When Julie had pushed through the hedgerow for the first time, she had found Mr. Peg standing in front of the shop surrounded by his plants. He stood inert, staring at the foliage surrounding him. Julie had subsequently found Mr. Peg in this state so many times that she now sometimes found herself believing that Mr. Peg only became animated in the presence of other people. When alone, he would stand among the plants as if he was one of them, soaking up the sun and doing little else.

Even now, Julie wasn't entirely sure how long the shop had been here for, nor had she ever spoken to anyone who could give her any real indication. Some of the old dears who came in regularly had been coming for years, but none of them could put a number on it. While she had never met any predecessor, she was sure that she couldn't have been the first of Mr. Peg's employees. The plants very much came first in his mind, with the need to generate income a secondary consideration.

Despite the fact that Julie and Mr. Peg saw each other three to five days a week, they really didn't have much to do with one another. Mr. Peg kept himself to the care of the plants, while Julie's remit was essentially everything else. There was the air of a disinterested marriage about their partnership, which suited them both just fine. Julie was curious to see how a third person would change the dynamic. Would Mike help to share the burden of looking after the old man and his plants, or would he take the role of their feckless son, who Julie would also be expected to care for?

Julie had watched the two of them from behind the till as Mr. Peg showed Mike around, explaining the inner workings of the shop. Unfortunately, the only thing that Julie had found for Mike to wear was a bright orange poncho, which she had located in the back of a cupboard. It covered his arms sufficiently, but the bottom inch of his midriff was clearly visible if he stretched in any direction.

Julie had soaked the t-shirt in soapy water and hung it out in the heat to dry. She had managed to remove the excess of chilli that had clung to it. The orange stains underneath had remained though, patchy and unsightly.

Julie was now sitting in the shop's small staff room, eating the ham sandwich that she had made the night before. There was still a clammy quality to her skin. Despite the inordinate amount of coffee she had drank this morning, her mouth remained claggy. She had been resting her head on the table when Mike popped his head around the door.

'Hullo,' he said, 'can I join you?'

Julie gestured for him to sit, before realising that she hadn't been in what they laughably called the 'staff room,' with anyone before. Come rain or shine, Mr. Peg always took his breaks outside. Julie supposed she would have to get used to this poky solitude being invaded from now on. With two of them in there, the small space now had the air of an interrogation suite.

'Mr. Peg said that we shouldn't take our breaks together normally,' Mike said, attempting to make himself comfortable on an upturned bin. His poncho made an obnoxious noise as he moved. 'But it wouldn't hurt on my first day.'

'Most of the customers we get come first thing, so it won't make much of a difference. Funny thing about old people, isn't it? Always wanting to get home as soon as they can.'

'I know someone who used to be like that,' Mike said. There was something sad in his voice as he spoke.

'Are we serving drinks now then?' Julie said, changing the subject. 'Is that why we need a pot boy?'

'Pot man, thank you very much.' Mike puffed up his chest, and Julie laughed. 'I still don't really know what he wants me to do. I think it's fetching and carrying.'

'I'm surprised he's letting you move the blessed things. We normally have to bend to their will.'

Julie took another bite of her sandwich before remembering that Mike's lunch was now spread down the front of his t-shirt. 'Did you want a bit of this?' Julie pushed the tinfoil towards Mike. He eyed the sandwich hungrily. She thought he might protest a little bit before taking half of her lunch, but he readily accepted it without a second thought.

'You don't move the plants and we've had, what? Three customers this morning? What do you normally do all day?' Mike spoke between bites of sandwich, covering his mouth with his hand to hide the masticated mass.

'Not a lot if I'm honest,' Julie said, folding the now empty tinfoil. 'He wants someone here just in case most of the time. Doesn't have a lot of time for the customers.' Julie absentmindedly rummaged through her bag as she spoke. 'It's more pastoral care than anything else ninety percent of the time. These old loves who come in rarely buy anything. They just want someone to talk to.'

'My Aunty Jean was the same. Got the bus into town every day so she could chew the driver's ear off. No need for it. I'd get her sorted before I left, make something for her lunch and everything.'

'My advice is to not do anything too quickly. Otherwise, you will find yourself bored stiff by lunchtime. Especially now that there's three of us.'

'He did mention some new big project, so maybe that will keep us all busy. That's probably what all the sand is for.'

Having finished his sandwich, he returned his full attention to Julie only to realise that she was now frantically pressing buttons on her mobile phone.

'Sorry,' she said, looking up at him briefly. 'My son called me, and I missed it.'

'Maybe he wants a lift or something?'

'I don't think so; he's in Thailand.'

'There you go then,' Mike said encouragingly. 'He just wants to let his old mum know how he's getting on.'

She winced inwardly at the phrase 'old mum,' especially given that Mike couldn't be any more than a few years younger than her but moved past it. 'I doubt it; he never calls.' Julie began to feel panicked. 'Christ, I hope he hasn't done anything stupid.' She attempted to call him, but it immediately went to the answer phone.

'Well if he's got some poor girl pregnant, a phone call isn't going to help much, is it?'

Mike reached for Julie's bag of crisps without asking. He opened the packaging and then ripped it all the way down the side so they could both easily get at its contents.

Mike attempted to give Julie a winning smile. Julie scowled at him and tried to call Harry again.

CHAPTER THREE

J ulie had spent the rest of the day in a low level panic. She still hadn't got through to Harry, despite having tried calling every half hour or so since lunch. When she pulled up outside the house, she convinced herself that this time the call would connect. She had proved to the universe that she could be patient, and this would be her reward. She had no such luck and the call once again failed. On further reflection, Julie thought the universe probably knew that she had been driving, so her small display of patience didn't count.

She rested her head on the steering wheel and tried not to lose her mind. He was a nineteen year old boy, away from home for the first time. Of course, he wouldn't be waiting in his hostel for stray phone calls from his family. He'd been out with his friends, that was all. She tried to channel her frustration into something constructive, although was struggling to think what that might be.

Julie picked up the flowers that Mr. Peg had asked her to throw away. He was always doing this, chucking perfectly good stock because of some imagined imperfection. Honestly, sometimes she didn't know what planet that man was living on. Fair enough if business was booming, but she doubted if they were even breaking even most of the time. He couldn't afford the luxury of getting rid of merchandise which didn't meet his impossible standards. She had wrapped them in brown paper and tied a piece of string around the middle. She didn't know why she had made the effort. For some unknown reason, it felt important. Even if she found it difficult to care about much in the world anymore, she didn't want other people to know.

When she lifted them off the passenger seat, she saw that they had left a horrible red stain on the fabric below. Not the normal kind of stain you would expect from flowers but something all the more violent and messy.

Looking at her hands, she realised that the pollen had made them look as if she was afflicted with some contagious skin disease. She let out a small groan of frustration before grabbing the flowers by their packaging and leaving the car.

She heard that someone was playing music. Not a car stereo but an actual guitar. The light melody soothed her, and the severity of her posture softened ever so slightly. It was the kind of music that you would expect to find in a picturesque restaurant overlooking the ocean, the setting sun on your face and the warm breeze in your hair. As Julie crossed the road, the music increased in volume, and she thought that her imagination was getting the better of her.

Having temporarily forgotten her missing son, Julie reached her own front gate feeling much more relaxed. The music was much louder now; it must be coming from somewhere in the direct vicinity.

Julie was so lost in her thoughts that she only looked up when she got to the front door, ready to put the key in the lock. She was so astonished to find the guitar wielding youth sitting in front of her house that she let out a small yelp and staggered backwards.

'Fuck,' the youth said, springing to his feet. 'Mrs. Giles, are you okay?'

Any Zen that she had found had immediately evaporated with the fright. Her heart was once again racing, her head swimming.

'Fine,' she said quietly. 'I'm fine.'

'Jesus, you look like you're going to faint. Here, why don't you sit down?'

Without thinking, she let him help her down to the floor so she could perch on the front step. It was only afterwards that she reflected on how stupid this was. Any number of rapists and murderers would be absolutely delighted with a victim who lay on the floor voluntarily.

'Can I get you something?' he said, looking concerned. She didn't feel like a woman in early middle age who had suffered a small fright. Instead, it was if she had adopted the persona of some old biddy who was one shock away from the pearly gates.

'No, I'm fine, thank you.'

'I think some water might help, Mrs. Giles.'

'I'll be fine in a moment.' He didn't challenge her, but continued to look at her intently, waiting for any change in her condition.

After her head had stopped spinning, she raised her eyes from the concrete and looked at him properly for the first time.

'How do you know my name?'

'Didn't Harry tell you I was coming?'

'You know Harry?'

He bobbed at the knees and rolled his shoulders backwards in excitement. 'There you are then, no wonder you were surprised.'

He took his phone out of his pocket and after pressing a few keys, put it to his ear. Julie made a token effort to get back to her feet, although almost immediately decided it wasn't worth the effort.

'Harry?... How you doing, mate?... Not bad, yeah. Listen, I've got your mum here... No dramas, here she is.'

He handed Julie the phone. His enthusiasm for God knows what was almost overwhelming.

'Alright, Mum, how you doing?

Julie's emotions were now indistinguishable from one another. She felt the relief that Harry was okay with the blind fury that this anonymous friend had been able to reach him so easily.

'Harry, what on earth are you playing at,' she said, already regretting how sharp she was being with him. 'I've been trying to call you all afternoon.'

'Bloody hell, Mum, calm down. How many times do I have to tell you? No signal here. You've got to do it through WhatsApp.'

Julie wanted to argue that she had definitely been trying to call him through WhatsApp, but she really wasn't sure.

Her voice lost all of its previous conviction. 'Well, it still shouldn't be this hard to get hold of you.'

'It's easy.' She thought of the several other times that Harry had attempted to school her in the use of technology and how quickly it had descended into a nasty squabble. She found it easier to muddle through alone, or not as the case may be. She now left the assorted icons at the top of her phone to look menacingly, their warnings going unheeded.

'I'll have another look then. How have you been?' She was struggling to hear him over the rhythmic beating of a drum and youthful laughter in the background.

'Yeah, fine. Listen, Mum. Is it okay if Jack stays for a while?'

She almost asked who Jack was before remembering the grinning young man standing in front of her.

'Is he a friend of yours?'

'No, Mum, he's a psychopath who I thought I would ask to stay in my old bedroom.'

'Very funny, Harry.' Jack was still standing over her, positively beaming. 'Are you enjoying yourself?'

'Yeah, Mum, all good. Listen, I'm in the middle of something, so I'll let you go. Talk soon, yeah?'

'But Harry...,' she started to say before realising that he had ended the call.

'All good then?' Jack said as she handed the phone back to him.

She didn't have the opportunity to answer him before the garden gate swung violently open. Julie couldn't see the cause, however the alternating scraping and tapping of a cane gave her a pretty good idea.

'What are you up to, lad?' Mrs. McGrath growled.

'I'm called Jack,' the young man said. She couldn't say for certain as he was facing away from her, but she was certain that he wasn't smiling anymore. Mrs. McGrath had that effect on people.

'That's your name, boy. It doesn't explain what you're doing standing over that wee old girl there.' Julie thought that Mrs. McGrath must be at least twenty years her senior and made a mental note to re-examine her wardrobe.

Jack attempted a response to no avail. To his merit, he did manage to splutter a few incoherent noises, which was better than most in the face of the belligerent Scot.

'I'm fine,' Julie said. She pushed herself up and her knees cracked. They gave way underneath her, and she fell back down.

'Shocked to an inch of her life!' Mrs. McGrath was near to shouting now. Jack had raised his arms in surrender, most likely in response to Mrs. McGrath brandishing her cane like a sabre.

'Mrs. McGrath, I'm fine.' With some unceremonious grunting, Julie managed to get to her feet. 'His name's Jack. He's a friend of Harry's.'

'They sound like a group of wronguns to me. Vagrants, are they? He's been out here begging for hours.'

'I was only playing my guitar,' Jack whimpered, recovering his confidence for a second. Mrs. McGrath responded by jabbing her stick in his leg. Jack gave a small cry, then once again fell into a submissive silence.

'Harry is my son. You remember? The tall boy with dark hair that used to live here?'

'I've seen a lot of people in my life. Can't remember them all.'

'What is it that you do?' Jack asked, trying to get the conversation onto friendlier terms. Mrs. McGrath responded with another stab of her stick. Jack was too quick for her this time and dodged to one side.

'Jack, go inside and put the kettle on.' Julie unlocked the front door. Jack gathered up his bags and took the first few steps towards the house backwards, no doubt so he wouldn't have to take his eyes off Mrs. McGrath. As he passed over the threshold, the old lady narrowed her eyes at him, giving him one last point of the cane before he disappeared over the threshold.

'Been keeping an eye out, ever since that toerag this morning tried that funny business.'

'You really can't attack people just because you don't like the look of them.'

'I'm doing a public service. Them bloody rozzas were no good. Half an hour it took them to turn up, and that's only because I wouldn't stop calling.'

'So he wasn't doing anything wrong? The telephone engineer?'

'Nothing that they can prove, lass. There's one hell of a difference.'

'Well I'm going to go in now. It's been a long day, and I'm hungry.' Julie raised a hand and turned to go.

'Wait.' Mrs. McGrath hobbled towards her. She took a small notebook out of her pocket and wrote something down in it. 'You're better off calling me if that boy of yours tries anything. Bloody pigs will only come if you're a corpse.' She ripped the page from the pad and handed it to Julie.

'I thought your phone wasn't working?'

'It's fixed now; don't know how.'

'You don't think it had anything to do with that telephone engineer?'

'I told you already, he wasn't a telephone engineer.'

Too tired to argue, she took the phone number from her neighbour and went into the house.

Jack was nowhere to be seen. His bags were still sitting in the front hall. Not only was she met with the general mayhem that she normally left the house in, but also the aftermath of Mrs. McGrath's primitive DIY. Julie's unwanted guest this morning had unsuccessfully attempted to lift one of the tiles off the ground, snapping it at an ugly angle. She'd left it where it lay, in a bed of the grouting that she had seen fit to try and dislodge.

Julie stuck her head in the lounge and considered whether she had the energy to tackle the mess in there. Compromising, she straightened the throws and the pillows on the sofa and collected the dirty plates. She placed the two empty wine bottles under the sofa, hoping she would remember to move them when she left for work tomorrow morning.

When she entered the kitchen with the dirty plates, she found Jack sitting at the table drinking a glass of wine.

'Hope you don't mind,' he said, giving her a hundred watt smile. 'Bit late in the day for tea.'

Happy to have an excuse, Julie took a glass from the cupboard and poured herself some. Jack had brought his guitar into the kitchen with him and was idly plucking at the strings as he stared at the far wall pensively.

'That's very nice,' she said.

'What? Oh, this? Thanks so much. It's not really about the music for me, you know? It's more about the state of mind that music gets me to. Do you know what I mean?'

Julie nodded, despite not having the first clue what he was talking about.

She got her first good look at him in the light of the kitchen. There was no denying that he was attractive. The temperature had started to dip outside, and yet he was still wearing a white vest with nothing over it. His body had the quality of a lithe cat, all muscle and grace. While his hair looked effortlessly quaffed, Julie expected it had taken quite a lot of time to get it to stay that way. He had his feet propped up on one of the other kitchen chairs. He wore a pair of dirty sandals on his feet that looked exhausted.

'What brings you to Brumpton? It's not exactly Paris,' Julie asked, trying not to sound like his mother.

'I've got a gig. Standing slot at a place in town, you know. This really trendy little bar.'

'And when you say town, you mean...?'

'Where else, the Big Smoke!' he said gleefully.

'You do know that we're an hour's walk from the train station, and even then, it's another half hour into London?'

'I don't mind cadging a lift off you. Harry said he used to do it all the time, no problem.'

Julie tried to stop her face from dropping. She didn't think she quite managed it.

'It will give us the chance to get to know each other,' Jack said, winking. He slid his hand across the table and placed it on Julie's forearm. In spite of herself, Julie's cheeks began to flush. He was obviously only interested in securing free transport to and from the station, and yet she had allowed herself to be immediately taken in.

'Yes, well,' she said, moving her arm away from him and picking up her glass of wine. 'I do have a job, you know. I'll help where I can.'

'Nice one,' he said, returning to his guitar.

'Do you want anything to eat?'

'I'm doing the whole vegan, organic thing at the moment, you know? Trying to do my bit for Mother Earth.'

Julie walked to the fridge and peered tentatively inside. 'I don't think I have anything like that.' She tried her luck in the freezer instead. 'Nothing in here but fish fingers.'

'Are they from a sustainable source?'

Julie turned the packet over a few times. 'They're dolphin friendly?'

'Yeah, that's fine. I normally have Wednesdays off anyway.'

Julie continued to play his guitar while she cooked their food. She took the flowers that she had rescued from Mr. Peg and put them in a vase. When she placed them on the table in the hall, she noticed that her hands were still stained.

'How do you know Harry then?' Julie said, putting the sandwich in front of her young guest. Jack swung backwards on his chair and grabbed another bottle of wine from the fridge. He opened it and topped up Julie's glass without asking.

'I met him at a Full Moon Party in Phuket. Great guy. Really got what it was all about, you know?'

Jack covered his fish fingers with tomato ketchup before sliding the bottle over to her. Julie smiled at him but didn't pick it up.

'He needed to get away from all this,' he said, gesturing to the room around him, 'to realise that it's bullshit.'

'What does that mean? He's not going to come home?'

'He's already home,' Jack said excitedly. 'That's my point. Your generation told us that this is what it's all about. The mortgage and the dog and the three sticky children who give you fuck all back. But it's not, is it? It's about the world you make for yourself.'

He asked this as if he wanted a response. Julie didn't think it was fair that she was being asked to answer on behalf of everyone born before 1970. She wanted to argue, but when you put it like that, it did all seem a bit pointless. She couldn't remember what she had wanted from life when she was young. She was sure this wasn't it.

'I'm used to not having him in the house now,' Julie said, changing the subject. 'It feels very strange to be eating dinner with someone else here.' It was for this reason that she had abstained from condiments. She couldn't even imagine how ridiculous she already looked to this polished face of youth, let alone if she had red sauce dribbling down her chin.

'Don't you have a boyfriend, Mrs. Giles?' Jack had finished his sandwich in three hungry bites. He was now running one hand through his long, brown curls. The other was tipping his wine glass back and forth on the kitchen table.

She felt herself flushing again. 'None of your business, young man.' He stared at her with an intensity that made her uncomfortable. He was used to making women feel like they were the only one who was important in the world, Julie was sure of it. 'It's a bit unusual for someone of your age to get steady work as a musician.'

'Well,' he said, offering a coy smile. 'I'm not technically employed as a musician. The manager said I could fill in when there's a gap in the lineup though.'

'What are you going to do the rest of the time?'

'You know, bar work, clean the bathrooms. Earning my stripes. All the greats do it.' There was definitely something artificial to his enthusiasm. Julie thought that he was trying to convince himself more than anyone else that this was an exciting opportunity.

'And that's worth moving away from home for?'

He shrugged his shoulders grandly in an affectation of nonchalance. 'There isn't much to do in Merseyside.'

'Couldn't you clean toilets in Liverpool? You might have ended up scrubbing the same bowl that John Lennon did back in the day.'

Jack didn't rise to it. 'What can I say? The music takes you where it's going to take you. You'll have to come down and watch me play.'

'Why not?' Julie said, immediately regretting it. She was starting to feel tipsy. The sandwich was so dry that she had been washing it down with the tepid wine. She pushed her chair away from the table and stumbled as she got to her feet.

'I should make the bed up for you before it gets too late.' She didn't feel too drunk, just happy.

Julie hadn't cleaned any sheets in a good long while. After much rummaging, she managed to find a fresh duvet set. It featured whatever animated character Harry had been obsessed with at the age of seven and had a suspect grey patch on the bottom right hand corner of the sheet. Julie contemplated putting a quick wash on and getting something nicer for her guest. She reminded herself that Jack had spent the last few months sleeping god knows where probably in a drug induced haze, so it was unlikely to be an issue.

Julie dropped the second pillow on the bed and made an effort to straighten the edges of the duvet. When she stood up again, her mood had changed entirely. She wasn't sure if it was the alcohol or the pressures of entertaining. All she knew was that she felt wearier than she had in a long time, and that she wanted to go to sleep immediately. She planned to say goodnight to Jack and then head straight off to bed. However, she was surprised to find him standing in the open door watching her.

'All done, are we?' He stood with one leg crossed over the other, leaning one elbow on the door frame. He still held his empty wine glass in one hand as he smiled at her coquettishly.

'There's clean towels in the cupboard,' Julie said, going to leave. She made a mental note to check that there were, in fact, clean towels in the cupboard. Jack didn't move out of her way when she approached the door.

'Are you sure I wouldn't be more comfortable with you?' Julie hadn't realised how close they were standing to one another until just then. 'Maybe I could keep you company?' Jack was a fair few inches taller than her, but she could still feel his warm breath on her neck.

She paused for a few seconds before responding. When she thought about it later, Julie wondered if she had seriously considered the request, or whether her wine soaked brain was so stunned by the situation that it had taken a few moments to process the information.

'I think you'd be better off in here,' Julie said, regaining her senses for at least the moment. She turned sideways and pushed herself up against the opposite door frame to pass him, afraid that he would be repulsed by her bulk.

'Maybe another time,' he called to her as she walked away from him.

'Goodnight, Jack,' Julie said, not turning around. She waited until the light in the hall went off before she went to brush her teeth.

CHAPTER FOUR

I f there hadn't been a sign announcing that the building was a care home, you still would have easily been able to guess that it had something to do with the NHS. That, or another bureaucratic giant. It had obviously been beautiful once. No doubt there had been a gravel drive complete with a member of the Household to greet you as you arrived. Great granite pillars still adorned the facade, with ivy creeping up them picturesquely. In its day, it must have been incredibly imposing, something terribly impressive to behold. Now, the illusion was almost instantly shattered by the watery green paint that someone had slopped on the front doors at some point in the last fifty years. Laminated notices were stuck in most of the front facing windows, reminding guests to wash their hands and that prior approval was needed to take residents out of the grounds.

'Alright, Tracy?' Julie said as she entered. She took a box of chocolates from her carrier bag and placed it on the reception desk.

'Julie, you shit,' Tracy said, already ripping the top of the box off. 'You know I'm doing Atkins.'

'You can have a day off though, can't you?' Although as Tracy was already cramming a second truffle into her mouth, she clearly hadn't needed much persuasion.

'You're too good to us, you know. There's no need to do all this. Betty's one of the good ones. Not like her in the room next door. Bloody nightmare.'

Julie folded the carrier bag neatly into four squares and put it in her handbag. 'Got to keep the head of the care staff onside. I promised Greg I'd look after his mum.'

Tracy stared at her, waiting for her to continue speaking. Out of respect, she even managed to refrain from inhaling orange creams for a few moments. Because of this, her most recent selection was starting to melt between her fingers. Julie had surprised herself, not having intended to share anything so personal. They knew about Greg's death, of course, but she had told some paper pusher in an unseen office somewhere. She had never actually announced that her husband had died. There was something much more real about it when you could see the reaction on the face of the person who you were telling. What were you supposed to say when someone told you that their husband was dead? It was uncomfortable for everyone involved. It was much easier to operate in the grey areas of language, and not to make things more awkward than they needed to be.

When it became clear that Julie wasn't going to keep talking, Tracy leaned over the desk. The health care provider wiped her fingers on the back of her trousers and put her hand on Julie's arm. The magazine that had been resting open on her lap fell to the floor with a small clatter.

'Don't you worry, sweetheart. She's in good hands here.'

In an attempt to bring the conversation round to a breezier topic, Julie nodded towards the poster advertising a summer fete that was pinned to the notice board behind the desk. 'That's a nice idea,' she said as Tracy craned her head around to see what she was talking about. 'Get them all outside and moving.'

'It's going to be a fucking shit show. Betty and her like will be fine. Happy to sit in their chairs most of the time. Her who caused all the trouble last night, running off, that's who I'm worried about.'

Julie gave her a small smile of gratitude. 'Who was it? Doreen?'

'No, Doreen died last Tuesday,' Tracy announced, returning to her chocolate. 'Found her in a puddle of her own piss next to the bathroom door. It's this new one. Keeps wandering off.'

'That's got to be tricky.'

'You're telling me,' Tracy said, sounding aggrieved. 'Only two of us on the night shift now. One for the desk and one on the rounds. If she gets out of her room, it's a fucking nightmare. Thought about locking her in a few times, but you know, health and safety.'

Tracy had looked up from her chocolate at that last comment, gauging Julie's reaction.

'Nothing that you can't handle, I'm sure. Is Betty in the day room?'

'Yes, my love. Being no trouble at all.'

Julie wondered whether Tracy would lobotomise residents on arrival if she had her way. With a small wave, she left her sitting on reception to polish off the rest of the chocolate. Before she turned the corner, Julie saw Tracy retrieve her magazine and return to its glossy pages.

Someone in the recent past had made an effort to make the day room slightly less depressing than the rest of the home. The enterprise hadn't been very successful. There were pockets of activity spread around the room where some token effort had been made to engage the more lucid residents in the hopes that it would help to slow the collapse of their consciousness in its entirety. Two younger workers were sat with one old person apiece letting them smear messy streaks of paint across the craft paper in front of them. The gentleman closest to Julie obviously had no interest whatsoever in the project. His carer had therefore taken to dipping his fingers into the paint for him and then dragging his hand across the page for him. After every second motion or so, she would coo something along the lines of, 'There,' or 'Isn't that pretty?' While he may not have been compos mentis enough to strike her across the face, there was definitely a spark of something behind his eyes that suggested that he wanted to.

Elsewhere, a group of residents sat around the television watching inane daytime programming. The woman sat in the far corner chattered over the dialogue in such a way that you would be forgiven for thinking the characters were in the room with you. None of the others seemed to mind. She was just another welcome distraction to the general beige aspect of the room.

Julie found Betty sat by herself staring out of the window with her hands crossed on her lap, the very picture of gentile submission.

'Hello, Betty,' she said, kissing her on the cheek.

'Oh hello, dear. Are you new?'

Julie sat on the seat facing Betty. 'I don't work here, Betty. I'm Greg's wife. Do you remember? We got married in 1994.'

'Of course, I remember,' Betty said, a little defensively. Her eyes remained vacant, so Julie didn't press the issue. 'Where's Greg? Parking the car, is he?'

'He's not coming today, Betty.' The first few times that they had ran through this pantomime, Julie had needed to remind Betty that Greg was dead. Each time Betty reacted with such horror and incredulity that Julie had to give it up. Either she continued to suffer through Betty's renewed grief every time they met, or she would stop coming altogether. Eventually she decided to stop telling her. Her mother in law received no benefit from being routinely reminded of her son's death anyway. She convinced herself it was a kindness, better for both of their sakes.

'That's not like my Greg,' Betty said, sounding affronted.

'He's got to work today. He'll definitely come next week.'

Her face lit up, as it always did when Julie mentioned Greg's job. 'He's a good boy. Always working hard for you and Henry. Where is my grandson?' She craned her neck to look at the other side of the room.

'He's away at the moment. Travelling.'

'He could have said goodbye before he went.' She looked more hurt than she was entitled to given that she had just called her only grandson 'Henry.'

Julie wanted to tell Betty that her son spent an entire day with her before he left. That Harry had started to look so much like her late husband when they had first met that Betty had spent their entire last visit calling him 'my little boy.' When the two of them had gone to leave, Betty had wept and clung to Harry with such severity that two orderlies had to restrain her.

That was one of the problems with Alzheimer's. It was a decade long argument where you were always right but could never explain to the other party why.

'What have you been doing today, Betty?' Julie asked, changing the subject. Betty refused to make eye contact. Instead, she looked out the window in a sulk. Julie knew she would only have to wait a short time until Betty forgot what it was that she was upset about and continued the conversation, yet she found the whole song and dance tedious.

'Nice outside, isn't it?' Julie inched forwards in her chair to try and impede Betty's eyeline. She didn't have much luck. She sat back in the saggy brown chair and let her head fall backwards.

Her eyes had only been closed for a few seconds when she heard a burst of raised voices from the other side of the room.

'What if she'd broken her neck?' a very tall man was shouting into the face of his squat counterpart. 'Would you be telling me to let her wander then?'

The little man was holding up his hands in submission. 'Alright, fella, calm down.' He was looking around anxiously now, assessing who could have overheard.

'Don't tell me to calm down, you bloody gold digger. I bet you'd love it if she wandered off and didn't come back.'

'Now, hold on, mate. That's beyond the pale, that is.' The further he was antagonised, the more pronounced his Australian accent became.

Julie tried not to look at the scene developing in front of her until she realised that everyone else in the room was staring unashamedly. First and foremost among the spectators was Betty. Her temper forgotten, she was now standing up to get a better look at the unfolding conflict.

The two men were standing over a much older woman sitting sedately in an armchair. As the fight between the two men reached fever pitch, tears had begun to roll down her face.

'You don't know what's best for her,' the tall man shouted. 'Who the fuck are you to her anyway?'

'I'm her husband,' the little man said, really raising his voice for the first time.

'No you're not.'

'I'm as good as. I love her.'

'There's not enough of her left to love. Why don't you just move on to your next mark?'

The smaller man looked properly mad now, his face flushing angrily. His big bauble of a nose approached the colour of beetroot. He moved to take a step closer towards his combatant when Tracy burst into the room.

'What the hell is this?' Tracy roared. Not only had all of the residents now turned their attention to the scrum in its entirety, a few members of staff had abandoned their duties elsewhere to watch the spectacle unfold. Julie gave up all pretence of pretending she wasn't watching and turned in her seat to get the best view possible. Only then did she realise that she recognised the tall man; it was her new colleague, Mike.

With the arrival of this figure of authority, both men immediately checked themselves and managed to rediscover their inside voices.

'I was trying to explain to this man...,' Mike started.

'This man? Who do you think you are, mate?' the other man interrupted. 'She's my bloody wife.'

Mike pulled his head back ready to launch into another spirited explanation of how the old lady wasn't, in fact, his wife, but before he could, Tracy intervened.

'Mr. Spencer,' she said, addressing Mike. 'This isn't helping. If you hadn't noticed, you've driven your Aunty Jean to tears.' Mike looked at her confused for a moment, before following her gaze to the old lady in the chair.

As soon as Mike comprehended the state that his aunt was in, he dropped to his knees and went to take her hand. Unfortunately for him, the other man was too quick.

'I think you've done enough,' he said with a nasty bite in his voice. 'You should go.'

Mike went to protest, but Tracy interrupted him. 'Please, Mr. Spencer,' she said in an official tone that Julie wasn't used to hearing. 'You're upsetting the other residents.' This didn't seem fair. The old dears assembled in the day room looked like they were having the time of their lives. Whatever the truth may have been, Mike gave the short man one last piercing look before exiting in a rage.

Now that the excitement was over, Betty returned to her seat. 'What do you think about that then?' Julie said, attempting to engage her mother in law in conversation once again. Betty was having none of it. Clearly, she hadn't forgotten her grump as originally thought. She had merely suspended it for the show. Now that it was over, she turned her head to once again stare out of the window with an impressive resignation.

Julie expected that Betty probably couldn't remember what it was that had upset her in the first place. However, when you are entering the winter of your life, any sort of sensation is better than none, so she clung to it for as long as she could.

Taking inventory of the rapidly perishing inhabitants of the room, Julie came to the conclusion that life was too short. She gave Betty a kiss goodbye and went to find Mike.

She found him outside the main entrance sat on the front step.

'Mike?' she said, approaching him from behind.

'I'm not apologising. He can fuck off.' He didn't turn around. Julie did a little cough, hoping that this would prompt Mike to take notice and realise his mistake. Unfortunately, this wasn't a Jane Austen novel, and Mike continued to sit huddled over facing forwards.

With considerable effort, Julie managed to lower herself down to the floor. The ground below her was strewn with small rocks. She had to prop herself up on her haunches to knock some of the larger ones away.

'You really need to be more careful with old people, you know. It doesn't take much to give them a heart attack. They have to turn the soaps off five minutes before the end in case the big reveal does one of them in.'

Mike turned his head incrementally towards her and realised it was Julie. 'Fucking hell,' he said, startled. 'Shit, sorry, didn't mean to swear. Shit, I mean...'

'Don't worry about it,' Julie said. She feared if she didn't cut him off immediately, he would get so wound up that he would start dropping c-bombs. 'It looked like a pretty stressful situation. Not surprising that you lost your temper.'

'Yeah. Well, he's not a nice man.'

'Do you want to talk about it?'

'Not really. I mean, I don't want to bore you.'

'It might do you some good,' Julie cajoled. If the display inside was anything to go by, the story was set to be sensational.

Mike let out a deep breath and launched into his story. 'Roy, he's the little bloke that looks like a radish, he arrives on the scene a few years ago and gets his claws into my Aunty Jean right off. Fifteen years younger than her if you can believe it.'

Julie couldn't, although that wasn't surprising. He had the complexion of someone who spent most of his life at the bottom of a pint glass and slept on the table it was served on.

'Anyway, all of a sudden he proposes to her. Jean's always been the maiden aunt. Courts all and marries none as my nan used to say. It's a bit quick, but it's not exactly like they're getting any younger. So great, we're all happy for them.

'About a year goes by without them setting a date. Aunty Jean has always had some money set aside. She's not rolling in it. She always had this plan though, spent her life working hard so she could retire at 55 and see the world. They can afford it, and as I say, the almighty might come knocking at any moment, so what's stopping them?

'I didn't know my dad, not really, and I lost my mum young. Now that Nan and Aunty Kath are gone, I'm all that she's got left, you know? I've got to look out for her.

'Anyway, one Sunday lunch, I press her on it. Force her to tell me what's going on. It turns out, they can't get married because he's got a wife back in Australia who won't give him a divorce.'

'Because she's religious?'

'That was my first question too. No, says he can't find her. Says that he hasn't spoken to her since he left ten years ago.'

'There isn't a relative who can put them in touch?'

'Not a dickybird. She keeps going on and on about how the wife is in Australia, and that it's understandable that he can't find her. I ask her why they haven't spoken to a lawyer. Surely, they could give them some advice if they're serious about getting married. Roy says he has, and there's nothing that they can do. She says she doesn't mind. They love each other, and a piece of paper isn't going to change anything.

'We had a few months of this. Me trying to convince her to look into it, and her having none of it. But then she starts getting forgetful. Wandering off at odd times of the night and causing all sorts of mischief. When she nearly set the house on fire, I knew something wasn't right. The doctor said that it isn't anything diagnosable, she's just getting old.

'So I got Roy to agree to put her in this place.'

He nodded his head backwards in a gesture towards the care home.

'He put up a fight, but what's he going to do? Of course, he wanted her to stay at home. She was cooking all his meals for him, washing his clothes. He's useless without her. Did you see him today? Egg caked down the front of his shirt. The staff probably won't let him leave. Duty of care and all that. You can only almost set your house on fire so many times before someone has to do something.

'Problem is, since she's been here, it hasn't stopped. She keeps wandering off. It's a bloody nightmare.'

'Don't they have someone checking that they're staying in their rooms?' Julie asked.

'Apparently not. Too few of them, they say. Got to focus on the high risk cases.'

'Higher risk than walking around by herself in the middle of the night?'

'They say that she's not likely to do herself any harm. She's not demented; she's just confused. That old berk Roy isn't helping either. The first time it happened, he agreed that we should keep Aunty Jean in her room. You should have seen it. The scene he caused was like something out of a Greek tragedy. How could we do this to her; it wasn't worth being alive if she couldn't be with her flowers. The woman lived in central London for ninety percent of her life. She's used to having a few potted plants on the windowsill. I said I'd get her a few daffodils and put them in a vase, but apparently that's cruel.

'So now we're in this ridiculous situation where the home are forced to let her run free like stig of the sodding dump because Roy somehow managed to wangle his way into getting her right of attorney, and he thinks keeping her indoors would be tantamount to incarceration without the chance of parole.'

Julie felt a bit bowled over by this flood of narrative. They sat in silence for a few moments before Mike said, 'Sorry, too much information.'

'No, don't be silly. I wouldn't ask if I didn't want to know. I was just thinking about how selfish I've been.'

'I doubt that.'

'Maybe not selfish then. More silly. Betty, that's my husband's mum, she's as good as gold when you think about some of the others. But I'm so bloody big and important that when I do occasionally take the time to come and see her, all I can think about is the inconvenience of it all. It's not right, especially when....' She paused and checked herself. 'Especially when she doesn't know any better.'

'I'm sure she appreciates it,' Mike said with a kind smile. 'Your husband too. It's not easy when they start to fade away.'

She thought about correcting him and instantly began to feel depressed. 'That's kind of you to say, thank you. Anyway, I should probably go back in for a bit longer. I'll see you tomorrow?' She attempted to stand but instantly fell backwards again. Mike jumped up with an embarrassing lack of effort and helped to pull her up.

'I thought you'd booked it off?'

'I had, yeah, but Mr. Peg said he had something important to tell us.'

'Oh yes, his big plan to put the garden centre on the map! How exciting. We'll be buying out B&Q before we know it.'

'And here we are getting in on the ground floor.' Julie said goodbye and walked back through the double doors. She left Mike standing there, looking a little lost.

When she walked back into the day room, she saw Jean and Roy sat together. Jean remained in her chair, with Roy perched on one of the arms. Her head was resting against his shoulder as Roy rhythmically stroked her hair.

Julie walked back over to Betty who was still looking out of the window.

'Oh, hello,' Betty said, as though noticing her for the first time. 'Are you new?'

CHAPTER FIVE

I n the three weeks Jack had been staying with Julie, they hadn't spoken about their almost liaison of the first night once. Julie expected that she had been relegated to the league of lost causes. Or perhaps Jack thought that it was too much effort for such a modest prize.

All in all though, Jack wasn't a bad house guest. Yes, she did find herself cooking for him more than she would care to. There was also often a definite smell of marijuana in the upstairs hallway first thing in the morning.

But Jack was always appreciative and never failed to be kind to her. More than that, Julie found that now there was someone else living in the house, she had a reason to make more of an effort. Gone were the days of her leaving empty bottles of wine on the living room floor for a few days at a time. Although truth be told, she and Jack often went through a fair quantity in the evenings when he wasn't working.

On one Saturday morning, she walked into the kitchen and was surprised to find Jack standing in front of the cooker. Normally, their paths didn't cross before at least eleven.

'I met this guy on the way to Machu Picchu a few years ago,' he said when he noticed that she had come into the room. 'He'd given up everything when he was properly old and moved to South America. Seriously, he was like forty or something.' He remembered himself for a moment. 'Oh, sorry. Only old relatively speaking, if you know what I mean. Anyway, he'd opened this restaurant, and the food in there was the fucking nuts.'

He hadn't started swearing in earnest until a few weeks into his stay. Julie wondered whether Jack spoke to his own parents like this and came to the conclusion that he probably didn't. It made the fact that she had brushed her hair and done her makeup before she came down for breakfast worthwhile. Of course, she wasn't actually trying to impress him, she told herself. She just didn't want to be ridiculous in his eyes.

'Anyway, he taught me how to make this amazing paella.' He'd set a place for Julie at the table and gestured for her to sit down. 'And now, Mrs. Giles, it is my small gift to you.' The dish slid from the pan onto her plate so perfectly that it was if it had agreed in advance.

Julie thanked him and began to eat. Jack stood over her, watching her take her first bite. She was reminded of many a disastrous Mother's Day breakfast that Harry had put in front of her and then instantly tried to banish the thought.

'It's really good, Jack, thank you.' Julie said between mouthfuls. Jack continued to stare at her in anticipation. She followed up with, 'The mushrooms are especially well done,' but thought it was unlikely that this was the specific feedback he was looking for.

'Some people have said that they think it's like professional standard.'

'Is that something you might want to do when you settle down?'

He harrumphed at this. 'What, be a chef? I told you, Mrs. Giles, it's all about the music. The only 9 to 5 I'm going to be doing is in my grave.' The line had been rehearsed, and he looked to her for a reaction.

She gave him a little laugh and hoped that would be the end of it. It was his ego rather than the man himself that she sometimes found exhausting.

JULIE WAS SITTING in the living room with a cup of coffee when there was a frenzied banging on the door. She wasn't surprised to find Mrs. McGrath standing on the front step. Julie had considered ignoring the incensed knocking. However, she thought that it was inevitable that the old woman would find her way into the back garden and then, through sheer determination, into the house.

'Where's the gigolo?' Mrs. McGrath said in the way of greeting.

'I'm sorry?'

'Your young man. Where is he?'

'He's over at Brian's. Helping him with the garden.'

'The pervert can't cut his own grass, is it? Or is he letching at small boys now as well?'

'He's had a broken leg for months. Didn't you notice?'

'Bigger things requiring my attention.' She shook the newspaper that she was carrying in the air. 'Need to show you something.' Without being asked, Mrs. McGrath pushed straight past Julie and walked into the living room.

Julie took a moment to compose herself on the threshold before closing the door and joining her unwanted guest. Mrs. McGrath had spread the newspaper out in front of her and was now leaning forward over it, inspecting the print.

'There,' the old lady said. She tapped a column of type in the bottom right hand corner of the page. 'Read that.'

Julie took a seat next to Mrs. McGrath and leaned in to have a closer look. The article detailed an investigation that the financial watchdog had started into a large telecoms company due to the misappropriation of funds. It alluded to the fact that several of the organisation's most senior members were currently suspended and would most likely need to resign.

Julie finished reading and turned to look at her visitor, waiting for some further explanation. Mrs. McGrath was leaning back on the sofa with her arms folded, looking smug.

It became clear that an explanation wasn't going to be forthcoming. 'I'm sorry, I don't understand,' Julie said, readying herself for the old loon's diatribe.

'It's them, the wrong 'uns who were tapping our phones.'

'The police told you that? They were definitely tapping our phones?'

'The bloody rozzas?' She made a dismissive noise, blowing air through her closed lips. 'Nothing but a group of glorified secretaries these days. Bobby Peel would sack the lot of them all off. It's all here,' she tapped the story again. 'You've just got to know what to look for.'

Julie looked at the story again as critically as she knew how, but there was nothing. No hidden meaning or surreptitious plots suggested themselves to her.

After a silence of a few moments, Mrs. McGrath became impatient and jumped into her explanation. 'That's what all that business with the phones was about. They were expanding their criminal empire.'

'How?!' Julie exclaimed, trying not to laugh.

'Why does everyone think I'm a bloody engineer? I don't know phones, but I do know crime.'

'Have you called the police?' Julie suggested, before realising her mistake.

'Haven't you been listening to a word I've been saying?!' She shuffled forwards on the sofa and stood up with the help of her stick. 'You can't wait for someone else to fix it for you. You've got to sort it out yourself.' She walked towards the door with such purpose that Julie was scared of what she was going to do next. That was until she heard Mrs. McGrath taking a mug from the cupboard in the kitchen and pouring herself a drink. Resigning herself to her fate, Julie followed her, in the hopes that there would still be some hot water left in the kettle.

It had taken the best part of an hour to get rid of Mrs. McGrath. She had spent most of the time contentedly ranting more to herself than to Julie. Even after so much vitriol, it still wasn't clear what slight the telephone company had inflicted on Mrs. McGrath, or what she intended to do about it.

Julie took the opportunity of being alone in the house to have a bath, spending an hour or so luxuriating in the tub. After she had got dressed, she had donned her summer dressing gown over her clothes. She felt relaxed and happy but a little hungry. Putting her slippers on, she made her way downstairs to make some lunch. As she walked past Jack's room, she went to look at the windowsill she'd given him a couple of quid to paint. Not the neatest job in the world. Then again, what could you really expect if you were going to pay your wayward lodger to do house repairs?

She found Jack standing in the front hall. The slippers had masked her footsteps, and he only noticed her when she was a few paces away from him.

'Oh, hello,' he said, not as sure of himself as usual. He was holding a wedge of bank bills that he tried to unceremoniously cram into his pocket. The volume of them was so great that it took two or three attempts. A few broke away from the spool and dropped to the floor. Julie picked the nearest one up and was surprised to see that it was a £50 note.

'Bloody hell, I think I'm in the wrong field,' she said, giving him a little chuckle.

Julie looked up at him from the note and smiled. He snatched the money from her hands before she knew what was happening.

'Yeah, well, I've been doing a lot, haven't I? Done Mrs. Sinclair's garden a few times too now,' he said, sounding a little sulky. He was so petulant that Julie felt like she had caught him doing something he shouldn't have been, although she didn't really know what. 'It's hard work, you know.'

'I'm not saying it isn't. Is that your money from the bar too?'

'Just leave it, yeah?' Julie didn't have a chance to question him any further. He pushed past her and went straight upstairs, his feet hitting each step heavily as he did.

Julie stood there slightly bemused, wondering whether she should go after him. Deciding that she hadn't, in fact, done anything that she needed to apologise for, she remained true to her original errand and went to see what they had for lunch. She was irritated to find an empty cheese packet in the place of the full block that she had picked up a few days previously, and a jar of pickle that only had the scrapings down the side available. Having someone else in the house may have its benefits, but this certainly wasn't one of them. Julie took off her slippers, replacing them with a pair of sandals and hung her dressing gown on the hook by the door before exiting the house.

The summer had been especially hot, and today was no exception. The sun beat down on her, and she immediately felt herself getting sweaty under the arms. The more nutritious meals that Julie had been making for her and Jack had been having a positive effect on her waistline but not drastically. When the days were warmer, she felt her bulk was something so disgusting that small children would point and laugh at her in the street. Luckily, there were none in sight currently, allowing her to make her way to the shops undeterred.

45

She stopped for a moment before crossing the road to let the mobility bus carrying Mr. Sinclair home to drive past. The two familiar orderlies unloaded the poor man from the vehicle and delivered him to a waiting Mrs. Sinclair outside number 32. Next door at number 30, Brian was closing his front door and struggling down the path on his crutches. He was so distracted that when he reached the street, he almost barrelled into Julie.

'Watch where you're going,' he spat instinctively. He then looked up and saw that it was Julie who he had almost knocked over. His face instantly softened. 'Sorry, my darling,' he said, his voice as clawing as ever. 'Didn't realise it was the most beautiful girl in the world.'

'That's alright, Brian.' It became clear that they were walking in the same direction. Julie attempted to speed up slightly in the hopes that Brian wouldn't be able to keep pace.

'What brings you outside on a lovely day like this?' he said. He placed a hand on Julie's arm so that she couldn't rush away from him without pulling him off kilter.

'Just up to the shop and back. Got to pick up a few bits.'

'It's my lucky day then.' He left his arm on Julie's but relented when it became clear that he wouldn't be able to maintain the physical contact and operate the crutches. 'You can help an old man to the bus stop.'

Julie would have been content to continue walking in silence together. However, from previous experience, she knew that Brian would continue to try and woo her if she left any gap in the conversation.

'What are you doing in town?'

'You know what it's like for a man of the world, my love. People to see, things to do, deals to put in motion.'

'I don't know what it is that you do for work. When you don't have a broken leg, I mean.' There was a suspect white van that remained parked outside of Brian's house most hours of the day. Now that Julie thought about it, she hadn't ever seen him arriving or leaving in it. It just remained there as a permanent staple of the street.

'A bit of whatever there is going, sweetheart. People like me make the world go round.'

'You think you're going to be well enough to work soon then?'

'I live in hope, my love. I live in hope.'

'But Jack's been helping you out in the garden? Helping you keep it tidy?'

'He is,' he said with noticeably less enthusiasm. An awkward silence followed.

'Sorry, did I say something wrong?'

'It's not easy to admit that you're getting old,' he said after a pause of a few moments. 'Especially when the fit young thing helping you is living with the girl of your dreams.'

Julie was surprised to find that she was feeling sorry for Brian. This was a new sensation for her. The only two emotions that she normally associated with him were irritation and revulsion. She paused on the pavement and waited for Brian to do the same.

'We all get ill sometimes. You just need to remember that it's okay to ask for help.'

'I'll do that, my darling,' he said, his normal bonhomie returning with a vengeance. 'Don't you worry, next time I need the slightest thing, I'll be knocking on your door straight away.'

Julie waited with Brian at the bus stop. It was not out of any desire whatsoever to spend more time with him, but because the idea of him undressing her with his eyes as she walked away made her feel physically ill. There was a delay after Brian had boarded.

He dislodged the elderly couple sitting in the first row, insisting that he wouldn't be able to reach the seats in the middle of the bus.

In front of the shops, there was a group of teenagers. They all looked like cheap facsimiles of one another in their jogging bottoms and designer caps. Their bikes were lying on the floor to their front, and they leaned with menacing intent against the wall behind them. One of their number, who appeared to be a few years older than the rest, was clearly their leader. He had the beginnings of facial hair, although it definitely still needed some work. It was patchy in most places and only really visible on the very bottom of his chin and his upper lip. There was also a splattering of acne on his brow, the remnants of his earlier, greasier years.

Julie could feel their eyes on her from a hundred metres away. Her clothes didn't feel large enough all of a sudden, and she pulled at the front of her top, hoping that it was covering her midriff adequately.

They continued to map her progress as she approached the shop. The group had positioned themselves in front of the ramp that led up to the electric doors of the shop front. It made it necessary for customers to pass within a few inches of them. It was only when Julie was directly in front of them that the ringleader started to make kissy noises, making her flinch. The others began to snigger under their breath and whisper what Julie expected were lude comments to each other.

Inside the front doors of the shop, Mr. Baker, the proprietor, was standing sentry.

'Did they give you any hassle?' Mr. Baker asked gruffly.

'Just kids being kids,' Julie replied. They didn't seem like the kind of kids who would react well to being reprimanded by an old shopkeeper. Besides, Julie came in here at least a few times a week and couldn't be doing with the hassle.

'Didn't used to be like this in my day. Children had a bit more respect.' Mr. Baker continued to chunter to himself, but Julie had walked out of earshot. She didn't expect that he needed an audience to keep up the diatribe.

On the way out of the shop, the eldest of them caught her eye and gave her a cocky little smile. She turned her eyes back to the ground. With cheese, pickle and the obligatory bottle of pinot grigio in hand, Julie returned to the house. She had barely had a chance to put her shopping bag down before Jack came running into the kitchen.

'Where have you been,' Jack said, walking towards her and wrapping his arms around her.

She was going to make a passive aggressive comment about having to buy some replacement cheese, but he didn't give her a chance.

'I've got big news.' Jack held Julie away from him at arm's length, beaming into her face. Jack's whole life sometimes felt like a performance, and this was no exception. It was clear that he wasn't going to tell her until she prompted him.

'Tell me?'

'Johnny just rang from the bar. Someone has dropped out for tonight.

They're going to let me go on.' She wondered how he would feel if his hip young friends could see him in such an obvious state of ecstasy over this marginal achievement.

His enthusiasm was infectious. Julie couldn't help smiling at him.

'That is fantastic. You must be so happy.'

'Well, you know. Not a big deal.' He disengaged from her and started to regain his original cool. 'I've told you before. It's not about performing. It's about the energy that you put into the world. If my music can help other people, then yeah, of course, I'm happy to do it.'

'Well, well done you.' She squeezed his arm, and then went about unpacking the shopping. 'You'll have to tell me how it goes.'

'What, you're not coming?' There was an anxiety in his voice that she hadn't expected.

'I don't think I would really fit in. I haven't been to a bar in years.'

'All the more reason then.' He moved to position himself in front of her.

'Jack, you don't want some middle aged woman hanging around embarrassing you in front of your friends. I've got work tomorrow. I can't go traipsing into London and getting home at God knows what hour.'

He moved half a step closer to her. 'So what if you're middle aged? You're not dead. What's the point in being alive if you're not going to live? Come on, when was the last time that you went to work hungover?'

Julie didn't want to admit how often this had been the case, so gave him a little smile in lieu of an answer.

'Come on, it won't be the same if you're not there.' He gave her another winning smile.

'I don't think I can walk to the station in this heat,' Julie said, grasping for any excuse now.

'I'll pay for the taxis. My treat.'

'I'm not staying out past ten.' Julie tried to instil some authority in her voice, although didn't think she managed it. 'And I'm only having two glasses of wine.'

'Great, great, great!.' He almost shouted the last word. 'I'll tell Johnny to put your name down at the door.' Jack left Julie standing in front of the open fridge wondering whether it was too early in the day to open the wine.

CHAPTER SIX

S o many different reasons as to why this had been a mistake presented themselves to Julie all at once.

As promised, Jack had paid for their taxi to the station and had even splashed out on some little bottles of wine for the journey. They had sat on a table of four, drinking and laughing together. It had made Julie feel young again. She had positioned herself so that she couldn't see her reflection in the window, not wanting the stark reminder of her aged face.

They had got off the train at Kings Cross and walked the short distance to the bar together. Before they walked inside, Jack had stopped her for a moment and taken her hand. Julie wasn't sure whether she felt like a mother or a lover or something in between. Regardless, it had been nice to be wanted in whatever guise.

As soon as they had walked inside, one of the most beautiful women that Julie had ever seen grabbed Jack by his shirt and tugged. She slid her hand down his arm until their digits were interlocked, leading him away from Julie into the modest crowd.

Initially, Julie had taken a few steps to follow but had lost him almost immediately. On reflection, she realised that they made such an incongruous pair that the young woman hadn't even noticed that they were here together.

Standing there alone, she felt painfully awkward. She decided to engage in the only activity available to her and made her way to the bar to get a drink.

The bartender gave her a small nod of the head upwards. He was much in the same ilk as Jack, except his hair was longer and tied in a messy knot on top of his head. Some parts of his face had metal studs through them. Julie thought the unpleasantness of suffering through the piercing was definitely not worth the resulting aesthetic.

'Could I have a glass of pinot grigio please?' she asked timidly.

Without giving her a second look, he went to fetch her drink. Wine in hand, Julie turned away from the bar and considered her next steps. She felt absolutely ridiculous. No, more than that. No one was even giving her the due consideration to make her feel ridiculous. She felt insignificant. Hoping not to make awkward eye contact with anyone, she stared down at her drink. The issue with that was that she was forced to look at the outfit she had chosen for the night's jollities. After much consideration, she had opted for a simple, white blouse and the most flattering pair of denim jeans that she owned. Only now, her shirt felt frumpy, and the jeans looked desperately tight. As soon as she was able to determine where the band would be performing, she would move to the other side of the room to keep herself away from any judging eyes.

Jack reappeared in front of her looking irritated.

'Emergency in the bathroom,' he said. 'Bloody hell, you think they could give me a night off. Do you want a drink?'

Before she could answer, Jack had turned round to address the man behind the bar. Julie finished the wine in her glass in one satisfying gulp and placed the empty on a nearby table.

'It's nice here,' Julie said to Jack as he put the large glass of white in her hand.

'Yeah, it's alright,' Jack said grumpily. She noticed a wet patch on the knee of his intentionally scruffy jeans but thought it was best not to mention it.

'Do you get on with people you work with?' She wasn't sure why she was desperately trying to coax a conversation out of him when he so clearly wasn't in the mood.

He started to answer her, but his response was drowned out by the heavy drum section of the first band. It had a sort of inoffensive indy rock quality to it. You could forgive the slightly rough and amateur aspect of anything when those who were performing it were so enthusiastic. The alcohol didn't hurt either. Julie found herself swaying to the tune, perhaps not quite in time but in a way that hopefully wouldn't embarrass Jack. She looked over to him. He was leaning against the bar, his face impassive.

The band cycled through their tracks, all of which sounded fundamentally the same. Jack made his way through his drink with a steady determination. Each time he bought another, he would place an accompanying glass in Julie's hand. She would have protested and offered to pay for a round, but she was too busy trying to finish the previous drink. By the time the first band had finished their set, Julie was much more vocal in her appreciation.

'That was great,' she said as the next act started to set up their instruments. 'Don't you think that was great?'

Jack turned to look at her. 'It was okay, Julie. They're not the fucking Beatles.'

'Oh, well I liked them.'

'You don't get out much though, do you?' Jack said, returning his attention to the stage.

Not really being able to refute that, Julie took a large sip of her drink.

The second band began to play in a very similar style to the first. Julie felt less elated now, more vacant. The novelty of the situation had worn off. She felt desperate to finish this sad little episode in her life and to go home.

A man of about Julie's age parked himself on the bar stool next to her. It momentarily wobbled dangerously on two legs before correcting itself with a bang. A few members of the audience in the direct vicinity jumped and then scowled at the responsible party before returning their attention to the band.

The man was wearing the garb of the city that had been the fashion 20 years ago. There were pin stripes on his suit, and his tie was fat. He still had a dark, full head of hair, which was brushed back and set with a lacquer of some type or another. On this bright summer evening, he was incongruously carrying a golf umbrella. The strap holding it together was disengaged, and she could easily read the words 'Jerryman Bloors,' printed across the dark, waterproof fabric with a white lion featured underneath them.

Julie was expecting a clumsy come on. After all, sloppy blokes like him were the only ones who showed any interest in her. But he was only interested in the music. Some prescient member of the serving staff had made the wise decision to only provide him with a plastic cup. At the end of every song, he would grip it between his teeth so he could applaud. After one number that he was especially keen on, he managed to splash beer down his front, the beaker bobbing up and down vigorously.

'Thank you,' the young man on stage said when they finished playing. He pushed the long hair out of his eyes, which immediately fell back into his face. 'This is our last number. But we've been the Big Town Cats.' He paused in anticipation of a modest round of applause, although the look on his face suggested it was more modest than he would have liked. 'Up next, we have the talented Jack Johnson.'

'Harper,' Jack shouted from where he stood next to Julie.

'Yeah, whatever mate. Everyone else, you've been great. This one is called 'My Baby Can Do No Better.'

They counted it off and fell into a track indistinguishable from their last. Jack turned his back on them and tried to catch someone's eye at the bar. The chap who had first served Julie was now chatting up Jack's lady friend from earlier on. Both were oblivious to him, casually flirting despite the growing crowd of customers waiting for drinks.

Jack slammed his hands on the bar. It was barely audible over the sound of the music. His hands curled into fists, and he banged them down once again. When this still failed to elicit the desired effect, he leant over the bar and began to serve himself. After he had filled up Julie's glass in haste, he started to pull his own pint. Clearly the young man wasn't as unaware of Jack's presence as he was pretending to be. He broke off his conversation, marched over to Jack and turned the tap off mid flow. Jack attempted to shove him but couldn't reach his shoulder. If their facial expressions were anything to go by, they exchanged a few angry words before the beautiful young woman could intercede. She put a hand on Jack's adversary's shoulder and leant in to say something in his ear. He gave Jack one last dirty look, and then disappeared into a back room. Jack and the woman then started to argue with one another.

The band on stage finished their last song. The perfunctory applause that followed was interrupted by the pair squabbling.

'That's what not together means. I can do whatever the fuck I like,' the young woman shouted.

'Do whoever the fuck you like, you mean,' Jack said, with a nasty sneer.

The look of disgust that she gave Jack transformed her pretty face entirely. Her nostrils became slits, and her eyes narrowed. At that moment, a slightly older and more respectable member of staff stepped out from behind the stage. He scanned the room until his eyes rested on Jack.

'Harper,' he said across the room. Jack didn't respond or look around.

Jack and the young woman continued to stare at each other.

'Get on stage now if you're coming.' All of a sudden, Jack lost interest in her. He leant over the bar again, picked up his half-filled pint and strutted over to the stage.

Julie watched Jack as he plugged in his guitar and began to position his microphone stand. She felt an odd sense of detachment from the events that had just unfolded before her. She reflected absentmindedly on how much she had actually drank this evening and how painful it was going to be to get up for work tomorrow morning.

Someone tapped her on the shoulder, and she feared that it was the boozy bloke next to her finally making his move. She was surprised to find it was the young woman, her eyes now wet. Even when on the verge of the tears, she really was very attractive. It was the kind of face that you would only expect to find in the company of celebrities or Greek statues. Its only off putting quality was a small, metal piercing directly in the middle of the bridge of her nose. The idea of the stud scraping on the bone below made Julie wince.

Expecting that she was going to be asked to pay for the drink that Jack just stole, Julie went to rummage in her bag for her purse. Before she could start looking, the woman tapped her on the shoulder again a little more insistently.

'Is he your son?'

'Not really. I mean, no. Sorry, I've had a bit to drink.'

The woman looked at Julie confused.

'He's my son's friend. He's staying with me.'

The woman gave Julie a slow nod, taking the information in.

'Jack's not very nice. You know, to women.'

'Did he hit you?' Julie asked, shocked.

'The worst ones don't have to hit you.'

Julie didn't have time to ask what she meant. Jack's music started and made any further conversation impossible. Unfortunately, being on stage hadn't improved Jack's mood. He had a face of thunder as he played the sweet introductory melody that he had showcased for Julie earlier that afternoon.

When she turned to look at the bar again, the woman was serving another customer. At some point in the recent conflict, her intoxicated neighbour had managed to source himself another drink. He started to knock it back as if the world was about to end.

Jack finished playing his introductory tune and those who had been paying attention gave a round of applause.

'Thanks very much,' Jack said, still not looking very pleased. 'My name's Jack Harper, and this is my music.'

When his hand connected with the strings again, something was obviously amiss. Not understanding the finer particulars of playing the guitar and having drank about a bottle and a half of passable wine at this point, Julie didn't know what it was, but it definitely wasn't right. The error was so severe that several of the patrons recoiled from the noise as it reverberated through the speakers unpleasantly.

The gent sitting next to Julie let out a snort of laughter. Luckily, it didn't evolve into a full out eruption of mirth, but for one very unpleasant moment, it definitely had the potential to. Jack looked up and shot a nasty glance in his direction. The man was clearly past the point of feeling any embarrassment, if indeed he had that capacity to begin with. He continued to smile happily as Jack attempted to recover his composure.

Jack eventually managed to find his groove. He looked incredibly on message sat on the stage. The young, beautiful musician with not a care in the world. Singing, not because it might make you rich and famous, but because it was a joy, and people wanting to hear your music could make you happy in a way that few other things could.

The lyrics were pleasant if only because you could let your attention wander while you were listening to them. Much in the same way that you can stop concentrating on bad television for up to five minutes and still not lose the thread of the plot.

'It's not easy when you have all this love to give.
It isn't fair when I don't have anyone to share with.
It's hard sometimes when you've been alone for so long.
How do you keep on giving, when you're always so alone?'
'So won't you tell me you love me, hey?' Jack cooed.

Julie had heard Jack practising this section from outside his bedroom door. Confident, if not arrogant, about most things, Jack had been surprisingly coy about this one particular song.

'So won't you tell me you love me, hey?' Jack sang again.

Julie could just about remember what happened next, and only because it had been an impressive departure from Jack's singing style more generally. After all, they were lovely little songs, but the lyrics weren't exactly inspired. Jack would take a deep breath, and then sing the last 'hey,' with all the gusto he could muster.

Except he didn't. He sang the first half of the lyric with no issue. When he reached the crucial line, his voice cracked. Not the small little imperfection that we all suffer from on the day to day, but the almighty failing of the voice that is usually reserved for boys entering the early stages of puberty. An embarrassment of this kind would normally be something to be laughed off with a group of friends. Awkward, yes, but nothing major. Unfortunately, Jack was literally standing centre stage in a room that was becoming increasingly more crowded.

It was too much for the man sitting next to Julie. He couldn't help it. He threw his head back and roared with laughter, pointing at Jack as he did for good measure.

Jack stopped playing and stood there, stunned. When the man failed to stop laughing, the young performer's face transformed from bemusement to rage. He let go of his guitar, jumped off the stage and began to push his way through the crowd toward the perpetrator. His instrument, now hanging from its strap over his shoulder, bumped into people at awkward angles as he went. He received a few shouts of protest but had already gone by the time anyone went to retaliate.

When Jack finally made his way across the room, he immediately launched at the laughing man. Julie was shocked that her houseguest didn't attempt any course of redress. He simply pulled back his arm and punched the man square in the face. It seemed so unlike the gentle soul who had been living under her roof for the past few weeks. He might have displayed a temper from time to time. It had been something more akin to a grumbling toddler than a brawling strongman though.

Jack got the first punch in no problem. There was a look of amazement on his face that it had actually landed. The recipient wobbled on his chair precariously and almost fell to the floor. Feeling encouraged by the success of this first venture, Jack pulled his fist back again, ready to land another blow. Unfortunately, the bigger man had come to his senses in the intervening half a second. He stood up to his full height and looked properly mad. Next to him, the able young man who was so sure of himself just a minute ago looked like a little boy. With one almighty smack, he hit Jack in the nose and sent him spinning to the floor face first. Julie winced as she heard an unidentified part of his face crunch sickeningly. The drunk chap, who had a rather impressive frame to support his substantial gut, took one stride forward and went to lift Jack off the ground.

Fortunately, before the matter could escalate any further, the manager had rushed over and stood between the two of them. Julie rushed over to Jack to see if he was alright. When she turned him over, he looked more dazed than anything else. The manager was now having an animated conversation with the bloke who had hit Jack. Julie couldn't hear what they were saying to one another. However, as the drunk man finally went to leave, she distinctly heard him say, 'Whatever, music is shit anyway.'

Jack, now seeming more alert, had propped himself up on his elbows. The manager was now saying something to Jack that was impossible to hear from where he and Julie were sitting on the ground. She took his guitar off of his shoulder before she helped Jack to his feet. She grabbed a few napkins from the bar and handed them to him to attend to the bloody mess below his nose.

'What are you playing at?' the manager said to Jack.

'Steve, I can explain. He'd been going at me.'

'Is that the explanation? Because it's shit.'

'You know what it's like. Some people are just looking for trouble.'

'Like you, you mean? That's the third scrap you've got into with a customer, and that's only the ones I've seen.'

'Yeah, well,' Jack said, the sulky teen voice once again making an appearance. 'I can't help it if people are giving me shit.'

'You can help acting like a dick though. I'm sorry, mate. I don't need this.'

'That's the last time it happens, Steve, I promise.'

'I can't take that chance. I'll pay you what you're owed at the end of the week.'

Jack first looked crestfallen and then furious. His posture changed again to a fighting stance. Before he could do any more damage, Julie put her hand on his shoulder.

'I think we should go, Jack.' He didn't look sure, but when he turned back, Steve had already gone. The effort to fight another doomed battle was clearly too great. His shoulders slumped and he let Julie lead him out of the bar.

JACK SAID nothing the entire ride home. They did get a few funny looks on account of Jack's nose. Thankfully, the trains were relatively quiet for a Wednesday evening. He sat with his head slumped against the window. His guitar was placed upright in the chair next to him. Every so often, Julie would glance over at him to see if there was any indication that he might want to talk. His eyes remained fixed and his expression vacant. At one point, he looked so zoned out that Julie was worried that he was concussed. That was before he nudged his nose with the back of his hand, and it instantly started bleeding again. She rushed to the bathroom and fetched him another wad of thin tissue. He took it from her without thanks and carried on looking out of the window.

When they got back to Brumpton, there were no taxis. Julie considered whether walking was an option, but the heat was still oppressive. The alcohol was no longer making her feel pleasantly giddy, just queasy.

She wasn't sure what she had expected tonight was going to be, but it wasn't this. She called a local taxi firm, and the two of them sat in silence at the bus shelter waiting for their lift to arrive.

They didn't talk at all, with one exception. 'You'll need to clean yourself up a bit,' Julie had said as an afterthought after she'd put the phone down to the taxi company. 'They won't take you like that.'

He left her sitting there as he ventured back into the station to use the bathroom.

When they got back to the house, the two of them staggered into the kitchen without much thought why. Jack went straight to the fridge and grabbed a bottle of wine from inside the door.

'Are you sure that's a good idea?' Julie slurred. Despite the sobriety of their journey home and a good bout of fresh air, she didn't feel any more composed.

Jack barely acknowledged her. He did an arm movement which may have been a shrug, but it was anyone's guess. He poured himself a glass and slumped down into one of the chairs around the kitchen table. Out of instinct more than anything else, Julie fetched herself a glass and took the bottle from him. Only when the neck was touching the rim did she realise that she had no desire whatsoever for another drink.

'It was beautiful, Jack,' she said, returning both to the table. 'The music, I mean. Before everything went wrong. I know you're probably disappointed with how tonight turned out, but you should be proud of what you can do.'

She went to the sink and poured herself a pint of water. She made a mental note that she must remember to get some paracetamol from the bathroom cabinet upstairs, hoping beyond hope that she hadn't polished them off the morning after her last binge.

'Goodnight,' Julie said. Having not received any response from him, Julie went to walk past him and out of the room.

'Wait.' He grabbed her arm as she walked past him. 'I don't want to be alone tonight.' Julie wasn't sure what the appropriate response was to this, so just stood still. Without letting go of her arm, he rose from his chair and stood close to her. Before she knew what was happening, he had brushed her hair away from her shoulder and had kissed her neck.

A combination of shock, indecision, and quite frankly, lust made her knees go weak. She placed one hand on the table to stop herself from stumbling.

'Jack,' she said in a whisper. She was afraid her voice would betray her if she tried anything more. 'I don't think it's a good idea.'

But it was already happening. Placing his wine glass on the table, he positioned himself in front of her. He put a hand on either side of her face, and they kissed with a frenzy that she hadn't known for many years.

There had still been an opportunity to stop there, Julie thought to herself later. They were in the kitchen, for God's sake. On the way to wherever they were going to do the deed, there was a chance that one of them could have come to their senses, and it was highly unlikely that it was going to be the teenage boy. But several bottles of wine and an evening of high drama don't normally lend themselves to good decision making.

Jack took Julie's hand, and silently led her upstairs.

CHAPTER SEVEN

J ulie wasn't able to say what exactly it was that had woken her up. It may have been the ringing in her head reaching fever pitch. Maybe it was how her parched mouth and throat were making it near impossible to swallow. Or perhaps it was the light streaming through the window and assaulting her eyes without mercy. If she had to make an educated guess, she would wager that it was because she was lying on her son's bedroom floor with nothing but the dinosaur blanket that he had owned since early childhood to conceal her shame.

After the debauchery had concluded, Julie had a vague recollection of shifting out of the bed. Unable to make it back to her own bedroom, she had set up camp on the floor with whatever coverings were available to her. She leant forwards and saw that Jack was lying on his front with one arm hanging over the bed frame.

The digital clock on the bedside table showed that it was 7.30. Julie tried to remember whether she had made the effort to put the clocks forward a few months previously. It was beyond her though. She collected her clothes from where they were bunched up in the corner and tried to leave the room with as little noise as possible. Having sex with your son's teenage friend was embarrassing enough. If she had to endure him seeing her naked in the unforgiving light of day, Julie thought she might just keel over and die.

Back safely in her own room, she checked the clock and managed to comprehend that it was definitely half past seven. At least she had about an hour to try and get herself into a fit state before she needed to be at work. There was a glass of stale water next to the bed which she downed without hesitation. In the top drawer of the dresser, the only medication she could find was an old tablet of something ground into dust. Deciding it wasn't worth the risk, Julie donned her dressing gown and made her way to the bathroom.

There was something comforting about the sterile environment that the cold porcelain provided, and Julie spent a moment with her head rested against the wall. Unfortunately, it wasn't enough to counteract the nausea resulting from the consumption of an overwhelming quantity of alcohol. She fell to her knees hard and crawled towards the toilet. Thankfully, she reached the bowl just in time. Initially, she couldn't find the strength to get back to her feet. She allowed herself to slide to the floor, holding her knees against her chest and wondering what in the world she had let herself become. If she didn't have anywhere to be, Julie thought that she would happily stay there all day, content to let the world keep moving around her while she slowly perished.

Without having any perception of an intervening period, Julie woke herself with a sharp intake of breath. Panicked, she looked at her watch and realised that it was now 8.55. She jumped to her feet and immediately regretted it. With time quickly running out before she needed to be at work, Julie splashed some cold water on her face and under her arms. It did nothing to help her feel more alert, but hopefully, it would at least partially address the cloud of alcoholic miasma which must have been emanating from her pores.

By the time she had got back to her bedroom, Julie had worked herself into such a frenzy that she couldn't see the clean uniform that she had left on the chair in the corner. Nor did it occur to her to check the pile of laundry downstairs waiting to be ironed. Instead, she began dragging dirty clothes out of the washing basket with wild abandon. In the very bottom, there was a scrunched and shriveled top that she must have worn several weeks before. With no time to source an alternative, she coated the offending article in a cloud of deodorant and a rather offensive Eau de toilette that Betty had bought her ten Christmases previously.

Once she had put it on, Julie caught sight of the clock in the corner and saw that it was now 9.05. She had no time to consider how ridiculous she looked. She ran down the stairs and slipped on the nearest pair of shoes before pulling violently to open the front door and running out into the street. Only when the door had swung shut behind her and the latch had engaged did Julie remember that she had forgotten her keys.

She sprinted round the side of the house and through the back gate, running straight into the back of the house. Luckily, her instincts had been right. Having no additional key for the front of the house, Julie had given Jack a spare for the back door. He had let them in last night, and Julie was elated to find that he hadn't locked the door after them. However, her excitement was short-lived. As she barreled through the door, she tripped on Jack's sandals which had been left directly inside the back door as usual. Her shin rubbed painfully across the linoleum and left a nasty friction burn where her trouser leg had ridden up. Her first impulse had been to shout for Jack to remonstrate him, before having to remind herself that he wasn't, in fact, her teenage son. The thought of this and her actions of the night before created a new wave of nausea that hit her with renewed conviction.

Her leg continued to throb, but she didn't have time for any self-pity. She grabbed her keys from her handbag which sat open on the kitchen counter and rushed off once again.

After Julie had been sitting in the traffic jam for about twenty minutes, she finally accepted that she was going to be horribly late, and there was nothing that she could do about it.

Looking at her reflection for the first time this morning, she saw that her hair stood at odd angles where she had slept on it. She grabbed at it and did her best to restrain it in a bobble. The problem was that she had intentionally cut her hair short to negate the need to tie it up. The resulting effect was something similar to the hairdressing styling of a toddler. Julie alternated between the two for a few minutes, trying to decide which one was ultimately worse. In the end, she wasn't sure whether she determined that they were both as bad as each other, or if she simply didn't care, but she took the bobble out and threw it in the foot well. She rested her head on the steering wheel until the car behind her pipped its horn to let her know that the traffic had moved on.

Julie finally pulled up in front of the shop at about 10.05. Under normal circumstances, she reckoned that Mr. Peg didn't have much of a sense of the passage of time. In fact, his devotion to his flora was so intense that Julie thought she could probably rock up in the middle of the afternoon, and he still wouldn't realise that anything was amiss.

But today was the day of Mr. Peg's big announcement. Whatever his grand new plan was that would herald monumental changes for the three of them. To that end, both Mike and Mr. Peg were stood outside looking concerned when Julie arrived. Even if they hadn't been, Julie also managed to knock over a sizeable pot on her way out of the car, announcing her arrival with an almighty clatter. Julie had a moment of realisation in which she understood that the look on Mr. Peg's face before had been irritation rather than concern, the latter having been reserved for the big pot which was now the wrong way up.

'Oh God, sorry,' she said, attempting to right it.

She had only made a token effort. Partly, this was because she knew that she wouldn't be able to lift it. Mr. Peg bustled over, and with Mike's help, managed to get the plant the right way up again.

Wanting to be helpful, Julie started grabbing handfuls of the soil that had deposited themselves on the floor and returning them to the pot.

'Julie, Julie, please,' Mr. Peg said desperately, waving his hands. 'You're putting clay into the soil.'

Julie stood there impotently still grasping two handfuls of dirt.

'It doesn't do well in clay,' Mike added helpfully.

'Oh,' Julie said, 'sorry.' She bent back down to the ground and tried to find somewhere discreet to put the soil. As the seconds ticked by, she felt herself becoming more and more flustered. As she walked over to the flowerbed and deposited the dirt, Mike and Mr. Peg stood watching like she was a madwoman.

'Right,' Mr. Peg said as Julie rejoined them, 'now that we've got that sorted, shall we start the team meeting?' He eyed her with irritation as she batted the dirt from her trousers. Julie knew he wouldn't say anything; he was much too passive aggressive for that.

When they got inside, Julie's heart sank slightly at the effort that Mr. Peg had made. He had moved the larger plants from the centre of the room and brought the table from the staff room through. In its centre was something small covered by a cloth. In front of each of the three chairs there was a notebook and a pen. 'We can only keep the shop closed until 11,' Mr. Peg said, shooting another angry glance at Julie, 'otherwise we're going to start losing business. But I wanted to talk to you both about a very promising idea that I've come up with.'

Mr. Peg leaned over the table and revealed a small container of sand that had been covered by the piece of fabric.

'Now,' he said with animation, 'what do you think of when you see this?'

In anticipation of being asked something ridiculous, Mike had looked down at the table as soon as the sand had been revealed. Julie had gone to follow suit but had been too slow. Mr. Peg made eye contact with such a ferocity that it was impossible to break it.

'Sand?' Julie asked, hoping it was the right answer.

'I'm not asking what it is. I'm asking what you think of when you see it.'

'Time?'

'Time? What on earth are you talking about?'

'Time goes through an hourglass.'

A look of exasperation crept over Mr. Peg's face. 'Can we only have sensible answers please?' He looked over to Mike, who was still looking down. With nothing better to work with, he returned his attention to Julie.

'When did you last see sand?' he asked in the tone of a teacher who was starting to realise his pupil was useless.

'You mean those big bags that have been outside of the shop for the last few weeks?'

'Away from work,' he said angrily. It wasn't clear whether he was enraged by Julie specifically or by the realisation that his pitch wasn't as winning as he'd originally thought. Either way, he was starting to look a bit pink.

'Probably Blackpool, about five years ago.'

Mr. Peg clicked his fingers and pointed at her. 'There you go,' he said, his eyes excited, 'and how did you feel when you saw it?'

'Not great,' Julie mumbled.

'Come on, I bet you were like a pig in mud.'

'Not really.'

His shoulders slumped, and he let out a great intake of breath. He made such a show of it that she felt the need to explain herself.

'It was our last holiday,' she said quietly.

'I'm sorry?' Mr. Peg said, sounding haughty now.

'It was my last holiday with Greg. Before he died.'

Mr. Peg looked mortified. He stood motionless for what felt like a painfully long time before his brain re-engaged.

'Michael.' He turned his attention to his other employee, no doubt reasoning that literally anything else would be better than this. 'What about you? When was your last trip to the seaside?'

'I took my Aunty Jean to Bournemouth.'

'There we go. Lovely family trip away,' Mr. Peg said, sounding excited again.

'Before we had to put her in the home.'

'Still a treasured memory together,' he said, sounding less sure of himself now.

'She took all her clothes off and went in the sea. Caught pneumonia. Weren't sure if she was going to make it."

'Christ,' he said instinctively, probably louder than he meant to. 'Could someone please tell me a happy memory that they have had at the beach?'

All three of them sat in silence. When it became clear that Mr. Peg wasn't going to let the topic slide, Julie said, 'We took Harry to Cornwall when he was a baby. He took his first steps on the beach.'

Mr. Peg held his hands up to the heavens. 'Fantastic, absolutely fantastic. Well done, Julie, that's exactly what we need. Think about that every time you're selling Backdoor Beaches.'

Dumfounded, Julie looked over to Mike, but he appeared to be as baffled as she was.

'Backdoor Beaches is the newest innovation in home relaxation. A way to ensure the pleasures of paradise in your own garden.' Mr. Peg recited the clearly memorised text with a worrying intensity in his eyes. 'Does anyone have any questions?'

Mike put up his hand and waited for Mr. Peg to ask him to speak. 'Are we doing the installation?'

'We will. Depending on demand, we may have to hire a few extra hands.'

'I don't know how to do plumbing though. What are we going to do until then?'

'We are only in the business of beach installation, although hopefully in time, we can build a partnership with a pool installer.'

'So, we're just going to be dumping a bloody great amount of sand in people's gardens?'

'Would you say that a waiter dumps food on people's tables in restaurants?'

Mike thought about it for a few seconds. 'I guess so?' he said, as if he wasn't entirely sure.

Mr. Peg sighed. 'If that's how you want to look at it, then yes, that's what we're doing.'

'It sounds a bit like fly tipping,' Julie said. She put her hand up as an afterthought.

'It's not fly tipping if someone asks for it.'

'How are you going to keep the sand in place?' Mike said, keeping his hand raised this time after he spoke. He was obviously anticipating that he would have further questions.

'I'm sorry?'

'How are you going to keep the sand in people's gardens?'

'How do you keep sand in place at the seaside?'

'You don't.'

'Exactly. An authentic experience in your back garden.'

'But that's not one of the good parts about being at the seaside, is it? Sand blowing in your face? Are we going to get a big dog to shit in the sand and encourage people to walk through it too?'

A little chuckle escaped Julie's mouth. Mr. Peg looked at her, unimpressed.

'Are we going to top the sand up? When it blows away?' Buoyed by Julie's amusement, Mike was more sure of himself now, and left his hand rested on the table instead of putting it in the air again.

Mr. Peg didn't answer him. Instead, he went to the table in the corner and came back with two thick paper booklets. He handed one to each of them.

'These are your scripts. Julie, I want you to spend the afternoon learning yours while, Mike, you set up the prototype out in the yard.'

'Mr. Peg.' Julie stood up and put a hand on his arm. She was speaking more kindly now. 'If this is all just because you don't have anything else to do with the sand, you really don't need to.'

'This is a winning business model, my girl. We need to get a corner on the market before everyone starts doing it.'

'Don't you think that's something to think about? That no one else has thought to do this before.'

'I'm sure they said that about Jacuzzis to start with. Sitting there, boiling in your own waters. Look at those chaps now. Millionaires.'

Julie thought that Mr. Peg fundamentally misunderstood what a Jacuzzi was if he thought it involved boiling in your own waters. She had to remind herself that this was a man who had just told her that he thought killing all life in your garden with half a ton of sand was a winning idea. With that in mind, she sat back down and picked up her script.

THE AFTERNOON HAD DRAGGED on much in the way that Julie expected it to. Once she had finished reading through his booklet, Mr. Peg had threatened Julie with having to make cold calls. She had therefore asked him to give her a bit more time to familiarise herself with the material. As soon as he left the room, she settled herself down on the table and promptly went to sleep.

'Big night, was it?' a voice said as its owner gently rocked her awake by the shoulder.

She sat up with a start before realising it was Mike who had woken her up.

'Something like that,' she said. Sitting up and rubbing her eyes, she looked at her watch.

'Christ, it's already lunchtime. I haven't made any calls. What am I going to tell the old man?'

'Tell him you've called everyone already.' He walked over to the kettle and filled it up. 'Not just the people on the return customer list. Everyone in the country. Tell him every one of them told you that it was a shit idea, and they were not interested.'

'I don't think that would go down very well.'

'Is this normal? These grand schemes?'

'He went through a phase of trying to sell jam once, but that was fairly short lived.'

'That, and it didn't put any of the customers in any real danger.'

'I don't think it's as bad as all that.'

'You tell that to Mrs. Brooks. He basically frog marched her into that so called prototype of his. To cut a long story short, she slipped on a wet patch, and Mrs. Fig is now driving her to A&E with a suspected broken hip.'

Julie shook her head. 'It's not a bad idea in theory. The problem is that the execution is absolutely horrendous, and no one in their right mind would buy it. Have you read this?'

Mike poured boiling water over the teabags and then returned to the table taking the catalogue from Julie.

'Common questions to expect from customers,' Mike read aloud. 'Will the sand kill my plants? Is this bad for the environment? How will I keep the sand clean?'

He flicked through a few pages and then returned to the page he had been reading from. 'Wait, where are the answers?'

'There aren't any! That's my point. He must have spent the evening writing a list of every conceivable criticism of his ridiculous plan and then couldn't think of any way to refute them.'

'Listen, I wanted to talk to you about the other day. At the home, with my Aunty Jean.' He handed Julie her tea, and she smiled at him in thanks.

'I'm sorry for unloading on you. It's just that sometimes, I feel like I'm the only sane person in the world, and I can't get anyone else to see sense.'

Julie took a sip of the hot, sweet tea. While it made her stomach lurch, it still made her feel better. There was something comforting about it that she wouldn't be able to define if someone asked her to.

'Are you sure you're not just being over protective? I get a bit like that with Harry sometimes.'

'Who's Harry?'

'My son. Sorry, I don't know why I thought you'd know that. I forget I've only known you a few weeks sometimes.' Julie said it instinctively and because she meant it, but immediately wished she hadn't.

'Oh, right. Well, that's nice. I mean, me too. I mean, I don't mean me, obviously. I feel like I've known you a lot longer too.'

'Well,' Julie said, feeling awkward. 'That's good then.'

They sat for a few moments in not quite an uncomfortable silence, but definitely one that had an uneasy air about it. Thankfully, it was broken when Mike remembered Julie's question.

'If your boy started copping off with someone who you thought was wrong though, you'd say something, wouldn't you? It doesn't matter how many people tell you that you're being crazy. If you thought that person you loved was going to get hurt, you would have to do something about it.'

'I suppose so.' Julie thought about when Harry had been a baby, and how true the sentiment that Mike was expressing would have been. How she would have happily murdered anyone who threatened to hurt her little boy. Of course, she still felt that instinct now, and if he ever needed her, she would instantly be there. But there was something more detached about their lives now. She wondered whether she would even know if he was in any serious trouble. Would it even occur to Harry to let her know? Probably not.

Mike said something to her that she'd missed.

'I'm sorry?'

'I said, you have a friend of his staying with you at the moment, don't you?'

In the odd parallel space that was Mr. Peg's shop, she had almost managed to forget the shame of the night before. With Mike's words, she felt her brain swell and rage at the realisation that in a few short hours, she would have to confront the living embodiment of her recent ridiculous behaviour.

She nodded meekly and felt a wave of nausea rush over her again.

72

'Must be hell having someone else living in the house after getting used to being by yourself.'

Julie made a small noise in the affirmative and pretended to return her attention to the printed booklet before her.

'Sorry, have I said something wrong?' Mike asked.

She smiled down at the pages but didn't look up. 'Just trying to give this another look before Mr. Peg gets back.'

'Okay then,' Mike said, looking confused. 'I guess I better get back to the prototype then.' He waved his hands mockingly and smiled as he said 'prototype,' in the hopes of recapturing the comradery of a few moments ago. Julie gave Mike another small smile but did nothing else to encourage him.

Disheartened, the animation fell from his face, and he headed out the double doors.

CHAPTER EIGHT

J ulie arrived home to find the cul-de-sac in its normal subdued state. The weather hadn't been unseasonably warm. However, there was definitely an awareness that it was the height of summer, and that no relief should be expected in the immediate future. Parking up in her normal space, the heat met her instantly when she opened the car door. Brian was leaning against the front wall of his garden, his crutches propped up against him. He had his arms crossed over his significant gut. He was staring across the road with a furrowed brow.

Julie readied herself against his normal seedy onslaught but was unexpectedly met by silence.

'Alright, Brian?' Julie said, wondering what on Earth was wrong with her for voluntarily entering into a conversation with the man.

'Alright, thanks.'

Julie was torn. She desperately didn't want to speak to Brian, but this sultry silence was so out of character for him that she felt she had no choice but to persevere.

'Jack's done a good job of the garden, hasn't he?' She peered over the wall and inspected the small rectangle of grass that lay beyond. If she was honest with herself, he had done a perfunctory job at best, but it served as a decent talking point.

Brian moved his head towards her with a jerk and gave her a dirty look. Before she could ask him what she had done wrong, he was limping back up to the house.

Unsure what had just happened but not entirely convinced that she cared, Julie crossed the road towards her own house. As she walked up the garden path, she could see Jack talking to someone across the threshold. When Jack saw her over the shoulder of his visitor, he looked startled. Julie couldn't hear what they were saying, but it was obvious from their body language that there was something furtive in their exchange. The man that Jack was talking to briefly turned to look at her, and Julie thought that she recognised him, although for the life of her, she couldn't think where she would have come into contact with such a character.

Julie got within a few feet of them, and the conversation abruptly ended. The other man gave Jack something in a cupped hand and then went to leave. His jogging bottoms were so loose that he kept one hand on the waistband as he walked. He leaned to one side as he went, and while he may have thought this gave him the air of a gangster, it did nothing but confirm Julie's expectations that he was a prized prat.

He passed Julie at the garden's narrowest point, coming within a few inches of her. With no warning, he jerked his head forward as if he was making a move to kiss her. Startled, Julie took a step away from him and slipped off the garden path. She stumbled as her foot hit the grass behind her at an awkward angle.

'Easy, sweetheart,' he said, sounding pleased with himself, 'just trying to be friendly.'

Before Julie could form a response, he was down the garden path and through the gate.

By the time that she reached Jack, who was still standing at the front door, Julie was no longer shocked, just irritated.

'What the bloody hell was all that about?' she said sharply.

'Don't mind him. He's a bit of a wind up merchant.' Jack's tone was playful. The casual observer would think that he was talking to a toddler who had smeared mashed potatoes down the kitchen wall. He took a step backwards, allowing Julie to enter the house.

'What are you doing messing around with people like that?'

'What do you mean people like that?'

'You know.' Julie struggled to define what she meant. The words 'chav,' and 'common,' crossed her mind, although she couldn't bring herself to say them. She became more irritated because Jack knew exactly what she meant, as anyone else would when faced with someone who was so unpleasant.

'People who make life harder for everyone else.' She noticed that the flowers that she had rescued from Mr. Peg had shed the majority of their petals, and yet were somehow still going strong. Thinking it about it again, Mr. Peg was probably right in his conclusion that they were a weed. No flower could last for almost four weeks in a dank hallway.

It was only after that she had picked the stray petals up that she remembered how they stained your fingers. She wiped her hand down the side of her trousers and wanted to yell in frustration as they left a messy mark on one side.

'Jesus, Julie. He's just a mate, and he didn't even come inside. I don't get what the problem is.'

'The problem is that this isn't your house, Jack, and you can't be inviting criminals round.'

'Oh, so just because he's wearing a tracksuit, that makes him a criminal, does it?'

'You know what I mean.'

'No, explain it to me, Julie. Does the urge to rob a corner shop come over every teenager in England when they put on their first pair of trainers?'

'Stop being ridiculous.' She walked away from him and into the kitchen. He followed her. At the sink, she attempted to wash the pigment from her hands. When that didn't work, she started to scrub at the stain on her trousers with a scouring pad.

'I'm not the one condemning an entire generation because they wear sporty clothes.' It was all such a joke to him; she could hear it in his voice. He thought everything she said was ridiculous. More than that, he thought she was ridiculous.

'What did he give to you then?' Julie spun around to face him, angry now.

He didn't look quite so cocky for a moment.

'What?'

'What did he hand you, just before he left? Are you telling me that was legal? Little packet of sugar, was it?'

A nasty grin spread over his face.

'Why are you getting so worked up, Julie? Are you having a hot flush? Bit of a problem for you old girls, isn't it?' He slowly looked her up and down.

All of Julie's righteous indignation left her. Her face flushed, and her legs felt weak.

'Are you having another one now?' he said, adopting faux concern. 'Do you need me to get you anything? Do you need to sit down; can I get you a chair?'

'Why are you being like this?' she said in a voice as small as she felt.

'I'm just trying to look after you, Julie.' He closed the gap between them and placed a hand on her arm. 'I'm here for whatever you need.' All of a sudden, she felt sick. She felt like if a man didn't touch her again until the rapture, it would still be much too soon. She shrugged her shoulder hard, and he moved his arm away from her.

'I don't want people like that in my house.'

'Easy darling, he wasn't in the…,' but Julie interrupted him before he could finish.

'I don't care, Jack. I don't care what clever line you've got prepared,' she said, much more loudly. 'I don't want people like that in my house.'

'Bloody hell, calm down, dear.' He went to the fridge and took a beer from it. She felt her fury anew, mostly because she had actually felt the need to buy beer especially for the little shit. 'I only usually see you getting worked up like that in the bedroom. Or is that the problem? You're feeling a bit frisky?'

'Don't talk to me like that,' Julie said in a raised voice.

'Or what?' Jack slammed his beer down on the kitchen table unopened. 'What are you going to do? Throw me out? Boo fucking hoo. Do you think I need anything from you? Do you not think there's a hundred others like you that I could get into bed just like that?'

'Why don't you go then? Why don't you take your little guitar and your bag of trendy clothes and fuck off?'

They both stood there in silence, eyes locked on one another. Julie couldn't believe that she had sworn. Jack, no doubt, was deciding whether to call her bluff when he had no job or anywhere else to go. The stalemate was broken with a knock at the door. He followed her back into the hallway when she went to see who was there.

'Julie, listen, listen,' he said following her. 'I'm sorry, alright? I didn't mean it.' He moved in front of her, blocking her way to the front of the house. 'Why don't I make us something nice for dinner, and we can talk about it?'

Julie was having none of it. She felt like his mask had slipped, and instead of the charming young man who had made her feel wanted and appreciated, she could now see who he really was. He was the cock that the woman in the bar last night had been talking about. Someone who got what they wanted and didn't care what the consequences were for the people around them.

'You can stay for as long as you like, Jack.' Julie's voice was still harsh and probably a bit too loud. 'But last night was a mistake. I'm your friend's mum, and that's it.'

In the way of a response, he scoffed in her face and stormed upstairs.

When she opened the front door, it was the last person in the world she expected standing on the other side.

'I have been knocking for a while,' Mrs. Sinclair said, 'but no one answered. I was about to give up.' A tall and slender woman with beautifully silky, long, black hair, she had made Julie feel incredibly frumpy once upon a time. Now though, the contoured lines of her face had a haunted quality about them, no doubt the result of having to surrender your life in the care of another. Mrs. Sinclair continued to wear her hair down, but it was now frizzy and lined with a few telltale strands of grey.

'Yes, sorry, I was at the back of the house,' Julie said.

Mrs. Sinclair held out the hedge clippers she was holding. Julie stared at them vacantly for a few seconds and then looked back at Mrs. Sinclair.

'The gardener left them on the patio yesterday. I thought he might need them for one of his other jobs.'

'Right,' Julie said. As she took them, Julie could hear Jack banging down the stairs. When she turned to look at him, she saw he had paused at the bottom step, holding his guitar and looking at the two women in conversation.

'Mrs. Sinclair was bringing your hedge clippers back,' Julie said, holding them out to him.

'They're not mine,' he said, pushing between them both. Julie had to move her head back to avoid being hit in his face with the guitar. Before Julie could question him any further, he was away from the house and out of sight.

Julie turned her attention back to Mrs. Sinclair, who was now making her way down the garden path.

'Excuse me,' Julie called, 'these aren't ours.' Mrs. Sinclair took no notice and continued to walk away from her.

JULIE SPENT the evening alone lying on the sofa. For her dinner, she had found something in the freezer and had microwaved it without much thought. Lying there with the television blaring unwatched in the background, she had felt defeated, both physically and mentally. This particular Sunday had taken everything she had to endure with nothing to show for it.

She had been craving her bed all day. As soon as she had showered and climbed into its soft embrace, she knew that it was going to be one of those days that despite being desperately tired, her sleep would be fitful and offering no real respite. She knew from past experience that you could be on the verge of collapse, but it didn't matter if whatever was happening in your life was keeping you wired. In those situations, like the one she now found herself in, there was no chance of real sleep.

Lying awake, Julie couldn't help replaying the events of the last few days. The argument with Jack had felt cathartic. There didn't seem to be any ambiguity between them any longer. Julie found it hard to recover the shame and regret that she had suffered from so acutely earlier in the day. As is often the case when you are able to analyse the events of an evening of drinking with some hindsight, it all now just felt a bit awkward. She didn't dread seeing Jack, but she didn't really want to. She knew that she had told him he could stay for as long as he wanted. Now though, she thought that she would have to ask him to leave. There was no real point in him staying in Brumpton anyway, now that he had ballsed up his job prospects entirely. This small point of decision gave her a temporary sense of peace, and she was able to drift off.

She was woken up by what she thought was the sound of the back door opening. The clock on the bedside table told her it was 1.15am. Part of her wanted to go downstairs and see if it had been Jack returning home. She thought about going to tell Jack now that she would like him to leave today. Wearing her middle aged lady pajamas in her duvet cocoon, she suddenly felt very vulnerable. The primitive part of her brain that craved the warm and comfortable was telling her that, of course, it would be a mistake to leave the safety of this room. What on earth had a hundred thousand generations of humanity toiled for if she was just going to put herself in danger for the sake of ejecting her unwanted guest half a day early?

On the edge of indecision, Julie then heard a noise that she thought was the front door opening. She lay there trying not to breathe so she could better hear the noises downstairs. Silence, she was sure of it. Turning onto her side, she attempted to put the whole silly situation out of her head and went back to sleep.

Julie was woken again by the unmistakable sound of the front door slamming closed. Irritated, she realised that it must have been Jack coming home from whatever he had been doing all night. She surprised herself by falling back to sleep fairly quickly. However, after what she was sure was only a short time, Julie realised that she was awake and facing the far bedroom wall. Nothing drastic had woken her this time. She hadn't been startled or thought that she was in any danger, but she was sure there was something not quite right. She turned over to look at the clock and saw that it was a little after three o'clock. Her eyes drifted to the other side of the room. It took her a few moments to process what she was seeing. Jack was standing in the doorway. He was backlit by the landing light, and she struggled to focus on him, her eyes still sleepy. The mess of his hair was still easily identifiable. She could also just about make out his bohemian uniform; the baggy grey vest hanging off his shoulders and the cargo shorts hanging off his hips.

'What do you want, Jack?' Julie asked groggily, shielding her eyes from the light.

Jack made some non-committal noises, hovering on the threshold.

'Are you drunk?'

He made a sort of deep grunting sound in the back of his throat which Julie thought was a yes. When she went to sit up, he took half a step backwards out into the hallway. She thought he might be trying to get her to come with him back to his room for a repeat of last night's antics perhaps.

Thinking of the best way to let him down gently, Julie said, 'It's really late. I need to go back to sleep.'

Jack didn't answer her.

'We'll talk in the morning, okay?' Accepting defeat, Jack left and closed the door behind him. The room was once again plunged into darkness. Julie felt a bit uneasy. She told herself that there wasn't anything to be afraid of. Jack wasn't dangerous, just a bit drunk. In a moment of panic, Julie jumped out of bed, took the dining room chair that was positioned in front of her dressing table and attempted to jam it under the door handle. She knew it wasn't logical. In fact, she appreciated that it was ridiculous behaviour. The only practical use would probably be to warn her when someone opened the door and it sent the chair clattering forward, but it made her feel better. She didn't think she would get any meaningful rest now, but still closed her eyes, happy to accept any small disconnect with consciousness that was possible.

A few minutes later, before she fell asleep for the last time, Julie heard something that sounded larger than a car driving into the street. A few seconds later, its engine was shut off and the driver's obnoxiously loud music died. Intrigued, Julie scrambled onto her knees and saw that the van belonged to a 24 hour plumber who was walking up Mrs. Sinclair's drive.

'Alright, love? Got a problem with your plumbing?' She could easily hear his jaunty cockney tones travelling over the dead of the night, although Mrs. Sinclair's response wasn't audible. Satisfied that she wasn't missing out on anything interesting, Julie lay back down.

AT EIGHT O'CLOCK, her alarm started blaring much too soon for Julie's taste. It took her longer than usual to find her phone and silence it. She heard an unusual hum of activity outside the window for this early in the morning.

Looking outside, she saw two paramedics returning their supplies to the back of an ambulance before getting inside themselves and driving away. The vehicle had been parked in front on the other side of the street. Mr. Sinclair must have had a funny turn in the night, Julie thought.

She didn't feel rested, just groggy. She could have happily gone back to sleep for another few hours. It felt like nothing in the world was worth achieving today, especially not selling great quantities of sand to unassuming pensioners. Why not tell Mr. Peg she wasn't coming in? Better yet, why not tell Mr. Peg that she wouldn't ever be coming back. She tried to remind herself that it was much easier to have a sense of perspective when you haven't spent all evening lounging around the house feeling sorry for yourself.

Dragging herself from bed, she moved the chair from in front of the bedroom door and walked towards the bathroom. The door to Jack's room stood ajar. Julie was about to avert her eyes, not wanting to catch Jack in flagrante delicto when she noticed something odd. She saw that Jack was lying on his back with his left arm hanging over the bed, hand facing up. Julie thought that lying in such a way couldn't be comfortable. He must really be out of it.

'Jack,' Julie said, pushing the door open. 'Are you okay?'

The smell of vomit hit her as soon as she entered the room. Her first reaction was not revulsion, but irritation that she would probably be the one who would need to clean it up. However, when she noticed that Jack's eyes were half closed and the source of the offending smell was still pooled in his mouth and crusted down his cheeks, that emotion soon turned to dread and then nausea. There was a red pinprick on his arm, and what she expected was the offending needle lying on the floor a few feet from the bed.

Julie ran to the bathroom, and for the second day in a row, she started her morning by retching into the toilet. In between the violent heaves of her stomach, she made the decision that she definitely wasn't going to work today.

CHAPTER NINE

Julie sat with her elbows resting on her knees. She had only drank a small amount of the coffee that had been given to her. Instead, she had clutched the mug with both hands wrapped around it as soon as it had been cool enough to hold. It didn't provide much of a comfort, but at least it stopped her moving her arms around every ten seconds.

'It's alright to be shocked,' the police woman said. She was sitting opposite Julie at the kitchen table. 'At least we know you didn't kill him.' She chuckled to herself and dipped her head in an attempt to catch Julie's eye, though she continued to stare at the surface before her. When she realised that her attempt at jollity hadn't quite hit the mark, she suddenly became panicked.

'Oh God, I shouldn't have said that, sorry.' There was an awkward pause when she searched for something to remedy the situation. 'This must be a very difficult time for you, and I'm here to help you with anything that you need.' This last line sounded as if it had been quoted verbatim from whatever official guidelines that she was working from.

'Thank you,' Julie said, purely because she didn't want this ridiculous person to keep yammering on. Julie had answered the front door in a haze. She told them where the body was and had then gone to the kitchen to wait for further instruction. Half an hour later, DS Winnington had arrived, insisting that Julie must call her Dawn. The silence between them had been punctuated by Dawn's occasional interjections of, 'How are you feeling?' and 'This must be really hard for you.'

'I'll put the kettle on again, shall I?' Dawn asked without really asking. Julie said nothing. She hadn't encountered a Family Liaison Officer before, but the making of hot beverages, either wanted or not, appeared to be a very key part of their role. 'Coffee is it?' Dawn stood over Julie who gave her no answer. She held out her hand for the cup. Julie didn't move. Of all the situations where you shouldn't be forced to socialise with irritating strangers, finding a dead body in your son's bedroom should really have been at the top of the list. For a moment, Julie thought that Dawn, standing next to her with her arm outstretched, might be considering wrenching the mug from her hands. She eventually thought better of it and went back to the kettle.

Julie could hear a constant bustle of activity from the hallway. People coming and going. A continued stream of invaders tramping up their stairs. She could tell by how heavy their footfall was that they hadn't taken their shoes off. What a mess they would be making. She reminded herself that she hadn't hoovered the stairs in months before she had someone staying in the house, and she would no doubt return to that mindset now that she was once again alone.

'Where do you keep your cups?' Dawn asked, already opening cupboard doors. 'Ooh, you've got that nice pasta sauce. Bit weird him looking round people's houses like that, wasn't it? You'll have to tell me what it's like. I've never had it before.' Even when she found the correct cabinet, she continued to rummage through the kitchen.

'Are you allowed to do that?' Julie suddenly thought to ask, looking at Dawn for the first time. 'Don't you need a warrant?'

Dawn spun around, terror plastered across her face. 'I was only looking for some sugar. I don't take it in tea, but I like a bit in my coffee.' Even faced with a possible abuse of police powers, Dawn managed to include some benign chatter with every sentence that left her mouth. 'My mum got me into it, you see. Horrible habit, isn't it?'

Julie wasn't really bothered. She just wanted the insufferable woman to be quiet. She turned back to the table and continued to sit quietly.

A few minutes later, she placed the hot drink in front of Julie. 'Were you worried that I might find the murder weapon?' she chuckled to herself again.

'He died of an overdose,' Julie said, without looking at her.

'Yes, of course, I'm so sorry.' There was a further pause in conversation that Dawn felt obliged to fill. 'I used to be a hairdresser, you see. People expect a bit of chatter there. Otherwise, it all feels a bit awkward, doesn't it? Sitting there, staring at each other in the mirror.' She did a little laugh. 'Set me up for this job though, didn't it? Listening to people's problems, giving them advice.'

Julie wondered how often Dawn had needed to support a customer who had found a dead body in her previous life. There were some fairly rough areas around here, so it was a distinct possibility.

Dawn made several more attempts to engage Julie in conversation. Not just about how she was handling Jack's death. She also asked where Julie had bought the kitchen blinds from, who 'that nice blonde boy was,' whilst pointing at Harry's picture on the fridge, and finally, whether she could recommend a good Chinese takeaway in the area because her usual one had recently been shut down by the Food Standards Agency. When none of that managed to draw Julie into a conversation, Dawn took her phone out of her pocket.

Julie had been lost in her own thoughts when she became aware of a man's voice with a bit more presence speaking from the hall.

'Where is it?' he asked with professional detachment. Someone muttered a reply.

'Very good. And the old lady?' The voice again responded, hopefully telling the man that she was, in fact, only forty two.

'Right, body first, witness second,' he said. Julie heard their voices becoming more distant as they made their way upstairs. Dawn remained oblivious, giggling at some innocuous content on her smartphone.

Julie listened to the police walking around upstairs. She wondered whether they had kept themselves confined to the crime scene, or whether they were moving through the house's upper floor indiscriminately. Her question was answered with the flush of the toilet. It was less the invasion of privacy that bothered her and more the realisation that she hadn't cleaned the bathroom floor in god knows how long.

After a further wait of about fifteen minutes, a middle aged man appeared in the doorway of the kitchen with a young constable behind him. He took a step into the room and went to greet her, before seeing Dawn still sitting on her phone with a dopey smile plastered across his face.

'DS Winnington,' he said threateningly.

'Mmmm?' Dawn said, without looking up.

'May I ask what it is that you are doing?'

'Best dog videos of 2019. Absolutely fantastic.' So engrossed was Dawn in these entertaining canines, the introduction of a male voice to the proceedings hadn't come as a surprise to her.

'Dawn? I mean, DS Winnington?' The tall officer said from behind the inspector.

'Yeah, in a minute.'

'DS Winnington,' the inspector shouted.

Dawn jumped in her seat, dropping her phone on the table with a clatter.

'Oh fuck,' she said scrambling to her feet. She stood to attention with her hands behind her back. 'Sorry sir. The victim, I mean, Mrs. Giles had expressed a wish to have some time to herself to rest so I...,' She paused to think. 'So I was sending an urgent email that I hadn't had a chance to before I came on duty.'

'Was it to the producers of 'Best Dog Videos of 2019?' He asked dryly. 'Do you have urgent business with them?'

'Right, yes, I forgot I'd said that. You see, after I'd sent the email...'

'DS Winnington,' the inspector interrupted, 'I'd very much like to get to the matter at hand. You might remember the reason we're here?'

He paused until Dawn answered, 'Yes, sir.'

'Perhaps you share my view that this may be slightly more pressing than your dog video?' He paused again.

'Yes sir.'

His eyes lingered on her a few more moments before he turned his attention to Julie.

'Mrs. Giles,' he said with the practised smile of sympathy. 'My name is Detective Inspector Morris. This young man here is Detective Constable Rowntree.' His eyes returned to Dawn, still standing with her back absolutely perpendicular to the ground. 'And I believe you have already met our Family Liaison Officer, DS Winnington. I know this must be a very distressing time for you, but I was hoping that you would be willing to answer a few questions.'

Julie tried to speak and realised that her throat was impossibly dry. She immediately started to cough. After being prompted by her superior officer, Dawn provided Julie with a glass of water. Only then was she able to tell the inspector that yes, of course she would answer any questions he had.

'Have you managed to get hold of his mum?' Julie said, chastising herself that she hadn't thought to ask before now.

The inspector nodded solemnly. 'Mr. and Mrs. Harper were notified by their local police force and are travelling now to view the body.'

Julie felt sick. It was impossible to imagine what it was like to lose a child, let alone finding out by some stranger knocking on your door. She realised that she would need to tell Harry. Maybe he would come home for the funeral. At least that was something to look forward to.

'How did you know the young man in question?' the inspector asked, all business now.

'He was a friend of my son's. Jack, his name was Jack. He had found some work in the local area and had asked to stay with me.'

The young constable took rapid notes in his police man's notebook. Julie was surprised to see it. She had expected that they would all carry those little computers around with them now.

'And how well did you know Mr. Harper?'

'Well, he was living in my house.' Julie began to wring her hands nervously in her lap. 'We'd eat meals together when he wasn't at work in the evenings, that sort of thing.'

'There wasn't another dimension to your relationship?' DI Morris stared at her with an intensity that made Julie feel uneasy. He looked short next to the beanpole constable standing next to him but was probably around the five foot ten mark. There wasn't a single hair on his pasty head, which made his dark, bushy eyebrows and the full mustache on his top lip even more distinctive.

'There were a few evenings when we would have a glass of wine together. Chat, that kind of thing.' Julie found herself nodding more than she normally would. She thought it might be a subconscious effort to try to convince the policeman that she wasn't holding anything back. Unfortunately, when she came to this realisation, she tried to overcompensate and then began to hold her head very rigidly facing forward and not moving it when it would have been natural to do so.

DI Morris struggled to find the right words for a few moments. 'What I am trying to ask you, Mrs. Giles, is..' He paused again. He looked pained even trying to get the words out of his mouth. 'Was there a physical component to your interactions?'

'I'm sorry, I don't understand what you're asking me?'

'Did you know one another carnally?'

'Are you asking me if we had sex?'

The inspector's face flushed with such severity and so rapidly that anyone who hadn't heard his preceding question would be forgiven for thinking that he was having a stroke.

'That's correct,' he stammered, averting his eyes for the first time.

'I don't see how that's relevant.' She tried to sound indignant despite feeling embarrassed. It led to her shouting slightly.

'It may have a bearing on our investigation,' said DI Morris, who was clearly mortified at having to press the point.

'If it ever does, I will answer the question.' Julie hoped she looked haughty instead of homicidal. She wasn't sure if she was pulling it off.

'I think it may already be.' He was recovering his composure now, remembering that it was, in fact, his job to ask such questions, and that he wasn't doing it out of some perverse pleasure. 'There is some evidence of sexual activity with the body.'

'You mean after death?' Julie said, horrified that she was even being asked the question. 'I'm very happy to give you a definite no on that one.'

'Heavens, no.' The detective became so flustered that he struggled to get his words out. 'What I mean is... What I'm asking is...,' He then started to cough uncontrollably, almost like he was allergic to situations this awkward.

'There is some evidence that Mr. Harper engaged in sexual activity shortly before his death,' DC Rowntree interjected. The Detective Inspector didn't look grateful for his young constable's help, more annoyed that it had been necessary. He scowled at DC Rowntree, no doubt making a note to admonish him later for his impertinence.

'Can I ask what evidence?' Julie said.

'There were some used… contraceptives in the waste paper bin,' DI Morris said, taking command of the situation again. His face had contorted when he was forced to say 'contraceptives.'

'Right,' Julie said. 'Yes, then.' She saw no reason to deny it, embarrassing as it may be. It didn't mean that she had killed him.

'Yes?'

'Yes, we had sex. Once, drunk, the other day.'

'And can I ask, did you pay Mr. Harper for his services?'

Julie once again looked agog. 'No!' she said, now feeling genuinely outraged.

'There was a large quantity of bills found in the victim's bedroom.'

'And because of that, you think he was a gigolo?'

'It isn't necessarily a ridiculous conclusion to come to,' the Detective Inspector said, now sounding a bit put out himself. 'A young man living in the house of a…,' he paused a second too long for Julie's liking, 'an older woman that isn't his relative. You can appreciate what the visual is like, I'm sure.'

Julie continued to stare at him aghast.

'Or perhaps you were helping the victim find clients within the local area.'

'I'm sorry, are you seriously asking me if I was his madam?'

DI Morris raised an eyebrow at her, the question hanging in the air between them. 'It's not as unusual as you may think,' he said finally.

'I work in a garden centre!'

'Not a very lucrative profession, is it? A little bit on the side would be very helpful. Fairly hard to afford a house of this size on a shop worker's salary.'

'If you must know, I used my husband's life insurance to pay off the remainder of our mortgage.' Julie had hoped that this would throw the inspector off balance, but his glare remained. Clearly, it was only bedroom matters that rendered him insensible.

'Were you aware of Mr. Harper's financial situation?'

'You mean all those notes? I asked him about it, and he said that he had been doing a lot of gardening for the neighbours.'

One of the inspector's eyebrows raised.

'I'm not saying it's true. I'm just telling you what he told me.'

'I see. Which neighbours was he providing gardening services for?'

'Brian at number 30, and Mrs. Sinclair at number 32.'

'Are they especially big gardens?'

'I have never had the pleasure of being invited into them, but if they're anything like mine, then no, not that big.'

'Make a note, Constable,' DI Morris said, despite the fact that DC Rowntree had been taking notes of the entire conversation.

'Can you think of anywhere else that Mr. Harper may have received the funds from? You weren't paying him for anything yourself?' Again the eyebrow was cocked.

'He did a bit of painting for me. The outsides of the windows and the sill in the small bedroom, but that's it.'

'And you don't know anyone with whom he associated?'

'The people he worked with, maybe? And well, there was this man here the other day.'

'Be specific please.'

'The day before yesterday. When I got home from work, Jack was talking to a man on the doorstep. He handed him something before he left.'

'An illegal substance?'

'I don't know. I didn't see.'

'Were you aware that Mr. Harper used recreational drugs?'

'I know that he smoked some…,' Julie paused, realising that she might be about to implicate herself in something that she was actually guilty of.

'Cannabis? Is that what you were going to say, Mrs. Giles?'

She looked down at her lap guiltily.

'Are you aware that Cannabis is a Class B drug, the possession of which can lead to up to 5 years in prison, an unlimited fine or both?'

She didn't know what to say, so remained silent.

'Is it your belief that Mr. Harper was selling drugs?'

Julie was about to answer before being interrupted by the sound of raised voices in the hall.

'I don't bloody care what this is. I'm coming through, boy.'

There was a noise that distinctively sounded like someone being jabbed in the stomach with a walking cane and then Mrs. McGrath appeared in the doorway of the kitchen.

A moment passed when all five inhabitants of the room said nothing to each other. Julie started to feel anxious, as if it was her role to introduce everyone present and apologise for the old lady barging in. Then she remembered that Mrs. McGrath wasn't her responsibility, especially when she decided to rock up invited.

'Hello, Maz,' Mrs. McGrath said, giving DI Morris a wicked little grin.

The police inspector looked so incensed that his mustache started trembling with rage.

'Mrs. McGrath, you know full well....'

'Oh, it's Mrs. McGrath now, is it?'

He took a moment to compose himself. 'Moira, I would appreciate it if you called me Detective Inspector Morris while I am undertaking official duties. Furthermore...'

Mrs. McGrath snorted derisively. 'Furthermore! Hark at you.'

'Now really isn't the time.'

Jimmy looked uncomfortable at this exchange, although there was something of a smile around the corners of his mouth. Meanwhile, Julie stared on with absolute incredulity. Dawn had also forgotten the stern professional stance she had taken at the arrival of DI Morris and instead was gawking with rapt abandon.

'Calm down, Maz, I'm not here for you. I'm here to be a good neighbour. Hello, Jimmy,' she smiled at the constable standing behind the Inspector. 'How have you been?' The constable looked up and gave her a friendly nod before looking away from the quarrelling pair again.

'Are the two of you well acquainted?' DI Morris asked Julie.

'Yeah, me and her go way back,' Mrs. McGrath answered before Julie could say anything.

'You and who, sorry?' he said, looking at her slyly.

'Her sitting at the table. Next door neighbours, aren't we?'

'Could you confirm her name please?' DI Morris said with a clever little look on his face. 'For our records.'

'Piss off, Maz.' she replied without missing a beat. 'Who do you think you're talking to? You don't need to know someone's name to know them.'

'It is of no interest to me whether you two are bosom buddies or if you don't know the woman from Adam. You have no rights in this house, and you are not entitled to be present when the police formally question a witness, whatever you may think.'

Mrs. McGrath folded her arms. 'Has she been arrested?'

'Well,' he said, the mustache rustling again.

'Because it would be very strange to arrest a suspect and then question them in their kitchen.'

The inspector failed to think of a winning retort, and the kitchen remained in silence.

'Okay, then,' Mrs. McGrath said, clapping her hands and looking about the happiest that Julie had ever seen her. 'While my neighbour is happy to aid your investigation, she is currently in shock. She will therefore be staying with me while you finish examining the crime scene. When she is feeling well enough, you can arrange a suitable time to meet with her again.' The words, professional and considered, sounded alien coming from Mrs. McGrath's mouth.

The inspector said nothing in response. He just continued to stare at the old woman with absolute fury. Mrs. McGrath took a step closer to Julie, and it was only then that she remembered that this farce was something that she was actually a part of. Events kept taking such strange turns that it was hard to reconcile them with real life.

She stood up from her chair feeling befuddled.

'Can you pack a bag?' Mrs. McGrath asked, addressing her for the first time.

'I can, but I don't really want to go upstairs again.'

'Right,' Mrs. McGrath said, charging off in the direction of the stairs.

'You can't go up there,' the detective said, finding his voice again, 'it's a crime scene.'

'Where do you keep your bras?' Mrs. McGrath said, shouting the last word in the inspector's face. He immediately started to redden. 'In your son's bedroom?'

Julie shook her head, although she didn't think the insane old woman really wanted an answer.

'What about your knickers?' Again, she directed the end of the sentence at the inspector in a voice slightly too loud for common discourse. 'Keep any of those in his chest of drawers?'

Julie once again shook her head, although Mrs. McGrath didn't look at her. 'We should be fine then, ey, Maz?' She gave him a smile which could be mistaken for pleasant if you didn't know Mrs. McGrath and left the room.

Julie took her keys out of her handbag and left them on the counter. 'Could you lock the door when you leave, please?' In their place, she picked up Jack's back door key that he had carelessly deposited on the side.

She left the three of them standing there in silence and went to wait for Mrs. McGrath in the hall. There was still a steady stream of human traffic coming in and out of the house, men in those white plastic suits that you see on the television mainly. She noticed that the flowers she had brought home at work were in a sorry state, some of their stems broken. No doubt they had been a casualty of some particularly clumsy policeman.

Mrs. McGrath appeared at the top of the stairs. In one hand, she carried a gym bag that she had unearthed from God knows where. She knocked a few pictures askew as she descended, the staircase being too narrow to accommodate both the bag and her cane. As they went to leave, Julie saw Jack's sandals on the rack by the front door. Shoes that this young man with his beautiful voice would never wear again. She felt unsettled, like something wasn't quite right. Maybe it was because her lodger had died in the house the night before, and now, the place was full of police officers. It was then that for the first time since she had found Jack dead that she didn't feel sick or panicked that there was a body in her house. She just felt sad.

CHAPTER TEN

Mrs. McGrath dropped the gym bag at the bottom of the stairs and stomped off towards the kitchen. Julie stood immobile, taking her surroundings in.

The positioning of everything in the house was an exact reflection of her own. Instead of the living room branching off to the left of the entryway, it was situated on the right, with the trend continuing for the rest of the house that was immediately visible. On this day especially, which was the strangest she had experienced so far, Julie found the effect incredibly jarring.

Much like her own house, there was no window in the hall, giving it a gloomy quality. Julie had counteracted this by painting the walls a shade of sky blue to give the impression that you could, in fact, see the sky. Mrs. McGrath had gone a slightly different route and elected to paint the walls a dark rouge. There was no dirt to speak of, but the entryway did seem to be incredibly dusty. On closer inspection, Julie saw that it was only the top half of the walls that were caked with this layer of dust. Throughout the day, Julie saw this was a common theme in the rest of the house and realised that it was because Mrs. McGrath couldn't reach the higher points in the rooms. Of course, the old woman couldn't ask for any help with the cleaning.

'What are you doing standing there?' Mrs. McGrath said, reappearing at the end of the hall.

'I wasn't sure where you wanted me.'

'In your own bloody house, ideally. You want a drink?'

She went back into the kitchen, and Julie thought it would be the wisest course of action to follow.

Much like the hall, the kitchen had been cleaned to the minimum standard required for hygienic living. No efforts had been made to improve the aesthetic of the room. It was the kind of kitchen designed for cooking, not entertaining. The sort of room you would expect to find in the galley of a boat or in a prison, not in someone's home.

'I'm sure I can find someone else to stay with, if I'm in the way,' Julie said, although she wasn't sure who. She could always go and stay with her sister, Amanda, but she lived just outside Birmingham. She thought of all those people who had been so kind when Greg had died and how she had disregarded their company with apathy, if not cruelty. She winced to think that many of them would likely still be willing to offer their homes to her, despite the years of neglect that she had subjected them to.

'Sit down, will you?' Mrs. McGrath said. She took a teapot off the shelf above the cooker and plonked it down on the side. Still holding her cane in her hand, she took the lid off the caddy and shook four bags into the pot.

'Actually, do you have coffee?' Julie asked, taking a seat at the oak table in the middle of the room.

Mrs. McGrath scowled at her. 'You'll find none of that Yankee nonsense here.' She lurched towards the table with the teapot in one hand. Julie could see the hot water inching dangerously close to the top of the spout. It took two further trips to bring the milk and the mugs to the table. She put them down with such force that Julie was surprised that the porcelain didn't break. Then, Mrs. McGrath took a bottle of a suspicious looking dark liquid and two glasses from one of the far cupboards, holding all three in one hand with surprising dexterity. She poured Julie a mug of tea and a small measure of the brown liquid.

'For the nerves,' Mrs. McGrath said, filling her own glass. She toasted Julie and downed it in one.

'But it's not even 11 o'clock.'

'More's happened to you today than would to most folk by midnight.' She refilled her own glass and held it aloft until Julie did the same. The hot liquid burned as it went down her throat and hit her stomach with a punch.

'Bloody hell,' Julie said, coughing. 'What is that?'

'My own blend,' she said, looking pleased with herself. 'Make it in the outhouses around the back.'

'Is that legal?'

'I'm not hurting anyone,' Mrs. McGrath replied, from which Julie took the answer to be no. 'What the tax man doesn't know won't hurt him.'

Without asking, Mrs. McGrath refilled Julie's glass. Julie took a big mouthful of tea, barely feeling it burn the roof of her mouth.

'Come on, then,' Mrs. McGrath said. 'Tell me what happened?'

'What do you want to know?'

'Did you kill him?' Mrs. McGrath asked the question and then kept her eyes fixed on Julie.

'What kind of idiot kills someone in their own house and then calls the police?'

'Lots of idiots around here.'

'Well, I'm not one of them.'

'So, you didn't kill him?'

'No, I bloody didn't.'

'That's good.' Mrs. McGrath said, having another shot. 'Don't think I'd want a murderer staying the night.'

Julie had only drunk her second shot after much coaxing from Mrs. McGrath. It had been more pleasant than the first. Despite still lighting her insides on fire as it slid down her gullet, she found herself enjoying the dizzying after effects.

The next on Mrs. McGrath's list of home remedies for shock had been a blisteringly hot bath.

Again, the focus had been placed on the medicinal rather than the therapeutic, with no bubbles added to the water. Her pale body was clearly visible directly under the surface, and Julie spent her forty or so minutes in the bathroom trying not to focus on her form made distorted by the clear liquid.

The temperature was just dipping to a point where the experience might have been deemed pleasurable when Julie heard Mrs. McGrath's cane wrapping on the outside of the door.

'Not good for you to stay in there for too long,' she called. 'Lie down is what you need.'

Much like Julie's own bathroom, two steep steps were located just outside the exit. As she went to leave, she almost tripped on a tray that Mrs. McGrath had left directly outside of the door. Julie nudged it hard, and the crockery positioned on it rattled loudly.

'Left some food for you,' Mrs. McGrath called redundantly from downstairs. 'Don't make a mess. Those sheets are clean on. The room to the right of the bathroom.'

Julie took the tray and put it on the bed in Mrs. McGrath's spare room. Her duffle bag was there waiting for her. She opened it and found a few oversized t-shirts and a pair of jeans that were so faded that they looked like they had been designed that way. In normal circumstances, these were the clothes Julie wore on the very rare occasion that she did jobs around the house. Thankfully, on further rummaging, Julie was relieved to see that Mrs. McGrath had thought to include a few pairs of underwear, although they were the most beige and sensible articles that her collection afforded. Julie took the largest t-shirt out of the selection of three and put it on. It had an indefinable smell that made her think of Greg and home.

Julie was unsure what Mrs. McGrath thought that she was going to be able to stain the sheets with as the tray only had a glass of water and two pieces of plain toast on it. It was just past lunchtime, and given that she hadn't eaten since the night before, Julie was surprised that she still didn't feel the least bit hungry. She chewed the toast methodically. Her mouth was still dry, and she had to take the occasional sip of water to aid her swallowing.

The bed wasn't plush. If anything, it most closely resembled a hospital bed, albeit without the due care to fold the sheet over the corners. But with the sun coming through the windows and a pleasant little breeze making its way into the room, Julie felt momentarily contented.

Just as she had come to really relish the idea of an afternoon nap, Harry popped into her head. All of a sudden, it occurred to her that her son didn't know that his friend was dead, and that there was no other way for him to find out. She thought about putting it off. Wouldn't it be better to wait until she felt a bit more steady? Afterall, she had found a dead body in her house a few hours ago. Julie didn't think that anyone would blame her if she put off notifying her son for a few hours. But no, it couldn't wait. She was sure that she wouldn't be able to sleep until she had got it over and done with.

Julie selected Harry's name from her contact list, remembering what he had told her about making the call over the internet. He wasn't going to answer, Julie thought, and that was absolutely fine with her. How many times did it need to ring before she could convince herself that she had made a good go of it? 5? 10? 10 seemed fair. Then she could go to sleep with a clear conscience then.

When her son answered on the ninth ring, she inwardly cursed him. 'Hello, love,' she said, attempting to hide her annoyance, 'everything okay with you?'

'Yeah, Mum, it's not a good time. I'm alright though. Eating well, not spending too much money, staying away from large bodies of water.' If she had been calling for a chat, this quick inventory would have obliterated any chance they had at a conversation. It remained a bit of a mystery to her what her son was actually doing on his travels, and she found herself not caring too much.

'I won't keep you,' she said, getting down to business. 'I'm afraid I've got something sad to tell you.'

'Nan, is it?' he said, even trying to move the news of a deceased relative on at a fair old clip. 'She had a good innings. Probably for the best.'

'Your nan is fine, although I'll let her know that her only grandson thinks it's time she gave it up. No, it's about Jack.'

'Christ, Mum. There was no need to throw him out.'

'It's not that.'

'You knew he was a musician when he moved in. A bit wild but harmless.'

'Well I didn't actually because you didn't tell me.'

'He shouldn't be punished for that though, should he?'

'Harry can you listen to me for just a moment?' she said, becoming impatient now.

'God, I can't believe you'd embarrass me like this in front of my friends. Honestly, you've always been like this.'

'He's dead.' There was a moment's silence on the other side of the line.

'Wait, what?'

'He's dead. He took an overdose. I found him this morning.'

Another pause followed. 'Are you sure?'

'Am I sure I found a body in your old room this morning?'

'Well it's a bit unlikely, isn't it? I only ever saw him smoking dope, and I don't think you can overdose on that.'

'He'd injected something into his arm, I don't know what.'

'You don't inject cannabis, Mum.'

'I never said he had.'

'I'm not saying I don't believe you…,'

'You think that my grip on reality is so tenuous that I would imagine a dead body in my house?'

'I'm just saying that sometimes you get confused.'

She wondered if it was normal to want to slap your own child. 'Thanks for that, Harry. Your friend is dead, and I thought you'd want to know.' With that, she ended the call before her son could ask her if she had managed to dress herself without any help this morning.

Her conscience entirely appeased, Julie placed the tray on the floor and lay on top of the bedding. Whether it was the alcohol, the gentle heat of the day or bathing in something akin to lava, Julie wasn't sure, but it was only a few moments before she had dozed off.

JULIE WOKE up with a thick head. At some point during her slumber, Mrs. McGrath had been in and taken the tray with her. She also noticed that she had left two paracetamol and a glass of water on the table next to the bed, which she took gratefully. She glanced at her phone and saw that Harry hadn't tried to get back in touch.

One of the adornments that Mrs. McGrath had thought it satisfactory to include in the room, with its otherwise spartan furnishings, was an old wooden clock. The actual face was so small that Julie had to get out of bed and move closer to read the time. She was surprised to find that it was almost six o'clock, and despite her lengthy nap, she didn't feel refreshed. She downed the rest of the water in the glass, but it seemed to make little difference to her pounding head. Looking for the clothes that she had arrived in, she surmised that her host had taken these too. She was forced to put on the faded jeans that Mrs. McGrath had packed for her and then ventured downstairs.

She found Mrs. McGrath in the kitchen standing over several bubbling pots on the hob.

'Shut that door,' she said as Julie entered the room. 'Bloody smoke detectors will be the death of me. Have a cup of tea that's too hot, and it will set the little bastards off.'

With real reluctance, Julie did as she was told. Whatever Mrs. McGrath was cooking was generating an unnatural amount of heat. That, coupled with the sun still blaring through the kitchen window, made the atmosphere almost tropical.

'I'll open the back door,' Julie said.

'Good luck,' Mrs. McGrath scoffed. 'Haven't been out there since 08.' Julie looked through the back window and saw how overgrown the garden was for the first time.'

'Or maybe open the window?' Julie suggested as a last resort.

'Had them painted shut. What's the bloody point? If you're inside, you want to be inside. Sit down, will you? All that moving about is making me dizzy.'

Julie wasn't aware that she had been moving about a great deal but sat down at the kitchen table obediently.

Mrs. McGrath heavy handedly put a glass of red wine in front of Julie.

'It's spag for dinner. If you're not happy with it then you'll have to go without. Haven't got anything else in.'

'Spaghetti bolognaise?' Julie asked.

'What else would 'spag,' be?'

'Spaghetti carbonara? Or spaghetti and meatballs?'

Mrs. McGrath turned around and had such a look of disgust on her face that you would have thought Julie had suggested pairing the pasta with human meat.

'I don't eat that slop,' she said.

Julie nodded, reasoning that it was easier to pretend that she understood the bizarre logic governing what Mrs. McGrath found objectionable. She took a sip of her wine and enjoyed the feeling of the alcohol hitting her bloodstream, even if the taste was slightly acrid.

Mrs. McGrath thumped the food down in front of her.

'That's quite a lot of food,' Julie said, letting out a nervous chuckle. 'I'm not sure if I can eat all that.'

'One big meal in the evening, and you'll make it through the whole of tomorrow.' Mrs. McGrath sat before her own meal and hung her walking stick over the back of her chair.

'Well, I'll eat what I can.'

'What you can is bloody all of it,' Mrs. McGrath said, cramming an impossible amount of spaghetti and sauce into her pinched mouth. Once she had swallowed, she said 'I'm not in the business of wasting food.'

For some unknown reason, Julie had expected the food to have some strange quality to it, most probably because everything else associated with Mrs. McGrath didn't conform to social norms in some not so subtle way. She had planned to take as many small mouthfuls as she could stomach and then push the remaining food to the edge of the plate, giving the illusion that she had eaten much more than she had in reality. What she wasn't prepared for was that the food would actually be fantastic. The sauce had a flavour that was so rich and satisfying that she found herself not being able to get it into her mouth fast enough. She began to eat in a frenzy, the fork bringing the delectable nosh up to her face almost mechanically. By the time she was finished, Julie was amazed to see that there were only a few odd strands of spaghetti left on her plate with the remaining pasta sauce.

Julie inched her chair backwards and contemplated undoing the top button of her jeans. Judging by the colour of them, she had probably purchased them somewhere around the year 2000, and she definitely wasn't still sporting her millennium figure. She had struggled to fasten them when she first put them on, and a few pounds of pasta and mincemeat definitely hadn't helped the situation.

Mrs. McGrath refilled Julie's glass and pushed it over to her. Julie, not yet feeling able to speak again, smiled at her appreciatively and took another sip. Even after the monstrous amount of food she had eaten, she still felt like the alcohol was still affecting her more than it normally would.

'Go on then,' Mrs. McGrath said, raising her glass to her mouth. Julie noticed she didn't sip her wine. Rather she wouldn't drink anything for maybe a stretch of ten minutes and then would then talk an almighty gulp in one go.

'I'm sorry.'

'The lad.'

'You mean Jack?'

'The dead one.' In retrospect, Julie didn't know why she had bothered to say 'Jack.' She had never heard Mrs. McGrath use anyone's name, or even to not address them with a pejorative, come to think of it.

'What do you want to know?'

'Enough to find out who killed him.'

Julie sat stunned, staring at Mrs. McGrath. She expected her to elaborate, but she seemed to think that the statement required no further explanation.

'What makes you think that someone killed him?' Julie said when no further comment was forthcoming.

'Had it coming to him, didn't he? Mincing around like that, getting up people's noses.'

'Mincing around?'

'In those skimpy little vests.'

'Are you saying that someone killed him because he was gay?'

'Who ever said anything about being gay?'

'You said he was mincing about.'

'Don't need to be gay to mince about. He thought he was pretty. People don't warm to that.'

'Most young people are sure of themselves, but they're not getting killed on a daily basis, are they?'

Julie took a sip of wine and decided to take another approach.

'Do you actually know something, Mrs. McGrath? Something that makes you think that he was murdered?'

'If I knew something, I wouldn't need you, would I? Sometimes you can just tell when something doesn't stack up right.'

Julie pinched the bridge of her nose and tried not to show her frustration.

'I'm sorry, I'm not quite following what you're saying.'

'What I'm saying, girl, is that I think that fancy man of yours was murdered, and I need your help to prove it.' She necked the last inch of wine in her glass and immediately refilled it. When she went to top up Julie, she tried to cover it with her hand, but Mrs. McGrath was too quick for her.

'Why didn't you tell the police this?'

'I could have handed them the murder weapon and the buggers still wouldn't know what to do with it. It happened here. Our street.' Mrs. McGrath rapped her fist against her chest as she said it. 'We've got to look after our own.'

'It's a very noble sentiment, but I think the police are better placed to look into a suspicious death.'

'The bobbies weren't the ones giving him a little nosh.' Julie instantly turned scarlet.

'Thought so,' Mrs. McGrath said, looking pleased with herself. 'You know the dirty then. Who he was hanging about with. What he was up to.'

Julie relayed to Mrs. McGrath what she had told DI Morris earlier in the day. She confirmed her and Jack's brief romantic liaison, even though the wise old coot had already figured that out for herself. Then, she told her about all that money that she had seen Jack with. That horrible little thug who she suspected of selling Jack drugs on her doorstep.

'Had you seen him before?' Mrs. McGrath interrupted.

'He did look familiar, but I can't think where I would have come across him. To be honest, I don't really go anywhere apart from work, and he didn't look like the type to hang out in a garden centre.'

'What about the playground? Or the toy shop? You might have seen him when you took your kiddies out.'

She wanted to point out that even when they had first moved into the close, Harry had been 14 and much too old for the park, but something Mrs. McGrath had said had sparked a memory.

'Mr. Baker's shop, that's it! He was standing outside with his little gang of hoodlums. Last Saturday, I went in to get some bread.'

'I know 'em.' Mrs. McGrath said. She picked up her stick, and Julie was worried that she intended to confront them immediately. Thankfully, she only went to one of the cupboards on the other side of the kitchen to fetch a fresh bottle of wine. 'Greasy hair under those grubby hats. Always trying to cause trouble until you let them know you're not going to take it.'

Mrs. McGrath reached over the table and pushed Julie's still half full wine glass towards her. Julie took a swig, but it didn't mollify her. She lifted it to her mouth again and drained its contents. She couldn't remember the last time her mind had been clear. She felt as if she had spent the last few days in a stupor. The fog that had accumulated from cooking the pasta still hadn't dissipated. Mrs. McGrath had continued to talk to her, but she hadn't taken the words in.

'I'm sorry?'

'I said that's where we need to start. Track that wrongun down and see what he was up to with the body.'

'Jack.'

'Not Jack no more, is he?'

'Yes, alright. But he was still Jack when the "wrongun" last saw him.'

'Not if he killed him.'

Julie had to concede that there was some logic in that.

'But what if Jack had just been buying a bit of dope or something? Nothing wrong with that, is there?'

'Nothing wrong with asking the question either.' She took another gulp of her wine. Despite having drunk enough to floor a small jungle beast, Mrs. McGrath seemed unaffected. Julie, in contrast, was struggling to keep her eyes open. The old woman continued to rant, but Julie found it harder and harder to follow the random progression of her thoughts. Feeling unsteady on her feet, she said goodnight to Mrs. McGrath and went to bed. She woke up at around three in the morning still fully dressed, absolutely parched with a pounding headache.

CHAPTER ELEVEN

Julie had managed to get back to sleep after raiding Mrs. McGrath's medicine cupboard for some paracetamol and sinking a few pints of water. She was momentarily roused by the sound of something knocking against wood. Dismissing it as some over eager neighbour embarking on an early morning DIY project, she let herself drift back to sleep. Five minutes later, she was awoken by something violently prodding into her side.

She flipped over in the bed and saw Mrs. McGrath standing over her. Her cane, which had acted as the prodding implement, remained raised and pointed at her, ready to strike again.

'What are you still doing in bed?' She asked, thumping a cup of tea on the bedside table.

'I didn't realise I needed to be up for anything.' Even with her trip to the medicine cabinet in the middle of the night, Julie's head still throbbed.

'Don't need to be up for anything? We've got a killer to catch, girl.'

Julie vaguely remembered some chatter the previous night about Jack's death.

'I thought we decided we were going to leave that up to the police,' Julie said, shifting her rear backwards and sitting up in the bed so that she could take a sip of tea. It had an ungodly amount of sugar in it.

'Not if we want something done about it, we won't.'

'For someone who has such a low opinion of the police force, you're on pretty friendly terms with their officers.'

'Not officers, that lot,' she said with venom. 'Cept Jimmy. He won't turn out half bad with a bit of work.'

Julie got half way through asking Mrs. McGrath how she knew them in the first place before she interrupted her. 'That's not for now,' she said irritably. 'We've got things to do. Downstairs in half an hour.'

Showered and dressed, Julie came downstairs to find Mrs. McGrath in the kitchen. Walking past the closed door to the living room, Julie realised that since she arrived, she hadn't actually seen inside. Mrs. McGrath was stood by the kitchen counters. She was dressed in a long, green mackintosh that had seen better days, with her customary red patterned scarf covering her head and tied under her chin. To complete the effect, she was wearing a pair of green wellingtons.

'Get your boots on,' she said impatiently. 'We haven't got all day.'

Julie put her empty mug down on the kitchen table. 'What, why?'

'You bloody know why. How many times do I have to say it? We're hunting a killer.'

'Yes, I understand the general sentiment, Mrs. McGrath, but what does that actually mean?'

'I'll tell you in the car.' She picked up Julie's keys and thrust them into her hand. Then the indomitable Mrs. McGrath put her arms up as if Julie was a wayward cow and hearded her towards the front door.

'Mrs. McGrath, I really can't.'

'Got a lot on, have you? Your social calendar is so pressing that you can't help out an old lady for a few hours?'

Julie wanted to protest. However when she realised that the only plans that she currently had were to attend a summer fete at the seniors centre, she begrudgingly climbed into the car.

'You sure you haven't been moving bodies around?' Mrs. McGrath said, pointing to the large, red stain on the passenger seat.

'It's pollen, or something else from some flowers I got from work. I tried to sponge it out, but I think I've made it worse.' Julie reached into the backseat to find a carrier bag for Mrs. McGrath to sit on. Before she could hand it to her, the old woman was already installed in the passenger seat next to her. 'Which reminds me, can I call my boss and let him know that I won't be in again today? Or will justice not permit it?'

'If you must,' Mrs. McGrath said, sounding unimpressed. Mr. Peg had been surprisingly compassionate, telling her to take as long as she needed. Julie felt sorry for Mike, being trapped alone with Mr. Peg and all his sand.

It was only as they were leaving the street that Julie thought to look at her house in the rearview mirror. There was still police tape in front of the front gate and a man in a white forensic suit was walking through the front door.

'Right here,' Mrs. McGrath said when they reached a junction. She sounded frustrated that Julie didn't know where they were going. To the chagrin of her fellow motorists, Julie crossed over the middle lane of traffic to allow her to turn as instructed.

'I think I've been more than accommodating,' Julie said after a few moments of no further instructions. 'The least you can do is tell me what we're doing.'

'I was down at the shops this morning. Getting some milk and bread in. Don't normally need to go until later in the week, but got another mouth to feed, haven't I?' Julie noted the angry glance shot in her direction out of the corner of her eye. 'Anyway, I came out of the shop and one of them was standing out there. Least, I think it was him. Can't tell one from the next.'

'One of who?'

'Those hoodlums. Part of that mob that sold your fancy boy his drugs.'

'Okay...'

'He got on the bus, number 9, so I did too. Rode it all the way to the terminal. Right sketchy neighbourhood it took us to. He heads off down towards those old warehouses. You know where the print works used to be before they shut it down? Didn't think it would be a good idea to go in alone. Not sure how many of them would be in there.'

Julie was incredulous. She was tempted to perform an emergency stop right here and now so that she could give her full attention to reprimanding Mrs. McGrath.

'You mean to tell me we're on our way to an old warehouse to confront a group of teenage gangsters? And you're not even sure whether one of them is who I saw talking to Jack?'

'What if he isn't?'

'If he isn't, then why are we doing it?'

'That's what police work is about. You try one thing, and if it doesn't pan out, that's the name of the game.'

'We are not detectives, Mrs. McGrath!' Julie said, exasperated. More than turning the car around, she was now fighting the urge not to veer across the central reservation into the oncoming traffic.

'And you're not going to be with that kind of attitude.' She folded her arms and rested her head on her shoulder.

The rest of the journey passed in silence. Luckily, Julie had a vague recollection of where the old print works were as Mrs. McGrath had now dispensed with her navigating duties. All of the buildings looked much the same, but one on the right hand side of the road had a dirty sign announcing that it was 'Spriggs and Co: Print Services,' which no one had thought to remove when they had gone out of business. It was the last factory in the business park. The road then met some overgrown thistles and beyond that, lay the dirty canal, full of old televisions and stolen shopping trolleys. There must have been another entry to access the car park because the only path that would take you to the front of the building was only suitable for pedestrians. Julie turned the car around and parked it on the left hand side of the road ready to make a quick getaway before waking Mrs. McGrath up.

'Good,' Mrs. McGrath said, and went to immediately exit the car.

'Hold on, hold on.' Julie said. 'Shouldn't we agree a plan of attack. What we're going to say?'

'There's too much thinking these days. If the lad who you saw on your doorstep is there, we want to know what he was doing. If he gives us any trouble, then we'll get him in the car and take him to that pillock, Maz.'

'We can't do that.'

'Why the bloody hell not? If he's guilty then someone needs to take charge.'

'Well...,' Julie searched for a reason that the old woman might accept. 'I've got stuff on the backseat.'

'He's better off in the boot anyway,' she said, opening the car door and heaving herself out with some effort. 'Can't be messing with you when you're trying to drive then. These criminals won't stop at anything.' Before she could protest any further, Mrs. McGrath was already making her way around the building to investigate further. Julie grabbed her phone, her purse, and her keys before running after her.

Julie had literally no idea what she had expected to find when she emerged on the other side of the path but was equally surprised at the scene that lay before her. A group of about seven teenagers were engaged in an assortment of activities in the concrete forecourt. The younger boys were doing lazy loops on their bikes, every so often trying to pull a wheelie or do a small jump, both of which were incredibly underwhelming.

In true Lord of the Flies style, the slightly older members of the gang were sitting behind a metal rubbish bin that they had managed to set alight.

'Any of them, is it?' Mrs. McGrath asked from where she stood next to Julie. They hadn't noticed the women yet from where they were assembled on the far side of the car park. Julie inspected each of them in turn as best as she could from such a distance. It was difficult, what with them all dressing almost identically.

'Oi, sweetheart,' one of them shouted, having spotted them for the first time. 'Come over and say 'ello.' One of the younger boys on his BMX was dispatched to escort the unlikely pair to his leaders. When they got a bit closer, Julie recognised him instantly. That rodential face, the little beady eyes peering at her from under his cap. Julie was surprised to see a girl who looked about five years his junior slumped over his lap looking up at him adoringly. Sat next to them was another girl of a similar age busy on her mobile phone. Unlike the other youths gathered around, she seemed to have no interest whatsoever in the scene that was about to unfold before her.

'What can we do for you, ladies?' He said when they were stood before him. He sat up a bit straighter as if he had illusions that he was in fact a reputable business man. He pushed his adoring companion off his lap without a second thought.

'We want to ask you some questions,' Mrs. McGrath said. She spoke to him in the same blunt tone that she had used on the telephone engineer, seemingly unphased by the situation. Julie remained half a step behind her, happy to allow the old bulldog to take the lead.

'It's all quality gear. If you two had rocked up last week, I would have been shocked. But I had another fancy bird down here yesterday, buying some of the hard stuff. Surprising the clientele you get these days.'

'We don't want to buy any drugs,' Mrs. McGrath said, again in clipped tones.

'Then what do you want? I'm a busy man.' He certainly didn't look like a busy man, Julie thought. In fact, he looked like a feckless teenager who had turned to dealing drugs for an easy buck.

'What were you doing with him? That lad who died.'

The youth looked away from her. 'Who's that then?'

'Jack,' Julie took a step forward, now standing next to Mrs. McGrath. 'Jack Harper. You were talking to him outside my house on Sunday.'

'I talk to a lot of people,' he said, not willing to commit. He took out a packet of loose tobacco and started to roll a cigarette.

'He was quite well spoken. Nice hair. Wore a lot of vests.'

'That posh boy. What a twat.' He switched to a surprisingly good imitation of Jack's plummy tones. 'Oh nice one 'guv, it's good some good shit this. I'll have to tell my boys about you.'

His cronies, who remained standing behind the two women a bit too close for comfort, laughed on cue.

'That sounds like him,' Julie said, nodding. She was going to attempt to defend Jack before remembering that he had, in fact, turned out to be a bit of a shit.

'And he's dead, is he? Shame, that. Can always overcharge those toffs a bit.'

'He was buying drugs from you then,' Mrs. McGrath said, returning to the proceedings.

'Couldn't say. Might have been a social call.' He put the roll up in his mouth, and his adoring young companion lit it for him.

'But you said he was a pillock.'

'Mix with all types of people in my line of work,' he said, shrugging his shoulders.

'What if we make it worth your while?'

The youth said nothing but lifted his head slightly to demonstrate his interest. Mrs. McGrath elbowed Julie. She looked in her purse and from the small selection of notes she had in there, she pulled out £5 and held it forward. Mrs. McGrath looked at it and then at Julie with obvious disapproval. She went to put the note back in her purse and select a different one but before she could, Mrs. McGrath snatched it from her hands.

'There.' She took out £20 and slapped it against the chest of one of the boys on the bikes who was currently in her orbit. He lost his balance and had to stick his foot out to stop himself from toppling over all together. He took the money over to his leader who stuck it in his tracksuit pocket without looking at it.

'Alright then. Yeah, he was buying some gear. Met him outside the shop. Asked if I could set him up.'

'He wasn't dealing drugs for you?'

He laughed. 'No, ta. He would have been a fucking liability.'

'What was he buying from you? Heroin?'

He laughed unpleasantly. 'Pretty boy like that, taking smack? Bit of weed, that's all. Nothing heavy.'

'You sure you didn't sell him anything else?' Mrs. McGrath said.

'Actually, I'll tell you what ladies,' he said, standing up. 'I think my fee's just gone up. 50 quid.'

'For what?'

'It's obviously information worth having. Why else would you be here?' The three goons behind them inched closer to them. The front wheel of one of their bikes jabbed into the back of Julie's legs and her knee briefly buckled.

'We paid for what you gave us, and you were lucky to have that,' Mrs. McGrath said, remaining firm.

'I think we've got a problem then.' He reached into his pocket and took out a short knife. Julie saw that it was in fact something that obviously belonged in a kitchen. Despite her terror at the current situation, she found herself wanting to laugh at how painfully amateur this whole set up was.

He took a step forward, but Mrs. McGrath didn't move.

'I wouldn't recommend that.'

'What are you going to do about it, granny?'

Julie was sure that Mrs. McGrath's eyes had narrowed at this last word. Without any warning, she threw Julie's purse back to her and the coppers in the bottom clattered to the ground. In a moment of frenzied activity, she placed her cane firmly on the chest of the yob closest to her and pushed her weight against it . He fell like a bag of potatoes, his bike falling heavily on top of him. Then, she swung her cane round, and it connected with the second of the gang's shoulder with a painful crack. For good measure, she rammed the stick into his ribs which left him clutching his body in agony. The final henchman was putting his foot onto the pedal of his bike to launch his counterattack. Before he could even look up, Mrs. McGrath had rammed the cane into his genitals with such force that the boy's eyes immediately began to water.

The older youth watched all this unfolding before his eyes with absolute bemusement. Not wanting to lose face, he took an incredibly tentative step towards his elderly combatant.

'Try it,' she said, holding the cane in front of her like a sabre. He didn't reply, but he also didn't make a move towards them. The dazed look on his face was now transforming into one of wounded pride and fury.

Mrs. McGrath turned away from him and walked with her usual limp towards the exit of the car park.

Slightly shell shocked, Julie started to collect the pennies that had fallen out of her purse.

'What are you doing, woman,' Mrs. McGrath called. She had already cleared a surprising distance.

'Right, sorry,' Julie said, dropping the few coins still collected in her hand and ran after her.

Julie was thrilled to find the car where she had left it. She was so giddy that she struggled to press the button to unlock the car. Mrs. McGrath didn't help by pulling at the door handle every few seconds.

'Get a hold of yourself,' Mrs. McGrath said with even less compassion than usual. Julie was alarmed to see their attackers emerging from the same path they had walked down a few moments ago. Their progress had been hampered by the need to bring their bikes with them. Julie noticed that the youth who had suffered the assault on his testicles was nowhere to be seen, but instead, the ring leader was riding his BMX.

'You can look at them all you like when we're in the bloody car,' Mrs. McGrath said, bringing Julie back to the moment. She managed to make her finger connect with the unlock button, and they both climbed in.

They pulled away, and the group immediately gave chase. Julie was so preoccupied with checking their position in the rear view mirror that she didn't pay attention to where she was going. The park was a mass of junctions and turnings that very quickly led to dead ends. More than once, Julie took a wrong turn and had to perform a very dodgy maneuver to get the car back on route. It did mean that despite her pressing want to affect a quick getaway, their assailants managed to remain within reaching distance of the car.

After having to, once again, correct a wrong turning, the young man got so close to the vehicle that he was able to grab hold of the wing mirror on Mrs. McGrath's side of the car. The little yob then started to throw his crooked elbow against the window. Julie let out a little yelp, more in surprise than anything else. While the assault on the vehicle appeared to be having no discernible effect on the glass, the muffled thud each impact made was fairly unsettling.

Now on the last straight stretch that led to the main road, Julie could finally speed up and make their escape, but was reluctant to do so while the youth was still clinging on to the side of the car for fear of inflicting some real damage. During the incredibly low speed chase that had ensued, Mrs. McGrath had remained sitting with her arms crossed looking bored.

As Julie slowed on the approach to the main road, one of the cohort burst from the pack and attempted to bring his body between the car and their salvation.

'What if he gets in front of us,' Julie said in a much too shrill voice. 'We'll be stuck.' Mrs. McGrath looked over at her with a look of stinging disapproval, and Julie realised that she had probably momentarily lost her sense of perspective.

Without looking around, Mrs. McGrath pushed the button to lower her window.

'Don't do that,' Julie said, her voice again piercing. 'They'll get in.'

Mrs. McGrath didn't answer her. Instead, she gripped her walking stick with both hands. With one decisive jab, she rammed it into the side of the youth closest to her, who immediately let go of the side of the car, toppling into his comrade who was attempting to impede their escape. Both fell to the hard ground. The final member of the party managed to slam his breaks on in time, narrowly avoiding a further collision. Not looking round to survey the havoc she had wreaked, she wound her window back up and returned her stick to the footwell.

In her haste to get away, Julie pulled into a gap in the traffic a fraction too small and received a long, resounding honk because of it.

'Not bad that,' Mrs. McGrath said as they came to a stop in the late afternoon congestion.

Julie looked at her passenger incredulously. 'We were almost attacked!' She sounded a lot more haughty than she actually felt. Yes, she had been in an almost constant state of panic since they first left the car, but it had been exciting. If she was honest with herself, it was downright exhilarating.

'Not that,' Mrs. McGrath said, disregarding Julie's concern for her safety, however contrived it may have been. 'I mean the information.'

'Was it? I didn't think it was very surprising. I was pretty sure Jack didn't take hard drugs anyway.'

'Injecting cannabis then, was he?'

'What?'

'What was the needle on the floor about if he was only buying dope from that dipstick?'

'Maybe someone gave it to him? Or he was at a party, and they had some left over.'

'How many parties have you been to where they divvy up the leftover drugs at the end of the night? It's not a bloody pasta bake.'

'Alright then, what are you saying happened?'

'Dunno yet. We've only just started investigating. I'm just saying I was right in thinking that it didn't add up.'

'One small part of it doesn't fit what you already know. It doesn't mean he was murdered.'

'What about the money?'

'What about it?'

'If he wasn't dealing drugs, then why did he have all that money?'

'He was doing some gardening,' Julie said. Mrs. McGrath looked at her like her brains were slowly dripping out of her ear. 'Quite a bit of gardening. And he was working in the bar.'

'They should get someone to go into schools and tell the kids it's not worth going to university. Much better money in landscaping and serving drinks.'

'Yes, alright,' Julie said, irritated.

'It's going to take a lot of work to make a detective out of you, girl,' Mrs. McGrath said, settling down in her chair to go back to sleep.

CHAPTER TWELVE

J ulie walked over the field towards the attractions with a Tupperware crammed full of biscuits.

She had convinced herself that it had definitely been her intention to make them herself. However, the police had only left her house late the previous afternoon. Therefore, she decided that their occupation gave her the perfect excuse to go to Tesco for her baked goods instead. In order to ensure that their authenticity wasn't questioned, she dragged them across her cheese grater, adding a more rustic quality to them.

On the journey here, Julie had spotted a few posters for the event billing it as a 'family fun day.' The only issue with them was that they were entirely posted on trees once you had turned onto the drive of the care home. Therefore, the only people that would see them would already be on their way here.

There wasn't a cloud in the sky, and the sun continued to bombard them with its ferocious heat.

Somehow though, there were sections of the field that remained abjectly muddy. More than once, Julie lost a flip flop to the saturated dirt and had to pause to reclaim it.

'Oh, very nice,' Tracy said, taking the container of biscuits from her from her place behind the cake stall. 'Nice to have something homemade. All we've had so far is Penguin bars.'

'It did say 12.30 on the leaflet, didn't it?'

'12.00 arrival for a 12.30 start, yeah,' Tracy said, placing the biscuits on a plate.

'There's just less people here than I would have thought.' Julie looked around again and confirmed her first impression. Only a handful of the 50 or so residents had anyone sitting with them.

'It's the smell,' Tracy said frankly. 'Granny piss. That's why we do it outdoors. Less chance of it getting into your clothes that way.'

'Oh yeah?' Julie said, wondering if Tracy had once again forgotten she was related to one of the residents.

'That's why we struggle to recruit too. Young people can't hack it.'

'I'll go and say hello to Betty then.'

'Right you are,' Tracy said, unwrapping a chocolate bar that she hadn't paid for.

Betty gave her the little sweet smile that she always greeted visitors with. Julie bent down to kiss her cheek, and her mother in law was gracious enough to pretend she knew who she was. For some unknown reason, she was wearing her coat and clutching her handbag. No doubt she had got the wrong end of the stick when they had told her she was going on a day out. It broke Julie's heart a bit to see she was wearing what she used to call her best hat.

'Well, aren't I popular,' Betty said smiling, as Julie settled in the chair next to her.

'Not as popular as me,' said another old lady sitting to their right. 'That's all my lot there.'

Julie looked at where she was pointing and saw a large group of people walking across the field. Unusually, half were in wheelchairs and the other half were attempting to push them across the uneven ground. On either side, there were a few stragglers who weren't wearing the uniforms that you would normally associate with health care professionals .

'It's my Robert and his boys,' the old lady said, leaning forward to make eye contact with Julie. Betty looked uncomfortable and focused on her shoes. Julie tried to follow suit, but the slightly manic woman ducked her head, so she had to meet her gaze.

'It is. Go and ask him.'

'I'm sure he is,' Julie said smiling placatingly and attempting to turn in her chair away from the nuisance. Before she could, the woman grabbed her arm and stopped her mid pivot.

'No, go and ask him.' The look in the woman's eyes was nearing deranged, so Julie thought it would be easiest to humour her.

'I'll be right back, Betty,' Julie said, getting out of her seat. Betty glanced up at her very quickly, like she didn't want to risk getting involved. She took a few steps to the approaching group before realising that she recognised one of the number on the far right fringe. Mrs. Sinclair was walking across the green with her arms crossed over her chest. It had taken her a moment longer to recognise her as she had done something rather drastic with her hair. Now in place of her dark silky hair that had once cascaded down her back was a rather severe, boyish style. It was the kind of haircut that women in the Autumn of their life affected when they finally realised that the daily maintenance of one's do simply wasn't worth the effort anymore. In spite of this, it still had the potential to be stylish. The natural wave could be teased into something resembling glamorous with the right inclination.

It was jarring to see it on Mrs. Sinclair, who was probably a few years younger than Julie. Despite looking worn, the beauty in her features was still obvious. Julie expected that the poor woman hadn't managed to recuperate from the events a few nights previously. First, needing to call an emergency plumber and then having to call the paramedics.

Julie's eyes wandered to the right, and she saw Mr. Sinclair. He looked none the worse for his ordeal earlier in the week, whatever it may have been. A powerfully built man pushed Mr. Sinclair's wheelchair, the rough terrain not even registering with him as an issue. His much weedier colleague was struggling several feet behind him, the back wheels of his patient's chair planted firmly in the mud. Even from this distance, Julie could hear the old gentleman in the chair shouting, 'Go on, lad, put some balls into it.'

'Mrs. Sinclair?' Julie said when the group reached her. Clearly lost in her thoughts, she looked surprised that someone was talking to her. So severe was the expression that it bordered on shock or even terror. 'It's Julie. Julie Giles. I live across the road from you?'

Mrs. Sinclair nodded. 'Yes, I remember.'

'I haven't seen you here before,' Julie said. 'I didn't know you had a relative in Thorneywood?'

'I don't,' Mrs. Sinclair said abruptly.

'Just fancied a day at the fair, did you?'

'They thought it would be good for Mr. Sinclair and the others to try something new,' she said with real reluctance and avoiding eye contact. She made Julie feel like it was an effort to talk to her. Of course, she knew the woman was reserved. After all, they had lived across the road from one another for many years now, and all she could usually muster was a slight incline of the head in Julie's direction. But this was taking it to the next level.

'Well, I won't keep you,' Julie said. She hadn't meant for it to sound sarcastic but had almost definitely failed. Without even a cursory goodbye, Mrs. Sinclair left Julie standing alone and went to rejoin her group.

Julie went back over to where she had been sitting, ready to answer the woman's questions, but she had lost interest. She was now trying to convince the old gent on the other side of her that she had 100 percent almost been chosen as a representative for the British shotput team in the 1976 Olympic games.

Julie and Betty had been sitting in companionable silence for a few moments when the old woman put her hand on her leg and squeezed it affectionately.

'Let's go and have a look at the stalls, shall we?' Betty said. 'It's been years since I've been to the fair.' It didn't matter to Julie that Betty likely had no idea who she was. It didn't even matter that three days previously, she had found a dead body in her spare room. Her warm little face made her feel wanted. Not because she was willing to cook and clean, but just because she wanted some company to go around the fair. Without a doubt, it made her feel happy in such an uncomplicated way that she experienced a sense of joy that would have felt alien to her a few moments ago.

As delicately as she could manage, Julie helped Betty out of her chair, and they went off to explore what wonders the Thorneywood Care Home Summer

Fete had to offer them. Betty wasn't interested in the tombola or the raffle. Nor could Tracy and her thin selection of baked treats tempt her. However, when she saw the hook a duck stand, she began to pull on Julie's arm like a dog straining on its lead.

'Hello there, ladies,' said the greasy man behind the stall. Julie had never seen anyone over the age of 16 with such severe acne. It was a shame that he had chosen a profession where he had to wear a money belt. It was fixed just under his enormous belly, further highlighting his enormous girth. His hair had gone without a thorough wash for so long that it actually looked wet to the touch. 'Welcome...,' he said and paused for dramatic effect, 'to reap a sheep.'

Julie looked at the attraction for the first time and saw that it wasn't actually plastic ducks, but sheep that littered the small pool before her. Weirder still, they weren't floating. Instead, they were standing still in about an inch of water.

'What's the aim of the game?' Julie asked.

He looked at her blankly. 'You've never played hook a duck before?'

'Of course I have, but... well, they're not ducks, are they?'

'Same difference,' he said, shrugging. He turned his gaze to Betty. '£2 please, love.' She handed it over to him without hesitation, and the vendor handed her a pole with a hook on the end.

'I don't understand. Why would sheep be swimming?'

'Why would you be picking up ducks from a hook sticking out of its head? Nothing makes much sense if you question it too much, love.'

Julie felt irritated that he did, in fact, have a point.

'Well there's not much sport in it, is there? They're not even moving.'

He nodded towards Betty who was struggling to capture one of the stationary sheep. The greasy man then turned back to her and looked smug.

JULIE SPENT five minutes watching Betty try to catch the wayward sheep and then another five minutes attempting to steady her hand and guide it towards the troublesome animal. When that failed, Julie snatched the pole out of her mother in law's hands and after taking a moment to calm herself down, managed to hook the thing herself. In reward of her efforts, Betty received a lump of cotton wool with a crudely drawn face in felt tip. As Julie took her mother in law back to the larger congregation of older people, she made a list in her head of all the things she could have done with the ten minutes she just wasted.

After all that excitement, Betty wanted a sit down, and Julie desperately needed some time to herself. She left her charge with her friends, proudly showing off her new pet sheep. Julie wandered through the dozen stalls and quickly came to the other end. Not wanting to return so soon, she carried on walking until she found herself standing behind the grand, grey structure that the old dears called home.

As she strolled, she had been thinking about Jack and what Mrs. McGrath had said in the car yesterday. Could someone have killed him? He had been a bit of a shit, but was that really reason enough to kill someone? Maybe he was a sweet boy who had been having a bit of an off period. If being a bit unpleasant was a reason to be killed, then the majority of the people at the local supermarket on a Saturday morning were in for an early end. He had been a veritable tsunami in Julie's own life. If anything though, that was testament to how humdrum and without incident her daily routine was. That being said, Jack had seemed to cause conflict wherever he went. His jilted lover at work looked ready to slap him, not to mention his rival behind the bar or the older bloke that he had the scrap with. And what about that great bulk of notes that he was carrying round with him? Maybe Mrs. McGrath was right, and Jack had a talent for trouble lurking below that charming facade.

Lost in her own thoughts, Julie turned the corner of the building, which took her to the side of the building farthest away from the fete, and she was surprised to see Mrs. Sinclair sitting on the back steps that led down from the kitchen.

'Oh, hello,' Julie said, trying to sound friendly. 'Sorry, I didn't mean to intrude.'

Mrs. Sinclair looked at Julie impassively. She didn't say anything. Instead, she appeared to be waiting for Julie to tell her what she was doing there, like she had some greater claim on the back steps of a care home through some unknown lineage. Julie saw anew the dark rings around her eyes. Her face was pale, and yet her hands were violently blushed as if she had recently fended off some horrendous skin condition.

'Listen, I saw the ambulance outside your house the other morning, and I just wanted to say… I wanted you to know that if you ever need anyone to talk to, I'm always here.' Afterwards, Julie realised this was the moment when she should have walked away.

Without placing her hands on the floor, Mrs. Sinclair stood up. She ran her hands down the back of her legs once to dislodge any lingering dust. 'Do you expect that you're the first gossip that has made themselves known to me, hoping for all the details of my life?'

Julie tried to protest. Mrs. Sinclair didn't let her. 'Are you so naive that you think I don't know how all of you all carry on, talking about my life? Who do you think you are? Not only did I need to deal with some cockney geezer in the early hours because the sink had decided to leak, but then I was forced to call the paramedics at half past five. And then, of course, the idiot plumber was still fumbling his way around the pipes because of his inability to work for more than five minutes without demanding another cup of tea.'

Julie once again went to speak and was immediately interrupted.

'Can you actually begin to comprehend how stressful it was to have all of those people in my house at once. Not only that but trying to come to terms with the fact that my husband could die any moment?'

Now Mrs. Sinclair gave Julie the opportunity to speak. Struggling to find any words that were adequate, she said, 'He made it through though, didn't he? Looks like he's enjoying himself.'

'You know nothing about my life,' she said with a muted fury. 'And you are not my friend. So please don't pretend that you are.'

Julie started stammering out an apology, but Mrs. Sinclair wasn't interested. The second that she was out of sight, Julie plonked herself down on the hard stone steps. She sat for a few moments trying to convince herself not to cry. Then the events of the past few days suddenly overwhelmed her, and she began gushing, her hands clasped over her face. In the past few days, she had experienced such a variety of emotions, and she now felt them pouring out of her. She was in jeopardy of becoming hysterical. It didn't matter to her. This week had seen a lifetime's worth of drama crammed into the space of a few days. She decided she was allowed to cry as much as she liked.

'Christ, are you alright?' a voice said. She peaked through her fingers and could just about distinguish the figure of a very tall man with dark hair. 'I heard someone wailing. Have you been mugged or something?'

'Who's going to mug me round the back of an old people's home?' She wiped her eyes on the back of her shoulder and was pleasantly surprised to find Mike standing in front of her. He was essentially wearing the exact same clothes that he wore to work. A pair of cargo shorts and a polo shirt, although this one wasn't branded with the garden centre's logo. The only noticeable difference was that his feet were adorned with a pair of sensible sandals, the ones with the strap behind the back of your ankle.

'I dunno. Never really gone in for muggings myself. You'd probably want to do it somewhere quiet though.'

'You'd still need a bit of foot traffic though. Otherwise there wouldn't be anyone to mug.'

'Well you're here, aren't you?'

She chuckled in spite of herself. 'Would you mind sitting with me for a bit?'

Mike rubbed his hand against the back of his head. 'Yeah, alright,' he said, lowering himself beside her. The step was so narrow that his left and her right thigh were pushed against one another.

'What was all that about then?' Mike asked. 'I saw some other woman marching off with a face like a slapped arse. Is it something to do with why you haven't been at work for the last few days?'

'No, it's nothing to do with that. She's my neighbour. It's not her fault. I was prying, and she doesn't have the easiest life at the best of times.' Her eyes were still moist, and she could feel that her nose was dangerously close to dripping. She sniffed loudly, and Mike handed her a hanky. She took it from him gratefully.

'Who uses a hanky in this day and age. When were you born, 1943?'

Julie had started wiping her face with it when Mike said, 'It was my dad's.'

'Bloody hell,' she said without thinking, throwing it back at him. 'How old is it?'

'He didn't come back from the war.' Mike looked down at his shoes with a sad look on his face.

'God, Mike, I'm so sorry.' She grabbed it back from him and continued to dab her eyes with it. 'It's really kind of you to let me use it. It's very…,' Julie scrambled for a word commonly used to compliment a hanky. 'Soft. Luxurious even.' She looked out of the corner of her eye and was horrified to see that Mike's shoulders were shaking as he silently wept.

'Mike, I'm so sorry,' she said, putting her arm around his shoulder. 'I didn't mean to upset you. Were you very close?'

Her colleague turned towards her and revealed that he was, in fact, laughing.

'Who inherits a hanky? Honestly, woman. I know I'm not exactly flush, but even my family could muster up a China bowl or something to leave to the grandchildren.'

Trying not to laugh, she threw the hanky back at him, and its corner hit him in the eye. He let out an exaggerated breath as if it had really taken him back.

'I don't care,' Julie said, attempting to look irritated. 'I've already apologised once.'

He managed to bring his chortling under control. 'Okay, I'm sorry, I couldn't help myself.'

'Shouldn't you be with your aunty anyway? What's her name again, Joan?'

'Jean,' Mike said, the expression on his face instantly souring. 'She's with that wanker- husband-not-a-husband of hers. We were having a lovely afternoon. I even managed to convince her to go on the helter skelter.'

'They have a helter skelter? Is that a good idea?'

'It's just a slide really. But they've painted the sides. Red and blue it is, same difference to her. Anyway, she was gearing up for her third go when Roy turns up with a bunch of flowers which he's clearly picked at the bottom of the drive. Those purple ones, you know? With the big hanging head on them?' Julie nodded. 'She wouldn't even give me a second look then, would she? Too busy with her fancy boy.'

'So you just decided to have a wander?'

'Well, truth be told, I saw you heading off, and I thought it would be nice to come and say hello. Because I haven't seen you in a few days, with you not being at work. I dunno, it's silly really, but...you know....'

'I know what?'

'You cheer me up. At least when you're not blinding me with a hanky.'

'Oh right,' Julie said, blushing slightly and looking at her feet. They sat in silence for a few moments, both waiting for the other to speak first.

'Listen,' Mike said. 'I was thinking, maybe it would be nice if we could...,'

'I'm sorry if I'm interrupting something,' a familiar voice said to their right. Julie looked around and saw DI Morris standing with the policeman that Mrs. McGrath had called Jimmy a few paces behind him.

Mike scrambled to his feet. The presence of these two police officers had momentarily made him forget that he hadn't, in fact, done anything wrong.

'Not at all, Detective Inspector,' Julie said with a perfunctory smile. 'What can I do for you?'

'We have a few more questions for you, Mrs. Giles. Would you be willing to come to the station with us?' Julie tried not to panic, though in her experience, telling yourself not to get agitated is about as useful as trying to swim on land.

'Yes, of course,' she said. 'How did you know where I was?'

'We are aware that you are related to a resident. When you weren't at your home or your place of work, it felt like the most logical choice.'

'Right,' Julie said, feeling slightly insulted that she was so easy to track down. 'Let me say goodbye to my mother in law, and I'll be right with you.'

She looked to Mike to say goodbye, but he was standing, looking at his shoes in a pose usually reserved for naughty school boys waiting to go into the headmaster's office. When she told Betty she was leaving, she was still holding her cotton wool sheep close to her chest and didn't appear to have an exact understanding of who Julie was. Then, for the first time in her life, she climbed into the backseat of a police car.

CHAPTER THIRTEEN

J ulie was fairly certain that the room they had put her in wasn't a formal questioning suite. There was no tape recorder on the table like the ones she had seen on police dramas. The chairs weren't entirely depleted of cushioning either, although you wouldn't be able to sit on one comfortably for a prolonged period. There was also some natural light coming through a very narrow rectangle of glass placed too high on the wall for Julie to look outside. Julie guessed that this was the place that they put people who they weren't able to formally question but that there was still something decidedly suspicious about. A person of interest was the phrase that came to mind.

She expected it was the middle of the three levels of comfort available. A slightly more accommodating room with worn out armchairs and a shallow sofa for grieving widows and the like must exist somewhere else in the building. It wouldn't do to put the dears in a room as depressing as this. Julie had been left alone while the young police officer had gone to make her a cup of tea. Much like her time at Mrs. McGrath's house, coffee was viewed as a fad only available in the colonies.

Jimmy entered carrying her tea.

'Where's DS Winnington?' Julie asked, hoping she wouldn't be part of today's proceedings.

'She had to er… go away for a bit,' Jimmy said.

Julie was intrigued. Before she could ask any more questions, DI Morris came into the room.

'Thank you for taking the time to speak to us again, Mrs. Giles,' DI Morris said, taking a seat across from her. He had been carrying a brown folder, which he placed on the table in front of him. 'I know your time must be very precious.' Julie thought she could detect a note of sarcasm in his tone, which was unsurprising really, given that they had collected her from a second rate summer fete.

'We were interrupted last time we spoke.' He looked irritated even at the mere memory of Mrs. McGrath. 'If it is alright with you, I would like to take some time establishing the order of events on the night that Mr. Harper died.'

Julie said nothing, rightly presuming that this question was entirely rhetorical.

'It is our understanding that Mr. Harper left his place of work at around midnight. Could you please tell us at what time he returned home?'

Julie could feel herself becoming flustered even at this most basic question. What was it about this nasty little man that filed her with such terror?

'I think… or was it…? No, I'm not sure.'

The inspector's top lip twitched. 'You're not sure?'

'I went to bed early. It had been a long day.'

'Then why did you start your previous sentence with 'I think'?'

'I'm sorry?' Julie's voice cracked.

'You must have been about to say something else. What was it?'

Julie really didn't want to go into the further particulars of her sorry relationship with Jack, but it didn't appear as if she had any choice.

'Jack came into my bedroom at about 3.15. I heard the front door crashing shut just before, so he probably got home around then.'

'Why would your young lodger be coming into your bedroom in the middle of the night?'

'You would have to ask him,' Julie said without thinking.

'Unfortunately, we can't, Mrs. Giles, because he's dead. Was there perhaps something more longstanding about your association than you first led us to believe?'

'Oh for goodness sake.' For the first time, Julie let her frustration overtake her panic at being in a police station. 'We've been over this. We slept together once. There was nothing more to it than that.'

'It's interesting that you say that, because we've received reports that you and Mr. Harper were arguing shortly before he died.'

This threw Julie. 'Who told you that?'

'Was it because you were angry that the victim had decided to end your affair?' DI Morris asked without answering Julie's question.

'I'm sorry, but how does that tally with your accusation that he came into my bedroom for a sexual encounter? Surely both can't be true?'

DI Morris shifted his weight in his seat. Julie was pleased to see that the reference to the matters of the loin were making him uncomfortable. 'I'll be asking the questions, thank you,' he said, averting his gaze for a moment. He fixed his spotlight eyes back on her and said, 'Did you ever want to hurt Mr. Harper?'

'No, of course not,' Julie said a beat too quickly.

'And there's no possibility that the victim returned to your address before 3.15?'

'I'm sorry, but I don't know. I heard a few things in the night, but nothing that I could be certain about. Oh, except I heard a 24 hour plumber arriving at Mrs. Sinclair's house.'

DI Morris didn't break his eye contact with Julie, nor did Jimmy make a note of what she would have expected to be new information. Well, Julie thought, at least that explains who told the police about the argument. Paraplegic husband or not, her sympathy for Mrs. Sinclair was reaching new lows.

'Could you shed any light on what the victim may have been doing between the time he left his place of work and returning home?'

'I really didn't know him that well.'

'Do you have any idea as to what he could have been doing between the time he left his place of work and when he came into your bedroom?'

'No, sorry.'

'None at all?'

'Maybe he went out to meet some friends.'

'A possibility,' DI Morris said, sounding momentarily conciliatory, 'except we checked his mobile phone, and there is no evidence of any communication with anyone else.'

Julie was starting to get annoyed, although tried not to let it show. 'He lived in my house for a few weeks, and yes, before you bring it up again, we did have a very brief and incredibly casual relationship. But he remains as much a mystery to me as he does to you.'

'Very well.' The inspector appeared to realise that this branch of questioning wasn't going to get him anywhere. His hand remained placed on the folder he had brought with him. Julie thought that it was more a prop than anything else. People were more likely to divulge something to you if they thought you already had the information.

'Did you see Mr. Harper again after he left your room at 3.15?'

'No, that was the last time.'

'Based on the state of the body then, that would place the time of death at some time between 3.15am and 6.00am,' the inspector said more to himself than anyone else. 'And have you given any further thought to where Mr. Harper may have been getting his funds from?'

Julie shook her head.

'You have no idea where a young man who only had casual employment had been able to acquire...,' he looked over to Jimmy.

'£320,' Jimmy said without looking in his notebook.

'And when we take into account that Mr. Harper had been unable to obtain his final wage from the bar in which he had been working on the night in question as he had planned, it is all the more peculiar.'

Julie shook her head again. That sounded very low to her. She hadn't had much experience of handling large sums of money, but that roll of bills that she had seen Jack with definitely looked like more than £320. Or even £320 plus the cost of the drugs that he had been buying. Especially if most of them had been £50 notes, like the one that he had dropped on the floor.

'We have found a set of fingerprints in some wet paint on the windowsill.'

'I told you I'd paid Jack to do a bit of work around the house for me.'

'I remember. Would you be willing to provide us with a copy of yours to eliminate them from our enquiry?

'I don't really understand what this is all about. Jack took an overdose, didn't he? No one killed him.'

The inspector continued to stare at her, although there was something evasive in his look. 'We are still open to all avenues,' he said. Julie thought he would make a good politician. Never really answering the question but making it feel like you should be thanking them for the scraps of information they threw your way. Mrs. McGrath might not be as tapped as she looks then. Someone may have murdered Jack. 'Your fingerprints would be very helpful, Mrs. Giles,' he repeated.

'Oh yes, sorry. Of course.'

'Very good. DC Rowntree can help you with that once we are done here.'

'Thank you,' Julie said and then felt silly.

'Mrs. Giles. Is there anything else that you can tell us that will help explain how a young man could come to this town and within a few weeks, end up dead?'

Julie wanted to be helpful, she really did, but she was so scared of sounding ridiculous in front of these professional people. Surely nothing that she could suggest would be of any consequence.

'I'm sorry. I just don't know what I could tell you that would be useful.'

'Did Mr. Harper have any other friends that you saw him associating with? Anyone that would have wanted to do him any harm?'

Before Julie could answer, the door slammed open, and Mrs. McGrath walked into the room. Julie found that for the first time in her life, she was actually pleased to see her.

DI Morris, whose back had been to the door, turned to admonish the intruder. His usual resolute persona dropped for a moment, and he registered clear unadulterated shock at seeing his adversary.

'What the bloody hell do you think you're doing here?'

'I'm here to support my neighbour.' She hobbled around the table and sat next to Julie without being invited.

'It's not Jeremy Kyle. You can't just come in and hold her hand because you feel like it.'

'I'm her appropriate adult,' Mrs. McGrath said, resting her stick against the table and getting comfortable.

'Her appropriate adult?'

'That's right.' Mrs. McGrath looked pleased with herself.

'Mrs. Giles, are you in some way vulnerable that you haven't disclosed to us?'

'She's just found a dead body in her house, you pillock. Wouldn't you say that would make most people feel vulnerable?'

'I was hoping that Mrs. Giles would be able to answer me.' DI Morris was attempting to act like a cool headed police officer again but didn't quite manage it.

'What's the point in having an appropriate adult in the first place if you're not going to let them do their job?' Mrs. McGrath managed to look inquisitive, as if this was a genuine question.

He turned to address Mrs. McGrath directly. 'As you are well aware, the Crime and Disorder Act of 1998 only allows for the provision of appropriate adults for children and those who are mentally vulnerable.'

'No it doesn't.'

'Yes it does,'

'It really doesn't.'

'Yes, it does,' the inspector said, in a voice that wasn't quite a shout but was getting there.

'The act says nothing about vulnerable adults or what constitutes being mentally vulnerable. If you would like to read an interesting study on broadening the definition, I would suggest looking at the National Appropriate Adult Network website.' The voice, informed and considered, sounded alien coming out of Mrs. McGrath's mouth. It was in such stark contrast to her normal belligerence and the spouting of little known conspiracy theories.

'And seeing as she hasn't been arrested, she can walk out of here whenever she likes.' Mrs. McGrath continued. Julie thought it was funny that Mrs. McGrath was willing to protect her from excessive police powers but still would not take the time to learn her name. 'So, either you let me stay, and you can carry on with the interview, or we'll go and get some chips.'

'Very well, Moira,' said DI Morris, conceding defeat. 'As you seem to be committed to hindering this investigation at every possible opportunity, I don't think there would be much point in continuing with this farce.' He left enough of a break that both women assumed he had finished talking. When they had just got to their feet, he said, 'However…,' and once again paused until they sat down again, 'I think this would be a good opportunity to remind you both that the investigation of crime is solely the remit of the police force. If any individuals were to take it upon themselves to attempt to circumvent the work of our hard working detectives, then they may find themselves being faced with a charge for the obstruction of justice.'

Mrs. McGrath started to argue with the inspector, but he interrupted her. 'The local youth that the two of you decided to pay a visit to earlier this week has already been eliminated from our enquiries.'

Julie looked dumbstruck. In contrast, Mrs. McGrath looked like a teenager who had been caught having a party at her parent's house and couldn't care less.

'Not only was he in police custody on the night when Mr. Harper died, but when he was arrested on a separate offence two days later, he disclosed to us that he had only sold cannabis to Mr. Harper and not the heroin that killed him. He did claim that he was subject to police harassment, given that two undercover officers had already spoken to him about the alleged position of class A drugs.'

Mrs. McGrath and Julie said nothing. DI Morris opened the folder in front of him for the first time and began to read. 'When he told us that one was a 'mean old bitch with a stick,' and the other was 'one of them old housewife types,' it didn't take much deducing to realise who he was talking about.'

'Moira, you may feel that you have a better understanding of how to run an investigation than anyone else alive, but there are proper ways of doing things. I don't care who you are or what relationship you have to this station. If I find that you acted illegally, I will not hesitate to arrest you. Do I make myself clear?'

DI Morris gave Mrs. McGrath a pointed look of such intensity that Julie would have instantly answered him if the question had been directed at her. After an uncomfortably long time of Mrs. McGrath not answering the detective, he said, 'Thank you for your time, ladies,' and left the room. Julie took a sip of her now cold tea before being taken to provide a copy of her fingerprints. When that was done, Julie hadn't found Mrs. McGrath in the reception area where she had anticipated that she would be. Instead, Julie was forced to wait a further ten minutes for the old woman to materialise.

'Where have you been?' Julie said when Mrs. McGrath emerged from the building. She had found a bench just outside the station and had been enjoying the afternoon sunshine.

'Saying hello to a few people, wasn't I?' Mrs. McGrath said, limping over to the bench.

'How did you even know I was here?'

'Jimmy gave me a call. Said they'd brought you in.'

I thought you didn't like policemen?'

'He's alright. Cod and chips for me. Mushy peas. Pickled egg.'

'Oh, we're actually having fish and chips?'

'Right weather for it.' Mrs. McGrath folded her arms and closed her eyes. With that, Julie tried to get her bearings and find a chip shop. In normal circumstances, it would have irked her that Mrs. McGrath expected her to buy her lunch, but she had actually been a very good neighbour recently. Not only had she given Julie somewhere to stay while the police were turning her house upside down, she had also stopped her from potentially incriminating herself in front of the police on two separate occasions now.

When she arrived back with the food, it wasn't clear whether Mrs. McGrath was asleep or just resting. Mrs. McGrath seemed to have a tendency to do this. Julie suspected that it had less to do with the old woman feeling tired, and more because she had become bored with whatever conversation was happening around her. Julie gave her a gentle prod in the shoulder to announce her presence. Without thanks, Mrs. McGrath unfolded her chips and began to eat.

'What did he tell you before I got there? Anything important?'

'It's hard to tell what is important, isn't it? It's like they've got three different versions of events in their head, and they're asking questions about all of them simultaneously.'

'Tell me it all then.'

Julie relayed the conversation as well as she could remember it.

'You're sure that he had more money than that when you saw him with it?'

'Not sure, no. But it definitely didn't look like as little as that. Unless there was one fifty pound note and the rest were fives or something.' Mrs. McGrath thought it over as she chewed. 'Do you think it could have been a robbery gone wrong or something?' Julie asked.

'Bit of a weird way of killing someone. You'd hit them over the head or something. How sure are you that the lad came in at 3.15?'

'That's when I heard the door, and he came into my room almost straight afterwards, so pretty sure.'

'And they think he was killed, what? Right afterwards?'

'The inspector said that he thought the time of death was between 3.15am and 6.00am, although god knows how they work that out.'

Mrs. McGrath nodded as she received this information, mulling it over.

They had been sitting, eating in silence for a few moments when Julie said 'Mrs. McGrath, why did the inspector say you thought you had a better understanding of how to run an investigation than him? And why do you know so many people at the police station?'

Not acknowledging Julie's question, Mrs. McGrath continued to eat her chips.

'When do you want to go?' the old lady asked finally.

'What, home? I'm happy to go now if you want.' Julie said, although the idea of getting the bus with Mrs. McGrath was a bit taxing.

'Not home, lass. To speak to the people your young man was working with.'

'What, why? They're not convinced it was a suicide now. They're taking it seriously.'

'Doesn't mean they're going to do it right.' She scrunched up the paper around the remainder of her chips, of which Julie saw there were a great deal, and threw them into the bin to her right. Mrs. McGrath then stood up with a 'harrumph.' 'Don't come into town much these days. Where's the train station?'

'You want to go into London now? I need to get home.'

'You just said that you didn't have anything on,' said Mrs. McGrath accusingly.

'It doesn't mean that I have the time to trek into London for no reason whatsoever.'

'Don't know how you normally live your life, but someone dying in your house isn't no reason whatsoever to me.'

'I didn't mean that,' Julie said, starting to lose her patience. 'If the police are looking into it already, then what good are the two of us going to do?'

'I've told you already. The people the lad worked with might be lying about what time he left, or they didn't have the wits about them to know when something was off.'

'I can't see why he even went in the first place. Not after all the carry on when I was there.'

Mrs. McGrath, who had been more interested in a map of the local area, now turned to Julie.

'What?'

'When I was at the bar with Jack, and he had that fight? I told you about this?' Julie said it with little conviction, realising that she had no memory of doing so.

'Who was he fighting with?'

'A woman first, but I don't know her name, and then one of the other bartenders. Oh, and then he had a punch up with one of the customers, and his boss sacked him.'

For the first time since she had known her, Mrs. McGrath looked incredulous. 'You're telling me that the lad you just found dead in your house had a fight with four different people a few days before he died, and you didn't think to mention it?'

'I don't think that's fair,' Julie said defensively. 'Up until this morning, everyone was saying that it was an overdose.'

'I bloody wasn't! Did you tell the police?'

'No I..., well if I'm honest, I'd forgotten about it. I didn't think it was important.'

'No doubt they know if they've been to the bar already.'

'There you go then,' Julie said, feeling vindicated. 'Nothing more for us to do.'

'Right.' Mrs. McGrath snatched the rest of Julie's chips from her lap and put them in the bin.

'I wasn't finished with those!'

'I don't bloody care.'

'You don't think we should just go back inside and tell DI Morris about it? Then he can look into it if he thinks it's relevant?'

'The bloody rapture will come before Maz Morris decides what's relevant. Look at the little thug who was dealing the drugs. We were a whole day ahead of them there.'

'You bumped into him outside the shops. It wasn't exactly the height of logical deduction, is it?'

'It's about putting yourself in the right situations. Where's the train station?'

'Mrs. McGrath, I really don't think it's a good idea.'

'I think you've proved that we can't trust your judgement. Which way?' She had such conviction in her eyes that Julie didn't dare to defy her. Cowed, she pointed to the direction of the station and then attempted to keep up with Mrs. McGrath as she marched toward it.

CHAPTER FOURTEEN

Julie looked on in horror as Mrs. McGrath pounded against the steel shutter of the bar. As she stood frozen in embarrassment, the normal selection of Londoners passed them. Some were used to living in the capital and wouldn't even think to give an old woman repeatedly bashing her stick against the front of a building a second look. However, there were some, particularly those passing with a friend or in a small group, who chuckled and looked over the shoulders to take a second glance at the spectacle.

'Mrs. McGrath,' Julie said once at a normal volume and then again louder when it became apparent that the old woman hadn't heard her. 'I don't think there's anyone there.'

'That's what they want you to think,' she said, giving the metal barrier another wallop.

'I think in this situation, it might actually be true.' Julie was petrified that one of the pedestrians was going to call the police. The inspector may be just about willing to forget about one indiscretion out of some mysterious loyalty he had to the mad old coot, but this would probably be the straw that broke the camel's back.

'Not bloody likely.' She took a pause from her thrashing and peered in through the bar's windows. 'Get away with murder that way, hiding behind a locked door. Cowards.'

'It's five o'clock. It would be more suspicious if there was someone there.'

'Not everyone is after a drink.' Mrs. McGrath said indignantly. 'Some people might just want a cup of tea or something.'

Julie noted the poster in the window for a performance by a band called The Clunge Hunters and thought that it probably wasn't the kind of place where people went for light afternoon refreshment. Before Julie could stop her, Mrs. McGrath started to smack her cane once again against the front of the establishment.

Absolutely mortified that she was involved in this scene, Julie started to walk down the street. She didn't plan on leaving Mrs. McGrath. Nor did she think she had any hope of plausible deniability should someone in a position of authority arrive. Julie just wanted a few moments respite from the gawping of those walking by. She was walking at a very gentle pace and had only planned to open up a gap of a couple of hundred metres between them before walking back the way she came. When she was just about to turn, she looked up and saw someone she vaguely recognised. It took her a few moments to place him before realising that he was the other bloke behind the bar that Jack had argued with. Having noticed Mrs. McGrath, who was continuing her assault, there was a look of real indecision on his face. Arriving to work and finding such a ridiculous spectacle to deal with even before the start of what Julie expected would be a very long shift wouldn't be ideal. The young man looked as if he was weighing up whether dealing with this situation was worth keeping his minimum wage job for.

'Hello,' Julie said before he could decide that it wasn't. 'Do you work at Nixons?' Being accosted by strangers is part and parcel of London life, but the man still looked startled that someone he didn't know was talking to him. His eyes passed from her to Mrs. McGrath and back. Julie asked the question again.

Something clicked in his brain, and he realised that he was still wearing headphones. 'Sorry, what?' he said, taking them out of his ears.

'Do you work at that bar? Nixons, is it?'

'I do, yeah.' He still didn't seem sure if he wanted to ask what it was that they wanted.

'Did you know Jack Harper?' she asked. His brow now creased, unhappy at the memory of his rival.

'Not really.' He was now looking over her shoulder, and Julie could tell that she had lost his attention. Mrs. McGrath materialised at her side, the conspicuous ceasing of the clanging now apparent to her. The young man put his weight on his back foot and held onto one of the straps of his backpack ready to retreat if necessary.

'This him?' Mrs. McGrath asked.

'This is…,' Julie said, leaving a gap for him to interject his name. When he didn't freely take up the opportunity, she said, 'I'm sorry, what was your name?'

'Oli. Oli Simms,' he said reluctantly. He appeared to think he didn't have any choice in the matter.

'He was just telling me that he worked with Jack.'

'That right?' said Mrs. McGrath. She hooked her stick over her left forearm and reached into one of the myriad of pockets in her great green coat. She pulled out a little notepad and a pen. Flipping the cover open, she made a note of something.

'Yeah. I mean, he was here for what, three weeks? Didn't know him well or anything.'

'We've got some questions for you. Better to do it inside if you don't mind.' Mrs. McGrath walked towards him and then stood half a step behind him. Obediently, he started walking towards the bar, giving the impression that he was being escorted.

Once the alarm was deactivated, chairs were turned the right way round, and the three of them seated themselves just inside the entrance. He still seemed very wary of them, as if he was unsure that this was all an elaborate plot to get the better of him in some way. The chosen table meant that they were visible from the street. His choice of seat was the one closest to the door in case he needed to make a quick exit.

'Can I get you a drink or something?' Oli said.

'We're fine, thank you,' Julie replied before Mrs. McGrath could order herself anything alcoholic.

'What's this about then?' Oli sounded more confident now that he was in familiar territory. His light grey t-shirt was a size too small, no doubt chosen on purpose to display his expansive chest.

'He's dead,' Mrs. McGrath said matter of factly.

'Jack? Yeah, I heard.'

'Why are you asking what this is about then? Not so ridiculous that people would come round and ask questions about a dead man.'

Oli looked nervous. His eyes darted between them.

'Heard there was some trouble here,' Mrs. McGrath said, scribbling something in her notebook. Julie looked over and saw that they were far from comprehensive. She had written 'dead,' in the middle of the page, circling it a few times for emphasis. Underneath, there was something else scrawled that was barely legible, although Julie was fairly certain it said, 'grey t-shirt.'

'He overdosed though, didn't he?'

'Drugs then, is it? A lot of that going on here, is there?' Mrs. McGrath said in a gruffer tone.

Oli shook his head nervously.

'You don't know where a young lad like that could have got his hands on heroin?'

Oli had started to look really flustered. 'No. Honestly, I really don't,' he said, bumbling slightly. 'I'm just saying if he overdosed then it won't have anything to do with the fight, will it?'

'Still need to look into it. Proper way to do these things.' She put another ring around 'dead.'

'What time did he leave here on Sunday night?'

His face visibly brightened. 'That's when he died, yeah?' Neither of the women said anything. 'I wasn't working. Spent all night with my nan at the hospice. Dying. Lung cancer.' Never before had someone been so giddy at the passing of a grandparent.

'Nurses can confirm that, can they?'

'Absolutely. Mum couldn't go because she's broken her toe, and Phil couldn't drive her. I was supposed to be working, missed a night's wages. Fucking nightmare.'

'What about this other bloke he was fighting with?'

Oli shrugged. 'Never seen him before. Your standard wanker from the city; they all look the same.'

Mrs. McGrath made another scribble on her pad. 'Who was working on Sunday?'

'It was Chloe. Covered my shift for me. Got a good chance of banging her soon, I think.' A smile spread across his face. He appeared to have forgotten who he was talking to, his eyes now focused on a random spot outside the window. 'She was sweet on that prat for a while. I'm in with a chance now though. Him being out of the picture at all.'

'Funny thing to say about a man to two people looking into his death.'

'Shit, no I didn't mean that.'

'Got an address for her?' Mrs. McGrath asked.

'Yeah...,' he hesitated. 'But I don't think she'd want me handing it out.'

Mrs. McGrath put one hand on the table and bent forward towards him. 'Got something to hide?' she said. Oli attempted to lean backwards to get away from her, but his chair only had so much give.

'It's in Hackney,' he said, the panic having returned to his voice. '33 White Fern Road. Second floor.'

Mrs. McGrath sat back in her chair. 'What line's that on?'

It still amazed Julie that regardless of the situation, she was perpetually rushing to try and keep up with Mrs. McGrath. With each step, she swung her cane out in a lazy circle before placing it back on the ground. This wasn't an issue in Brumpton, where the old woman was such a presence that most people had learned to steer well clear of her. The throngs of London presented something of an issue. More than once on their walk to the tube station, Mrs. McGrath's stick had managed to make contact with the shin of an unsuspecting pedestrian.

There was a rare break in the foot traffic, and Julie was able to walk alongside her troublesome neighbour for the first time since they had left the bar. 'Do you really think that was a good idea?' she asked.

'Didn't do anything wrong.'

'We did exactly what DI Morris told us not to do.'

'No, we bloody didn't. We asked that daft lad some questions. Not our fault if he thought we were something we weren't.'

'Are you surprised? Who else carries a notebook except journalists and police officers.'

'Concerned citizens.'

'I really don't want to get into any trouble. Maybe we should go home,' Julie said, and really meant it. Her feet were tired, and she really didn't see what good any of this would do. Surely, the police were best placed to investigate Jack's death. If the past few days were anything to go by, Mrs. McGrath wasn't much of a detective, and Julie certainly wasn't. If she was honest with herself, she wasn't even much of a shop assistant. She felt like she'd been useful once as a mother and a wife, but what was she now? Someone who did the bare minimum at work to then come home and drink too much wine.

Mrs. McGrath abruptly halted in the middle of the pavement, causing those immediately behind her to make an emergency stop. Harsh words were muttered slightly too quietly for them to hear before the slighted parties carried on their way.

'If you want to go home, then go,' she said. There was something to her tone that Julie hadn't heard before. She didn't sound merely cantankerous or belligerent, but truly irritated. 'Doesn't mean much these days, does it? One more dead teenager.'

'You didn't even know him,' Julie said, trying to defend herself. 'And if you did, I don't think you would have liked him very much. Not that you really seem to like anyone.'

'It's not about liking people,' she said. 'It's about doing what's proper. If you don't look after each other, then what's the point?'

Julie didn't know what to say. She just stared at the old woman and felt a bit guilty for wanting to give up.

'What do you need me for though?' she asked. 'You've got it under control.' Or at least as under control as an old woman who clearly isn't qualified to be investigating crimes can have it, Julie thought.

Mrs. McGrath shrugged. 'I dunno. It's better with two people. Someone to talk to. Bounce ideas off. Besides, if you're not here, that wazzock Maz is going to say I'm just a mad old lady.'

'I'm not convinced you're not.' Mrs. McGrath scowled at her. 'Are you ever going to tell me what you have against him?' Julie asked.

'Not if you have a paddy every time we hit a dead end,' she said, and charged off into the station.

Despite the tube being absolutely rammed, something of a buffer zone formed around the two women as they stood in the middle of the carriage. The first gentleman who had tried to be chivalrous and offer Mrs. McGrath a seat had been given a look so venomous that no further attempts were made. 'Didn't like his hands,' the old woman had said loudly enough for the entire compartment to hear. 'Looked like a strangler to me.' Those sitting closest to the poor gentleman had given him nervous glances before attempting to shuffle a little further away.

The overground from Highbury and Islington to Hackney Central was less busy, and they were able to sit next to each other. Once they arrived, Mrs. McGrath managed to get directions to White Fern road from one of the station attendants.

'How are we going to check on his alibi?' Julie said as they left the station. 'You didn't take any details. The name of the hospice or anything.'

'Don't need it. You can just tell by looking at them.'

'You can tell by looking at someone if they're a murderer?'

Mrs. McGrath made a grunt which Julie took to mean yes.

'That doesn't seem very thorough.'

'The only reason he had to kill the lad was because of this girl. His head wasn't bashed in, he was pumped full of drugs.' Julie conceded that Mrs. McGrath had a point. 'Besides, a great ninny like that wouldn't have the stomach for it. He'd have shit himself as soon as he'd stuck the needle in, and I don't remember seeing any of that on the carpet.'

Again, Julie thought that the old woman had a point. 'What about this bloke from the city? How are we going to find him?'

'Don't need to,' Mrs. McGrath said. 'It just doesn't fit.' And that was that.

They reached the door of 33 White Fern Road and rang the bell for the second floor flat. When they rang the third time and there was still no answer,

Julie was worried that Mrs. McGrath's stick would once again spring into action. Luckily, the door was opened by a cyclist in a hurry. He looked at them both dumbly standing on the top step.

When a few seconds passed and Mrs. McGrath said nothing, Julie stammered, 'Delivery, for the second floor.' She began to pat her pockets looking for something to act as a parcel for delivery.

'Yeah, whatever,' he said, uninterested. 'Just leave it in by the postboxes. Can you move please? I'm late for work.' The two of them stood to one side, and he hurried out.

'Not bad, ey?' Julie said, feeling pleased with herself.

Mrs. McGrath made her usual noncommittal noise in the back of her throat.

'Quick thinking, wasn't it? Telling him that I was delivering something.'

'Word of advice,' Mrs. McGrath said, knocking on the only door on the second floor, 'if you're going to pretend that you're delivering something, actually bring something to deliver.'

'It wasn't bad for a first attempt though, was it?' Julie said, but Mrs. McGrath wasn't willing to give her any praise. On the other side of the glass, they could see a figure approaching them. 'Let me do the talking this time, will you? We don't have to treat everyone that we talk to like they've murdered someone.'

The door opened, and they were met with the face of Jack's erstwhile beau. She was just as beautiful as Julie remembered. Her hair, dark and wavy, was not unlike Jack's, albeit longer. It was piled on top of her head in a messy bun. She wore an oversized t-shirt which was hanging off one shoulder and a pair of pyjama bottoms. Even though it was late in the afternoon, she looked as if she had just got out of bed. Despite not wearing any makeup, Julie thought that she looked better than she herself would have done if she had spent all afternoon preening. She wondered whether Jack had actually slept with this young beauty. The idea that he would have compared the two of them almost made her physically cringe. She gave Julie a puzzled look, like she recognised her face but couldn't place where from.

'Chloe?' Julie said. 'We met at Nixons.' Chloe still didn't look sure. 'I was a friend of Jack's.'

'Oh yeah,' she said in an airy voice.

'He was staying with me.'

She nodded slowly as if she was taking the time to take this information in. It was the kind of reaction you expected when you surprised someone with the knowledge that you were, in fact, their biological parent, not that you shared a mutual acquaintance. Mrs. McGrath shot Julie an unimpressed look.

'Listen, we have a few questions about Jack. Would you mind if we came in?' Chloe turned and looked back inside the flat for some unknown reason.

'Yeah, I guess?' She said it in that irritating way that young people do where they turn every statement into a question.

They followed her inside and were billeted at the kitchen table. No offer was made to provide them with refreshments, although looking at the pile of dirty cups and mugs in the sink, Julie thought that this wasn't necessarily a bad thing.

'Need to ask you a few questions,' Mrs. McGrath started when Julie didn't immediately jump into action. Cleo looked taken aback by the old woman, as if she was some great, wild animal that she had discovered in her flat.

Julie smiled and adopted the voice she normally reserved for difficult customers. 'If you don't mind, that is.'

'I guess?'

'Can you tell us what time Jack left the bar on Sunday night?'

'Maybe 11.30? Or 12?' Mrs. McGrath sat up straighter in her chair, the lack of uncertainty irking her.

'Could you be a little more precise?'

'Yeah, I think it was 12.00. Because we'd just called last orders?'

'Why is that a question?' Mrs. McGrath said, unable to stay silent any longer.

'I'm sorry?' Chloe said, her first actual question since they arrived.

'Why is 'because we just called last orders,' a question?'

Chloe looked confused. Julie didn't wait for her to attempt an answer or for Mrs. McGrath to alienate her any further. 'What was he doing there in the first place? What with the manager sacking him a few nights before.'

'He'd brought his guitar with him. I guess he thought that John would figure that he was missing something good and ask him to play? I guess when that didn't happen, he just sat in the corner drinking. He was flashing his money about, you know?'

'Do you know where he got his money from?' Julie asked.

Chloe shook her head. 'He always had a lot? But he wouldn't say where from.' Her face turned sad all of a sudden. 'I think there could have been something really special between us, you know? Like, I know he wasn't always nice, but someone who sings like that, can't be all bad, can he?' Her eyes started to become moist, and Julie moved a bit closer so she could put her arm around her. 'I just think, if we'd had some more time together...,'

'He definitely left at midnight?' Mrs. McGrath interrupted.

'What?' Cleo said, again looking a bit shell shocked. 'Yeah, like I said, I saw him leave as they were calling last orders.'

'Right,' Mrs. McGrath said, and walked out of the flat without another word to either of them.

CHAPTER FIFTEEN

'I know what she was saying wasn't useful, but that doesn't mean we can't be nice to her.'

Mrs. McGrath looked unconvinced. 'Who are we to her? Why would she care if we were nice?'

'Sometimes you just want someone to be kind to you. They don't have to be someone you know.'

Mrs. McGrath made a derisive noise. It was a little past rush hour and so they hadn't struggled with getting seats. They sat on either side of a table of four. The two commuters next to them tried to focus on their smartphone and their newspaper, respectively. The train was stuffy and yet Mrs. McGrath continued to wear her ubiquitous mackintosh.

'You took your time in there. Stood out on the bloody street for hours.'

'I was in there for maybe 10 minutes after you left, Mrs. McGrath. There's no need to be so dramatic.'

'Didn't feel like it.' Her tone was moody, petulant even.

'Do you want to know what she said about the drugs? Or where she was for the rest of the night?'

'No,' she answered bluntly.

'Why not?'

'She didn't do it. What's the point?'

'You know, I don't think you can get all high and mighty about the police not investigating properly if you're not willing to fact check the alibis of even the most obvious suspects.'

'That's not proper detection. Anyone can do that.'

'Enlighten me then; what is proper detection?'

'You know, being able to tell if someone's done it.'

'So what you're saying is that it doesn't matter how hard DI Morris tries? If he doesn't have the instinct for it, then he's never going to be able to catch killers.'

'Well you've got to find the killer first. Got to be able to look him in the face.'

'And at that point, the case is closed?'

'Pretty much, yeah.'

'And how are you going to find the people in the first place if you don't actually ask any questions?'

Mrs. McGrath stared at her dumbly, and Julie gave her a reproachful look. 'Go on then,' said Mrs. McGrath, as if she was doing Julie a favour. 'What did she say about the drugs and where did she go after she left the bar?'

Julie reached into her bag and pulled out the receipt that she had scribbled her notes on the back of. 'She didn't know anything about heroin. Her and Jack used to smoke a bit of dope in the alley behind the bar sometimes on their breaks but nothing harder than that.' She flipped over the receipt and read the other side. 'Straight from work, she went home. Bit of a party going on apparently. Spent the night with one of her flatmates who just so happened to be home.'

'You needed to write that down?' Mrs. McGrath said derisively.

'You took notes too.'

'To put the screws into that muppet. I could just about remember 'was with my dying nan,' even at my age.' She snatched Julie's notes from the table. 'At it like rabbits, these young people.'

Unsure of whether Mrs. McGrath included Julie as a 'young person,' she felt her face start to redden. As ever, the old woman took no notice of the effects of her words on others. She reached into her coat and drew out a bottle of the brown spirit that she had plied Julie with on her overnight visit and a plastic cup. She filled the vessel about two fingers full and slid it towards Julie. She then raised the bottle in a 'cheers,' motion and then took an almighty gulp. Thinking she should really know better by now, Julie took a sip and immediately winced.

'What do you think he was doing then?' Julie said when she caught her breath again. 'Between when he left the bar and when he got back to the house.'

'Dunno. Maybe he came back and was knocking around downstairs. Doesn't mean that he couldn't have opened the front door again just because he got back earlier on.'

'But why would he be opening the front door again? It's not like he knew anyone else around here.'

'You don't know that.'

'That's true. DI Morris said he'd checked his phone though. No calls or texts that night.'

'There's always something going on; haven't you realised that yet? Like your lad who was fiddling with the telephone box. Looks innocent on the face of it, but there's always something murkier underneath. Have a proper think about when he was staying with you. Anyone you saw him speaking to or that didn't feel right.'

Julie thought for a few seconds and then said, 'Nothing springs to mind.'

'What about the day before he died? You said you found him chatting to that yob when you got home from work. What about before you left in the morning?'

She cast her mind back to that morning. 'I don't know, Mrs. McGrath. I was hungover and late. I forgot my car keys and had to run back into the house in a panic.' Mrs. McGrath continued to wait expectantly. 'I tripped over his shoes? Is that something?' The old woman looked unimpressed. 'Don't look at me like that! I'm clutching at straws. I can't think of anyone who he got on the wrong side of that we haven't talked to already.'

'Doesn't mean someone couldn't have travelled to kill him.' Mrs. McGrath said, and Julie nodded, although she couldn't help feeling that this plot was getting more farfetched by the second. 'Who was it that he was gardening for? That sour faced cow at number 32?'

'Mrs. Sinclair with the very difficult life due to caring for her severely disabled husband,' Julie said with more than a hint of admonishment in her voice. 'But I already know what she was doing. I heard a plumber arrive just after Jack came into my room, and then the paramedics were there. Her husband had a funny turn. Alright now though.'

Mrs. McGrath suddenly turned her attention to Julie. 'Where's this plumber come from all of a sudden? You haven't mentioned him before.'

'Didn't I?'

'If you'd mentioned it, we'd have been to see him already. First the punch up in the bar, now this. Anyone else you want to mention while we're at it? A drug baron living in your cellar maybe?'

Julie ignored the slight and said, 'Is that how we're approaching this from now on? Speak to whoever was the nearest to Jack before he died and work out from there?'

'Seems about right, yeah.'

'But what are we saying the motive is? You don't just get people going around committing murder for no reason.'

'What about Harold Shipman? He had a good reason for knocking off all those old ladies, did he?'

The man with the newspaper stopped reading at this and cocked his head towards them.

'You need something?' Mrs. McGrath asked him loudly. He gave her a dirty look and went back to his newspaper. 'And we've talked to everyone who might have actually had a motive. If you don't know the why, you've got to focus on the what. Who had the opportunity, and this lad did. Could have been her who he was doing the job for too. What did the rozza say, time of death between 3.15 and 6? Either one could have done it after he'd finished.'

Julie shook her head. 'She said she called the paramedics at around 5.30. She said he was still there when they arrived and then I heard them leaving when I got up at 8. Not sure about the plumber though.'

'There you go then. Worth a conversation with him at least.'

Julie gave a theatrical sight for effect. 'How are we going to find him? I didn't get the licence plate or anything.'

'You'll have to talk to her over the road and ask. The miserable one.'

'Again, the woman who is the primary caregiver for her severely disabled husband out of the goodness of her own heart.'

'Why do you keep telling me what she does?'

'Because you keep calling her miserable.'

'I'm not saying she doesn't have a good reason to be.'

'And why do I have to talk to her?' The memory of the altercation at the fete was very fresh in Julie's mind, and she didn't expect that Mrs. Sinclair would have forgotten either.

'Had a bit of a falling out a few years ago about a conifer tree.'

'What a surprise. How do you fall out with someone who lives on the opposite side of the street as you about a tree?'

'Bloody ugly thing, it was. Couldn't look out the front bedroom window without seeing it. You can go round when we get back and then we'll go to the plumbers first thing tomorrow. The office is probably closed now, bit late in the day,' she said, looking at her watch. 'Can talk to a few of the other neighbours tonight too. Who else on the street looks a bit dodgy to you? What's his name, always chatting up the ladies.'

'Brian at number 30.'

'Put him on the list.' Julie said, wondering if she should now be taking notes. 'Actually, it wouldn't hurt to speak to the rest of the neighbours as well. See if any of them are hiding anything.'

Julie inwardly groaned. Not that she knew from previous experience, but she was sure that one sure fire way to get on your neighbour's bad side is to casually accuse them of murder.

She put the top back on the bottle and returned it to her coat. 'That's enough of this,' she said sternly, 'we can have a bit more when we're done for the night.' Mrs. McGrath said, taking Julie's silence for agreement. At some point in this mad endeavour, the decision had been that she would be included in these investigations indefinitely. She didn't exactly mind, but it would have been nice to be consulted.

'It's too late to go about knocking on people's doors.' Julie protested.

'Better chance of catching them at home in the evenings. That's how the Jovies work.'

'Who, sorry?'

'Those neat religious types that are always turning up uninvited.'

'You mean Jehovah's witnesses?'

'That's what I said.'

'People aren't going to want to talk to you if you bother them after being at work all day.'

Remarkably, Mrs. McGrath conceded the point. Julie felt disproportionately elated at winning this small battle with the curmudgeon. 'Alright then, we'll do that tomorrow too.'

'Oh wait, I forgot,' Julie said, suddenly remembering, 'I've got work tomorrow, sorry. We'll have to do both on Friday instead. The plumbers and the conversations with the neighbours. If there's not enough time I'll come with you on Saturday morning.'

Mrs. McGrath threw her arms up in the air theatrically. 'Should we just wait until there's another murder?'

'If anyone gets murdered between now and then, I promise that I'll hold myself accountable.'

Mrs. McGrath glared at Julie. She must have realised that she wasn't going to change her mind because she said nothing. She folded her arms and turned her attention to the countryside streaming past the window.

WHEN JULIE ARRIVED for work the next day, she wasn't able to get through the entrance. Thankfully, she had been paying attention, otherwise she would have collided head first with the two bags of sand blocking the gap in the hedges. She groaned at the sight of them, remembering Mr. Peg's winning 'Backdoor Beaches' scheme before driving her car as far down the layby as she could and proceeding on foot.

Walking up towards the garden centre, Julie saw that the massive bags littered the drive. So encumbered was the narrowed tarmac that at one point, she had to turn sideways in order to squeeze through. She reached the greenhouse, and Mr. Peg was nowhere to be seen. Mike was sitting at the small table in the staff room eating an apple.

'Hello,' he said with a concerned smile when he saw her. 'Everything all right with the police? Sorry for not saying much, not very good with the rozzas. You want to talk about it?'

Julie dropped her bag on the table. She filled the kettle and turned it on. 'I'm fine,' she said, not wanting to go through what had happened with Jack. 'But what on Earth's going on here? I thought we'd got rid of the sand.'

'Mrs. Wilkin's order? That got rid of the two that we had, yeah.'

'What do you mean the two that we had?'

'Mr. Peg was so encouraged by how quickly we got our first customer that he decided we needed some more sand as soon as we could get it. Problem is that he was worried about getting a flood of orders and not being able to fulfil them because we didn't have the product. So what you're seeing here is the result of that winning logic.'

'What about the rest of the beaches?' she asked. Mike looked at her quizzically. 'I don't know, whatever else it is that you're putting into these gardens to make them look like beaches instead of a lawn covered in sand.'

'The sand's it. Oh no, I tell a lie, each Backdoor Beach comes with a complimentary bucket and spade. But that's all.'

'So you're just arriving at the people's houses...'

'Person's house. Remember we've only had one customer so far.'

'Of course. Arriving at this person's house and distributing a bloody great load of sand over their garden.'

'And even then, I'm not really doing that. He sent me with two of those bags, and Mrs. Wilkin's garden was the size of a postage stamp. I spread around the first one and even then, it was a foot deep in some places. But the lorry had unloaded the bags and left me there so there wasn't much I could do with the other one. I tried to push it to one side of the garden. Bloody heavy though. I didn't have much luck. I had to leave it blocking one side of her french doors.'

Julie laughed and put a cup of tea in front of him. 'And I thought I'd pulled the short straw doing sales.'

'Mrs. Wilkin was very nice about it. Bless her, I don't think she's all there. She probably thinks that she's at Bournemouth seafront in 1982 or something.'

'Well, there you go then, at least we have one moderately happy customer. Where's Mr. Peg?'

'Out the back with the peace lilies. Said that he needed to think out the next part of his strategy.'

'Can't he just get the sand company to come and pick it up?'

'Why would he? He ordered it on purpose. He doesn't realise that no one else thinks this is a good idea.'

'Aside from his one existing customer of course.'

'And there's the problem. The lunacy of Mrs. Wilkin has convinced him that people would be interested if we publicised it more. He was talking about radio adverts this morning. I at least managed to make him cancel the repeat order until we get rid of the stuff that we've got.'

Julie laughed. 'It's good to have you back,' Mike said, becoming awkward all of a sudden. 'I er... well, I missed you, truth be told, Julie.'

'Oh...,'

'Only a few days that you were away for, and I saw you yesterday at Thorneywood, I know. But still. Sorry, is it alright that I'm saying that?'

'No, yes of course.'

'I didn't want to make you uncomfortable or anything.'

'It's fine, honestly.'

'Because I know we have to work together, but I just really like talking to you.'

'Mike...,'

'Sorry, I'll stop now.'

'I've missed you too, Mike. Talking to you, I mean. I've missed your company.' She was surprised to find that she really meant it.

He looked shocked for a few seconds and then he gave her a smile. His face was so wide that it went on for days, stretching from ear to ear. He looked down at his cup of tea.

'It would be nice... if we could see each other outside of work. Sometime soon maybe. A drink, or something to eat?' He peeked up at her to gauge her reaction, his face still turned to the table.

'Yes… I think I'd like that. How about Saturday night?'

'Okay, then,' he said, looking pleased with himself. '8 o'clock? We can go to the Italian on the market square?'

'Okay, then,' Julie replied, allowing herself to smile. They sat in silence, neither of them sure what to say next. It was on the verge of becoming awkward when a voice said, 'Excuse me,' a bit too loudly from inside the main shop. 'I'll go,' Julie said, pushing the table against Mike so she could extricate herself from the small room.

Standing before the till was a man of about middle age. If his pinchy features were anything to go by, he looked like he had already worked himself up into a state. This was fairly impressive, given that he was standing in a garden centre by himself.

'Sorry, we're not open until 10, but you're free to wait outside until then.'

'I don't want to buy anything,' he said angrily. 'I want to return something.'

'Oh, right.' Julie looked down to his hands and saw that he wasn't carrying anything. 'Well that's no problem. Is it still in your car? We can help you carry it in if you like.'

'I couldn't get it in my car because it's two fucking tons of sand.'

The smile on Julie's face became fixed. 'Could I take your name please?'

'Wilkin. Bob Wilkin. Although it's my poor old mum that you duped into buying the stuff from you. Carol Wilkin.'

'And just to confirm, you are wanting to return your Backdoor Beach?'

'What the bloody hell is a Backdoor Beach?

'The product that your mother bought?'

He looked at her blankly for a few moments. 'You mean the sand?'

'Why don't I go and get the manager.'

She found Mr. Peg in the rear yard with his head in his hands. As ever, he had the vacant look of someone who lives in their own little world.

'Mr. Peg?' Julie said. He didn't immediately look up, and she wondered whether he had actually managed to nod off. When she put her hand on his shoulder and squeezed it slightly, he looked up. 'There's a man who wants to speak to you, Mr. Peg. It's Mrs. Wilkin's son. He wants to talk to you about returning the beach.'

'Returning the beach?' he said, as if this was an existential question. 'It's a way of living, Julie, a state of mind. Did you make it clear to him that he can't return a state of mind?'

'We didn't get round to that, no.'

'Well can you go back in there and make him see sense, please?'

'He's quite upset. I don't think that would help much.'

Mr. Peg got to his feet looking very agitated now. 'Really, Julie, this is why I employ people. I have much more important things to be thinking about than dealing with customers right now.' He paused on the spot, waiting to see if Julie would take the lead and leave him alone.

'If you want to tell me what the returns policy is, I'm happy to go and relay the information?'

He looked at her like she was losing her mind. 'How many times do I have to say it? It would be the equivalent of asking for your money back after a profound religious experience. It's priceless.'

Julie hoped that Mr. Peg would get all of this nonsense out of his system before they went inside and talked to Mr. Wilkin. Otherwise, she was sure the old man was very likely to get a thump. She thought about giving him a quick slap herself. Not only for her own gratification but also to knock a bit of sense into him.

When it became clear that Julie wasn't going to act as his champion, Mr. Peg walked back towards the garden centre with his employee following behind him. They found Mr. Wilkin standing next to the counter where Julie had left him. Even in the few moments that he had been kept waiting, his anger had intensified. His fists were now clenched at his sides, and as soon as he saw the pair entering through the back doors, he moved to confront them.

'Are you the manager?' he said before Mr. Peg could speak.

'Yes, I am,' Mr. Peg said proudly, which given the current state of affairs, was absolutely at odds with reality.

'What are you going to do about this fucking sand?'

'If you could perhaps explain why it is that your mother is unhappy...,' Mr. Peg started before the angry man interceded.

'Listen, I don't want any of your salesman bullshit. I want you to get over to my mum's house this afternoon and get rid of it.'

'I'm not sure your mother would thank us for that, sir,' Mr. Peg said, still smiling politely. Mike joined them, still holding his cup of tea.

'And this must be your hatchet man,' Mr. Wilkin said pointing angrily at Mike. 'If he's got enough time to drink tea then he's got enough time to fix my mum's garden.'

'Let's not be hasty,' Mr. Peg said, holding his hands up. 'Does your mother really want to give up her new lifestyle? Have you talked to her about it?'

'If by, her new lifestyle, you mean not being able to go out into her garden, then yes. I think she'd very happily give it up.'

'But have you spoken to her about it?' Mr. Peg said.

'The woman is 82. Her entire house is carpeted, and she bought a mop last week. She has given up her right to an opinion.'

'Well then, sir,' Mr. Peg said as if he had won some great victory. 'Unfortunately, we will be unable to process the return unless the purchaser themself is unhappy with the product.'

Mr. Wilkin's face turned white. He closed the gap between himself and Mr. Peg. They were much closer now than the norm for polite conversation. 'Listen to me. I don't give a shit about anything you have to say to me. That sand will be out of my mum's garden by the end of the day. If it isn't, then I'll be back again tomorrow with a few of my friends. Do I make myself clear?'

Mr. Peg raised a digit in the air to make a further point. Before he could, Mr. Wilkin grabbed his finger. If the colour of the angry man's knuckles and the little yelp of pain that came out of Julie's employer were anything to go by, he was squeezing fairly hard. 'Do I make myself clear?'

Bizarrely, the affront against his person hadn't seemed to phase Mr. Peg. However, Julie saw that when his eyes rested on a small signet ring that the man was wearing on his little finger, Mr. Peg's face immediately lost all colour. He gave a feeble nod, and Mr. Wilkin let go of his hand. Before Mr. Peg could say anything else, the angry man had stormed out of the shop, slamming the door behind them.

'Fucking hell,' Mike said, forgetting himself for a second. 'That was like something out of a mafia movie.'

'If a mafia movie involved selling sand to unwitting pensioners,' Julie said.

'Will you both be quiet, please?' Mr. Peg said angrily. Although both Julie and Mike had both been laughing, they immediately stopped when he spoke, disconcerted by how stern his tone was. Usually, he just sounded mildly annoyed with them. This was something more. 'I need a moment to think.' He perched on the edge of one of the benches displaying their summer flower range and put his fingers to his temples. After a few minutes of them all standing around awkwardly, he turned to Mike.

'Mike, do you think you could get the sand back in the bag? The stuff you've already spread around the garden.'

'Not all of it, but most, yeah. It will probably take the rest of the day though.'

'Don't worry about that. Julie, can you give Mike a lift down there?'

'That's fine, I can stay and help him if you like?' Julie said.

'No, I need you back here.'

'It would be easier with the two of us working on it,' said Julie. She had no great desire to collect sand all day, but the prospect of spending the afternoon with Mike in the sunshine was surprisingly appealing.

'Someone will have to man the fort. I need to go out.'

They both looked at him incredulously. Neither of them had ever seen Mr. Peg outside of the garden centre before. It was akin to seeing a teacher outside of school. Absolutely incomprehensible.

'I can't move those bags Mr. Peg,' Mike said, 'even if I can get the sand back in them.'

'Just get the sand back in the bags, and I'll do the rest. Julie, take the spare keys. I won't be here when you get back.'

'Okay, Mr. Peg,' Julie began, but he was no longer paying attention to her. Without another word, he stormed out of the front door. A few moments later, Julie and Mike heard an engine and were shocked to see Mr. Peg going down the drive on a small, red motorcycle. Much like its owner, it looked like it had seen better days.

CHAPTER SIXTEEN

For the first time in a long time, Julie had woken up that morning feeling refreshed.

Aside from the drama of the morning, it had been a day devoid of any real stress. Somehow, the wine had seemed superfluous for once. Out of herself, Mr. Peg and poor Mike, she felt like she had drawn the long straw. After dropping Mike off at Mrs. Wilkin's house, Julie's working day had largely consisted of her reading a trashy book that she had taken from a rack by the counter and occasionally tidying the shop. She suspected that the few customers that would normally have come in were deterred by having to abandon their cars on the side of an A-road. They had probably rightly concluded that going to the superstore just down the store would be a better use of their time. By the time she had closed the store, Mike hadn't returned from his impossible task. However, as she had been walking down the drive back to her car, Mr. Peg had passed her on his motorcycle. She stopped to speak to him, but he didn't seem interested. He merely raised his hand as he passed. She reasoned that he must just be feeling stressed about the sand and nothing else.

So when she got home the previous evening, it hadn't been a conscious decision not to open a bottle of wine. For whatever reason, it hadn't appealed to her. Instead, she had made herself a simple dinner and then gone to bed almost immediately after it was finished.

The door to Harry's old room, or Jack's room as Julie found herself thinking of it, had remained firmly closed since she had regained sole possession of her house. The policemen had dropped the keys through Mrs. McGrath's letter box, and no one had taken the time to explain what the rules were to her. It might still be considered an active crime scene. What with all the attention that DI Morris had given her recently, she didn't want to bumble in and disturb something by accident, only to be accused of intentionally interfering with the investigation again. If Julie was honest with herself, she was a bit relieved.

The last week had been so surreal, so outside her experience of everyday life so far, that she had more or less managed to convince herself that it wasn't something that was happening to her. She had a horrible feeling that when she saw Jack's room again, it might bring it all back and make it real for her. With everything that had happened, she had constantly been in a state of some extreme emotion, whether that be lust, shock, or excitement, that they had become confused. Giddy felt the best way to describe it, a heady thrill. As she sat in the kitchen that morning eating her breakfast, she made a small confession to herself that she might even like it. Not Jack's death, of course; that was horrendous, and her brief liaison with the younger man made her cringe if she thought about it too much. It was more about experiencing things again. Even if it didn't feel enjoyable at the time, it felt like it had value.

However, the thrill that she had experienced felt like something entirely remote as she approached Mrs. Sinclair's door. She had only seen her once since their last exchange. Julie had stumbled across her in the local shop, giving poor Mr. Baker a right tongue lashing due to a ten pence increase in the cost of canned beans. Julie hadn't attempted to speak to her as she walked away from the shell shocked shop keeper, although her neighbour had shot her a caustic glance before making her way to the check out.

Forget it, Julie said to herself. Nothing to do with me, any of this. If the plumber had something to do with it then the police will route him out. She had turned her back on the front door and was ready to go home when she remembered Mrs. McGrath. The personification of tenacity herself was very unlikely to let the whole matter drop just because Julie didn't want to have an awkward conversation. She stood immobile, torn between deciding whose wrath she would rather face. Fortunately, the decision was made for her when Mrs. Sinclair opened her front door and curtly said, 'What do you want?'

'Hello,' Julie said in an overly friendly tone.

'That doesn't really answer my question, does it?'

'It's Julie Giles from across the road?' Julie ventured.

'I know who you are. Why do you feel the need to remind me every time we meet?'

'Because you're always so rude to me,' Julie said under her breath.

'What was that?'

'I said I wanted to ask you about the plumber who came to your house the other night.'

Mrs. Sinclair's stiff upper lip became even stiffer. Julie waited for some verbal acknowledgement of her question, but when none was forthcoming, she carried on. 'I'm guessing you already know that Jack died the other night, the night that Mr. Sinclair wasn't well.'

'I gathered something had happened to him when he didn't turn up to cut the grass.'

'And that's why I wanted to talk to the plumber. To see if he had seen anything unusual.'

'I take it you are qualified in some way to conduct these investigations?'

Julie hesitated. 'Not really. If I'm honest, I'm only really helping Mrs. McGrath.'

If Mrs. Sinclair's face hadn't been friendly before, it was nothing compared to how hard it was now. 'I have no interest whatsoever in helping that crackpot old lady in her endless pursuit to harass everyone she comes into contact with. If you bother me again, I will be reporting you to the police.' And with that, Mrs. Sinclair slammed the door in Julie's face.

Walking back to the street, she felt exhausted at the mere anticipation of the battle she would have to have with Mrs. McGrath. The old woman would insist that she keep trying until she got the information she needed, even in the face of an impassable witness and potential arrest.

Julie was brought back to reality by the sound of Brian calling, 'Hello, beautiful,' at her from where he sat in his front garden. The sun had burned his arms and face badly so that the crimson of his skin stood in stark contrast to the white vest and cargo shorts that he wore. 'You wanna come and share a few tinnies with me, sweetheart?' He pulled the can of beer from a bucket that was resting on the floor next to his feet, holding it out to her even though she was still standing on the street. Another bucket was overturned, and his injured leg rested on top of it.

'Sorry, Brian. I really can't. I've got stuff to do today.'

'You can only put me off for so long, my love.' He put the can down on the ground and began to unfold a second deckchair for her. 'At some point, you're going to have to realise that we're meant to be together.'

Julie was considering finally putting Brian in his place once and for all by telling him how foul he was and that no member of the opposite sex would ever be able to tolerate him for a prolonged period, let alone the rest of their lives, when a thought struck her.

'Actually, Brian,' she said, walking through his garden gate. 'I was hoping you could help me with something.'

'Need a strong man to help you with something around the house, do you, sweetheart?' The comment was all the more farcical being made in front of Brian's ramshackle abode with his chubby arms clearly in view.

'If I do, then I know where to come,' Julie said, giving him what she hoped was a coy smile and taking the seat next to him. 'No, it's actually about Jack. More specifically about the night he died.'

Brian had been lifting his cold can of beer to his lips but stopped dead at the mention of Jack. 'Not your job to do that,' he said with none of his usual bravado. 'Leave the police to do it.'

'Normally, I'd agree with you. Only Mrs. McGrath has got it into her head that his death wasn't an accident and maybe someone else was involved.'

'Didn't think you could stand her. Since when have the two of you been so close?'

'We're not; she just needed some help. She wants us to talk to anyone who might have been involved.'

'I was here,' Brian said immediately. 'And before you ask, I was by myself, but that doesn't mean anything, does it? Anyone who was up and around at that time of night would have been up to no good. Just because I was alone and asleep in my bed doesn't mean I have anything to hide.'

'Actually, I was just going to ask if you saw what company the plumber that was at Mrs. Sinclair's house was from. She won't tell me; you see, she and Mrs. McGrath don't get along, and she thinks that the old woman is poking into her business.'

'Ohhh,' Brian said, his voice instantly brightening. 'That twat with the loud music, you mean. Yeah, what was it?' He scratched the top of his head. 'Wainwrights, was it? No hold on, it was Cartwrights. I remember now. I used to have a girlfriend called Maggie Cartwright. Nice thick legs she had.' A creepy smile spread over his face, and Julie felt the need to pull down the hem of the dress she was wearing.

'I'M JUST SAYING, if you didn't owe me a favour before, you do now.'

'What, because you had to talk to some slimy old man?'

'And that dragon! She threatened to call the police, you know.'

'You've said already.'

'I know that, you just don't seem to care.' Mrs. McGrath grunted in response. 'So I intend to carry on saying it until you acknowledge the fact that I keep having to do your dirty work for you.'

'It's not for me. It's for the dead lad.'

Julie couldn't really be doing with Mrs. McGrath's self-righteousness. They had been sitting in her car outside the portacabin that served as Cartwrights head office for the last half an hour. Despite having the front windows down, the temperature in the car had become uncomfortable. 'Honestly, how long does it take to eat a sandwich?' Julie said, looking at her watch. 'Why don't you go and try the door again?'

'I went last time; it's your turn.'

'I've done enough today.'

'I can't go.' Mrs. McGrath folded her arms and slumped down in her chair. 'I'm disabled.'

'You didn't look very disabled when you were clobbering those teenagers with your walking stick.'

'Adrenaline does amazing things to the human body.'

Julie sighed, which elicited no reaction from the old woman whatsoever. She was half way out of the car when she spotted a woman of about her age approaching the portacabin. 'Mrs. McGrath, I think we're in business, look.'

Mrs. McGrath's eyes snapped open, and before Julie could say anything further to her, the old woman was halfway across the road towards the office entrance. She looked over her shoulder before she went inside. 'Come on,' she called to Julie who was twenty paces behind her, 'they'll be on their tea break if you don't hurry up.'

'Do you want the car to get stolen?' Julie said a bit too loudly as she entered the office. She hadn't appreciated that the space inside would be so compact and found herself shouting the words almost directly into the face of the woman they had just seen entering. 'Oh, sorry,' she said, blushing, and then attempted to move behind Mrs. McGrath to remove herself from view. Luckily, the woman behind the counter didn't appear to be very interested in them, or anything else for that matter.

'We need to talk to one of your boys,' Mrs. McGrath said to the receptionist who was routing through a drawer in her desk.

'Oh yeah?' she said, without making eye contact with them.

'Did a job in Brumpton in the early hours last Monday.'

The receptionist made a non-committal noise and continued with her rummaging.

'Nothing dodgy or anything, just need to have a word with him,' Mrs. McGrath continued. In spite of herself, Julie felt grateful for this rude receptionist and her clipped tones, giving Mrs. McGrath a taste of her own medicine. Still the receptionist continued to largely ignore Mrs. McGrath. 'We could make it worth your while, give you a little something for the effort.'

The receptionist looked up for the first time. 'How much are we talking?'

There was a moment of inaction in the small room before Julie realised that Mrs. McGrath was looking at her.

'What, me?' Julie said.

'I've not got anything, have I? I'm a pensioner.'

Julie tutted audibly but reached into her handbag regardless. She had two five pounds notes in her purse. There was also the last bit of shrapnel that she hadn't dropped on the floor when fleeing from the little thugs on their bikes. She held out the notes to Mrs. McGrath who snatched them from her grasp without any ceremony and placed them on the counter in front of the receptionist.

She looked at them distastefully before saying, 'You got anything else?'

'Not unless you want my coppers,' Julie said.

She shrugged and took them off the counter. 'Better than nothing. Last Monday you said?'

Mrs. McGrath nodded, and the receptionist proceeded to wrap a few keys on her keyboard. 'It's Kurt that you want. Older bloke, white hair, bit of a belly. You should catch him if you're quick, he'll be in the back finishing his lunch.'

The receptionist refused their request to show them where the canteen was but was willing to give them some almost adequate directions.

'She was friendly, wasn't she?' Julie said, after they had gone back outside and into another one of the cabins clustered around the main office.

'About as friendly as I would be,' Mrs. McGrath said.

'I can believe that. Do you have any idea where we're going?'

'It's this one,' she said with absolute certainty, pushing one of the doors open. They were met first with the overwhelming smell of urine and then the sight of a twenty something year old man relieving himself into a urinal.

'Bloody hell,' he said, immediately trying to get his appendage back into his trousers.

'Sorry,' Julie called as Mrs. McGrath slammed the door shut again. 'I thought you knew where you were going?'

'Silly cow gave me the wrong directions, didn't she?' Mrs. McGrath said, charging forward towards another one of the cabins.

'Why am I always paying for the bribes by the way? First those hoodlums and now her.'

'You've got money to burn.'

'How do you work that one out?' Julie asked.

'Living in that big house all by yourself. Only working a few days a week.'

'Last time I checked, your house was exactly the same size as mine, and you don't work at all.'

'Yeah, well, I'm a pensioner, aren't I?'

'How does that even make sense?' Julie started to ask. The question died in her throat as Mrs. McGrath flung open another door, and they were met by a dozen faces craning their necks to see who had entered the room.

'We're looking for Kurt,' Mrs. McGrath stated plainly without any further explanation.

'Which one?' the man sitting closest to them asked.

'Not sure.' When neither (or indeed none) of the Kurts got to their feet, Mrs. McGrath said, 'White hair, older bloke, bit of a belly.'

A rumble of laughter ran through the room. 'That will be you then, Winnie,' someone called from the other side of the room.

'Fuck off,' said a man sat at one of the nearer tables. 'It's definitely Pinhead.'

'Which one of you did a job in Brumpton last week? Early hours of Monday morning, Lexington Avenue.'

'Fucking hell,' said the man who thought they were describing Pinhead.

'We need a word with you.' Mrs. McGrath said. The man, now looking sulky, nodded to the pair of what looked like garden chairs on the other side of his table. While several of the diners had returned their eyes to their lunch, it seemed unlikely that their conversation would remain between the three of them if it was conducted here. 'In private,' Mrs. McGrath said, coming to the same conclusion. Winnie didn't look happy about it, but he obliged and followed them out into the forecourt.

In the full light of the day, his droopy jowls were now clearly visible. Julie thought that he was older than she originally thought. Or maybe he was the type of bloke that had spent all of his youth drinking and eating whatever he liked, only to have middle age crash into him like a freight train. Either way, he was not an attractive man. He had the beginnings of a beard, not out of design, Julie guessed, but through inattention.

'Who said I had a bit of a belly?'

'Her on the front desk,' Mrs. McGrath said.

'Was it Trisha or Debs?'

'Dunno. She didn't say her name.'

'Fuck, I bet it's Trisha. Not happy with me at the moment. Caught me down The Bulls Head with another bird.'

'We want to ask you about the job you did on Lexington Avenue.' Mrs. McGrath said, characteristically taking no interest in this man's private life whatsoever.

'Oh yeah? What about it?'

'How long were you there for?'

'I dunno, maybe two hours.'

'Long time to spend on a bit of plumbing.'

He shrugged. 'The job takes as long as the job takes, love.'

'What after that? Where were you?'

'Had another job down the road, can't remember the name. Some kind of bird, Sparrows Walk or some bullshit like that. All of them are called something like that round there. Can't keep them separate in my head.'

'Crows Way?' Julie interjected, speaking for the first time.

'Yeah, that's it.' He eyed her suspiciously. Up until this point, he hadn't given her a second glance. His attention had entirely been absorbed by Mrs. McGrath. 'Posh people love that kind of shit. Naming all the roads after the same thing. What's this about anyway?' he said, only now thinking for the first time to ask why these random strangers wanted to know where he spent his Monday evening.

'Some dodgy business. Trying to figure out if anyone saw anything.'

'And who are you two? Funny looking bobbies.'

'Neighbourhood Watch,' Mrs. McGrath said. 'Got to look after yourself these days.'

'Too bloody right, love. Pigs will do nothing for you.'

'How long would you say you were there for? At your next job?'

'I left that first job at about ten past six and then the next one was a couple of hours too. Something wrong with their washing machine. Flooding the cellar, fucking nightmare.'

'And the office could confirm that, could they?'

His eyes passed from one to the other of them. 'They can, yeah. I haven't got anything to hide if that's what you're trying to ask.'

'Didn't say you did.'

'Alright,' he said, as if the matter was now entirely closed. 'What's your story then?'

'I told you. We're Neighbourhood Watch.'

'No, I mean, have you got a fella? Are you married?'

Mrs. McGrath didn't say anything. Julie thought absently that Winnie and Brian would get on very well.

'Shame if you don't. Beautiful woman like you.'

Julie now hoped that he was a bit older or had a penchant for women who were in the Autumn of their lives. She didn't generally consider herself to be a beautiful woman. She did think though that surely, she was the more objectively attractive of the two. Mrs. McGrath looked as if she had entered the world by being pulled through a bush backwards and had lived the rest of her life there.

Somehow, Mrs. McGrath continued to resist Winnie's charms and said nothing.

'Are you married?' he tried again.

'He's dead.'

'You must get lonely.' His eyes conveyed an empathy that Julie was certain he didn't feel.

'Not really. You didn't see anything funny that night, then?' Mrs. McGrath said, all business.

'Nothing springs to mind.'

'Alright, then. Thanks.'

'Wait,' Winnie called as Mrs. McGrath turned to go. 'Better take my number, in case you've got any more questions for me.'

'You're alright. We know where you are.'

'You never know, you might need something when I'm off duty.' He patted down his pockets and after some fumbling about, he managed to find a crinkled up piece of paper. 'You got a pen?' he said, suddenly remembering Julie's presence. She had to remove her purse from her bag to locate one in its very depths and then handed it to Winnie. He took it from her without a word of thanks.

Mrs. McGrath snatched the note from him and immediately stuffed it into her pocket. She began to walk away before Julie had a chance to reclaim her pen or put her purse back in her bag.

Julie had presumed that they would be going straight back to the car.

However, once they reached the street, Mrs. McGrath made a beeline for the office. Walking straight up to the desk, she said, 'I need to know whether that bloke was at another job after the one on Lexington Avenue.'

'I'm not sure if I...,' the receptionist started to say.

Mrs. McGrath grabbed Julie's purse from her hand and before she was able to protest, the old woman had unzipped it and tipped all the remaining coins onto the desk.

'You can have all that. Haven't got anything else.'

The receptionist stared at her for a moment in disbelief before coming to life again. She laboriously scraped the coins off the counter into her cupped hand. Only when they were all collected did she bring the computer to life again and pull up the requested information.

'He went straight to his next job from the first one you asked about. He invoiced them for two hours, and they paid it, no hassle.' Having everything that she needed, Mrs. McGrath turned and exited the small building at her normal speed. Julie followed the best that she could and closed the door behind her.

'That's not like you,' Julie said when they were both sitting in the car again.

'Mmmm?'

'Checking an alibi. What happened to being able to tell if they were a murderer just by looking at them?'

'Sometimes you can tell they're dodgy, but you don't know why.'

'It isn't a different look, then? Murderers don't look any different to people who rob post offices?'

'It's not an exact science, is it?' Mrs. McGrath said a little testily.

'Alright, I only asked.'

'You're always going on about how we need to ask more questions, and when I do, you give me grief about it.'

They arrived at a red light, and Julie slowed the car to a stop. The silence that ensued felt all the more charged because of their inactivity.

'Shall we leave the neighbours until tomorrow? Approach it with fresh eyes in the morning?'

'Yeah, alright,' Mrs. McGrath said, once again closing her eyes and allowing her head to slump to one side.

CHAPTER SEVENTEEN

On Sunday morning, there was a bang on the door a full half an hour before she and Mrs. McGrath had agreed to meet. On her way to answer it, Julie tripped over the hedge clippers that Mrs. Sinclair had dropped off the day before Jack had been killed. If they weren't hers and they weren't Jacks, they must be Brian's. Julie made a mental note to return them to him later this afternoon.

'I thought we said nine o'clock?' Julie said, opening the door to the old woman. She grunted in reply and pushed her way into the house. 'We can have a cup of tea though? Agree on an approach.'

'What are we agreeing on?' Mrs. McGrath said, taking a seat at the kitchen table. She undid the buttons of her coat but didn't take it off. 'We ring people's doorbells and ask them if they've killed anyone lately.'

'Have you ever thought that the most direct approach might not always be the best one?' Mrs. McGrath looked at her blankly. 'You know, like maybe people won't confess to killing someone just because you knock on their front door and ask them?'

'Done much police work, have you?'

'Well no, but it seems like common sense.'

'Doesn't matter if they don't admit it. I'll be able to tell.'

'Yes, that's all well and good, but they're not being tried in the court of Mrs. McGrath, are they? We need to have some evidence to give to the police if they're going to take us seriously.' Mrs. McGrath let out a deep breath and rolled her eyes. 'What's the point if your snooping isn't actually going to lead to an arrest?'

'Fine. What do you want to do?'

'Who is it that you actually want to talk to?'

'I did a bit of work last night when you were having your evening off.' Julie let the comment slide, already feeling her enthusiasm for this mad enterprise waning. 'Managed to speak to everyone apart from that mad biddy at number 2, the hermit at number 40. Oh, and your other young thing across the road.'

Julie processed this information and said, 'You mean Mrs. Stuart, John Taylor and Brian?'

'That's what I said, yeah. She's got something against me, and him at number 40 was too scared to open the door. Your man across the road wasn't in.'

'Sorry, why is he my man?'

'Always chatting you up, isn't he? See him when I'm putting out the bins sometimes.'

Julie found it amusing that despite admitting she was running a full investigation into the inhabitants of the street, Mrs. McGrath still felt the need to invent a story to excuse her day to day snooping.

'Why will they talk to us today if they wouldn't yesterday?'

'You're going to knock. When they answer, I can come up the path and have a good look at them.'

'Well, as long as we've got a plan.'

'Got to be one of them. I can feel it in my waters.' Despite having not touched the cup of tea that Julie had put in front of her, she necked the whole thing in one great swallow before marching out of the house.

When Julie left her house a few minutes later, she saw that Mrs. McGrath was already standing outside of Brian's door. Clearly, she had forgotten that Julie was supposed to be taking the lead. She had been rapping the handle of her cane fairly discreetly against the wood. Discreetly for her, that was. In fact, it was an almost gentle gesture which surprised Julie. However, the Zen approach didn't last long. After thirty seconds of waiting, she lost her patience and resorted to her usual banging.

'I don't think this is getting us anywhere,' Julie said about a minute into the assault.

'Got to be persistent. The bugger has to come out sometime.'

Julie saw the curtains next door twitch. She could really do without another uncomfortable confrontation with Mrs. Sinclair. 'Why don't we come back later?' she said when there was a brief pause in the thudding. 'Go and speak to the other two and then circle back around.'

'We're letting him get away with it then,' Mrs. McGrath said. She pulled back her arm to continue the onslaught.

'Get away with what? You don't know he's done anything.'

'Not doing his public duty.'

'I think his public duty can wait until this afternoon.' The old woman thought for a second and then raced down the path at her usual tempo. Julie managed to catch up with her just as she stationed herself behind the big fir tree at the bottom of Mrs. Stuart's drive.

'Go on then,' she said, giving Julie a little nudge with her cane.

'Oh, I'm taking over again, am I?' Julie said, taking a peek up the drive at the ominous looking black front door. She hadn't had much to do with Mrs. Stuart in the past. Any early attempts at a friendly exchange had always received a frosty reception, so she had quickly stopped trying.

'Keep up, I told you at the house. Good for your training anyway, isn't it? Do a few of them alone.'

'My training?'

'On how to run an investigation.'

'I can't think of any situation in my life where that would be an advantage.'

'What about if you found a dead teenager in your spare room?'

Julie gave Mrs. McGrath an unimpressed look that Mrs. McGrath promptly ignored.

'Anyway, what makes her any different from everyone else on the street that you've...,' Julie took a moment to search for the right word. Alienated was likely to be the best fit, or harassed maybe. She settled on, 'questioned.'

'I'll tell you later. Come on,' Mrs. McGrath said, giving Julie a firmer jab with her stick, 'While we've still got the daylight.'

As Julie rang the doorbell, an overwhelming sense of dread overtook her. She suddenly realised that she hadn't the faintest clue what she was going to say. She was on the verge of going back to speak to Mrs. McGrath for some guidance when the door was opened.

Mrs. Stuart was of a similar age to Mrs. McGrath. However, the two women couldn't have been more different in appearance. Mrs. Stuart's hair was white from root to tip, but smartly. That, paired with her respectable blouse buttoned up to her neck and a long, black pencil skirt, gave her an air of gentility that Mrs. McGrath couldn't hope to match even on her most reserved days. As soon as she had opened the front door, she crossed her arms, just in case her visitor was in any doubt as to how much of an irritation her visit was.

'Yes?' Mrs. Stuart said when no explanation as to Julie's presence was forthcoming. Julie continued to stare dumbly at her. It suddenly occurred to her that she couldn't explain why she knocked on this estranged neighbour's door because there wasn't any sensible justification.

'I was hoping to ask you some questions,' Julie spluttered.

'Were you now?'

'About Jack. Jack Harper.'

There was a pause that made it clear that Mrs. Stuart had no idea who Julie was talking about.

'You might have seen him on the street. About 19. He was staying with me.'

'All the young people look the same to me,' Mrs. Stuart said curtly.

'He'd only been staying here for a few weeks. You might have noticed him because you hadn't seen him before?'

Again Mrs. Stuart said nothing.

'So you haven't seen anything unusual over the past few days?'

'Aside from a nuisance visit from a little known neighbour?'

Julie began to apologise for bothering her before she was interrupted. 'I may be old, but I'm not blind. Of course, I took note of the fleet of police cars that were parked outside your house. Is that what you came to ask me?'

'Yes. Well, no. What I wanted to know. I mean, what I came to ask was…,'

'Get to the point, will you?' Mrs. Stuart said, interrupting again. 'I haven't murdered anyone in their sleep as of late, nor do I have any idea of who might have felt the need to if that's what you're trying to ask.'

Julie could feel her face burning, the little composure that she had now lost to her. 'I didn't mean to suggest you'd done anything wrong. We're just trying to find out if anyone saw anything.'

Mrs. Stuart was smiling now. She seemed to be enjoying Julie's discomfort, almost revelling in it. 'And who is we?' she asked.

That moment, Julie heard the telltale tapping that told her that Mrs. McGrath was making her way towards them.

'No,' Mrs. Stuart said. 'No, no, no, no, no!' With each repetition of the word, her voice became louder. 'You are not to step foot on this property.'

'Calm down, you old goat,' Mrs. McGrath said. 'It's not about all that.'

'I don't care what it's about,' Mrs. Stuart shrieked, losing all her previous haughtiness and becoming quite insensible. 'There is nothing that you could possibly have to say to me that I want to hear.'

'There's no need to shout.'

'I am not shouting,' Mrs. Stuart shouted. 'I am explaining that I have no interest in whatever nonsense you and your little friend here have dreamt up.'

'Can't really dream up a dead body, can you?'

'Wicked people come to wicked ends,' Mrs. Stuart said in a very convincing impersonation of a religious zealot. 'You'd do well to remember that,' she said, pointing at Mrs. McGrath accusingly. Any further discourse was immediately halted when Mrs. Stuart slammed the door in their faces.

'What was all that about?' Julie asked when they were safely back on the street. 'I didn't realise you knew each other so well.'

'Who says we know each other?'

'You must have had quite a bit to do with her if she feels that strongly about you.'

Mrs. McGrath shrugged. 'Can't help it if people take against me.'

They had started to walk towards John Taylor's house for their next interview. 'No, I'm sorry, Mrs. McGrath, that's just not good enough.' Julie stopped in the middle of the pavement. The old woman either didn't realise, or she didn't care and continued alone. Only when Julie called her name again did she stop and walk back towards her.

'Got to get on,' Mrs. McGrath said, irritated.

'I'm not going anywhere until you explain to me why that woman dislikes you so much.'

Mrs. McGrath took little interest and began to scrape at something on the pavement with her stick.

'You say jump, and I say how high. Then when I ask you one little question, you won't tell me anything.' Julie folded her arms in an attempt to display her indignance. Still, the old woman didn't seem to be taking any notice. 'You don't always have to act like you're under siege. If you want my help, then this has got to go both ways.'

A further interval elapsed without any explanations, and Julie had just resolved to go home when Mrs. McGrath mumbled, 'Cats.'

'Cats?'

'I was coming back from the shops one day when I saw her chasing a stray off her front garden with a broom. It wasn't doing anything to hurt anyone, just sitting there minding its own business. Didn't seem right, so I started feeding it.'

'Right...,'

'Next thing I knew, her highness was at the door telling me I was ruining the neighbourhood. Encouraging vermin, all that bollocks.' There was a pause which suggested that Mrs. McGrath had finished her story.

'That can't be the end of it, surely? The woman was ready to have a coronary when she saw you.'

Mrs. McGrath's attention on the patch of pavement that she had been prodding intensified.

'Mrs. McGrath?'

'Bit later on, she found a load of rats in her cellar. Exterminator said that they'd been attracted by some nuts that had been put down there. Her nibs threw a fit at me. Said she wouldn't have bought them because she's allergic.' Mrs. McGrath sounded so wounded that someone who didn't know better may have been willing to accept this little fiction.

'Christ, what were you thinking?' Julie said.

Mrs. McGrath looked at her, stung. 'You just believe her straight away?'

'You're not exactly known for being reasonable.'

'Name one time I haven't been reasonable.'

'What about that poor telephone engineer that you chased off with your conspiracy theories?'

'I was right about that. I showed you the newspaper.'

'You showed me a story about dodgy accounting! It had nothing to do with the lad trying to fix your phone for you.'

'I don't think she did it,' Mrs. McGrath said, willing to accept at least temporarily that her case was fundamentally lacking. 'The woman is evil, but I'm willing to say that she didn't kill the lad. Can't get much fairer than that, can you?'

Despite it only being midmorning, it felt very late in the day to Julie. The unpleasant exchange with Mrs. Stuart had made her see herself and Mrs. McGrath as the rest of the sane world did. They weren't the intrepid seekers of justice that she had allowed herself to imagine. Instead, she was the woman who was deluded enough to follow the whims of someone so unhinged that they were willing to fill someone's house with rats.

'Let's get this over with,' Julie said, taking the final few paces towards Mr. Taylor's house. She would keep her word and conduct this one final interview and then that was it. Her previous life may have been mundane and more than a little bit pathetic, but at least it was private. No one would see it and laugh at her for so woefully trying to reach above her station and absolutely failing.

Julie walked up to Mr. Taylor's front door without looking back to check that Mrs. McGrath was following her. She knocked and waited for a response. Mr. Taylor appeared in the gap between the door and the jamb, the chain still firmly attached.

'Hello,' he said with a nervous smile.

'Oh, hello there,' Julie started. Before she could get any further, she saw the man's gaze move past her to something in the distance. His complexion now ashen, he said, 'Sorry, no,' before closing his front door again. Julie heard the distinctive sound of several locks being engaged on the other side.

Julie turned and saw that Mrs. McGrath hadn't bothered to conceal herself behind the hedges at the bottom of the garden. Instead, she was standing in plain sight.

'I don't think he's coming back,' Julie said, walking back towards her neighbour.

'What did you say to him?'

'I said hello, that was it.'

'You must have said something else.'

'I don't think I'm the problem here.'

'Bit rude.'

'I'm just saying I've never had a problem with anyone on this street before I started knocking around with you.'

'I'm the problem then, am I?'

'Well he answered the door, didn't he? It was only when he saw you that he bolted.'

'Right.' Mrs. McGrath walked towards Julie with such vehemence that she would have knocked her over if she hadn't moved out of the way at the last second. The banging that Julie had witnessed up to this point was a gentle tapping compared to the onslaught that Mrs. McGrath was now subjecting Mr. Taylor's front door to.

'Mrs. McGrath,' Julie shouted, but the old woman took no notice. She moved closer and repeated herself, but again, there was no response. She seemed to be in a mania, totally past the point of appreciating how extreme her actions were.

It was only when Julie physically pushed her shoulder and put herself between the door and its assailant that she finally stopped the banging. Even then, the look in Mrs. McGrath's eyes made her think that there was still a real danger that she would attempt to go through her to continue in her frenzy.

'What are you doing? He's going to call the police!'

'Need to talk to him, don't we?' she said, her voice as steady as it ever was.

'He's a little old man who barely ever goes out of his house. What is it that you think he's going to be able to tell you?'

'Never know, do you? Sometimes it's the quiet ones.'

'And that's justification for scaring him half to death, is it? Almost knocking his door in because he's too scared to talk to you.'

Mrs. McGrath gave her usual shrug that she reserved for when people pointed out her inappropriate behaviour.

Julie felt something past simple annoyance now. Mrs. McGrath felt like a low consistent hum that had been building in her brain slowly over time to the point where her noise was now on the verge of splitting her head open. She was so incensed that she couldn't speak, couldn't even take the time to consider how she could make this ridiculous old coot understand how mad her view of the world was.

It had all become too much. Without saying another word, she walked around Mrs. McGrath and back towards her own house.

'Fine,' Mrs. McGrath said, following her. 'We can leave him until afterwards.'

Julie didn't trust herself to speak. She just kept walking.

'Got to be off first thing though. Can't be waiting around for you to get out of bed.'

Still, Julie said nothing.

'Had a look on the maps, and it's about 200 miles, I reckon.'

Julie turned on the spot. By the time Mrs. McGrath had followed suit, they were less than a foot apart.

'What are you on about?'

'Liverpool. That's where you said he was from, wasn't it?'

It was all so absurd that it made Julie feel like she was the mad one.

'I'm not going to Liverpool with you,' she said, trying to keep her voice steady. 'I'm not going anywhere with you.'

'Who else is there to talk to around here after him? Got to go back and talk to your lad over the road when he gets home, but that's about it. And he didn't know anyone else around here, did he? So it's got to be someone from back up north.'

'Don't you get it?' Julie said a bit too loudly. 'I'm done. I'm not traipsing around the country asking a group of people random questions just so you can get a look at them and decide if they might be a murderer.'

'That's not right,' Mrs. McGrath said, 'We've all got a duty to see right done.'

'What duty?!' Julie positively bellowed in her face. 'Who do you think you are? I think we've safely established that you're not a detective. Why don't you just go home where you belong?'

'It's not for you to tell me where I belong,' said Mrs. McGrath indignantly. 'I've still got a part to play.'

'And what is that part? The crazy old woman who scares half the neighbourhood to death. Go back to your house. You're making us both look silly.'

Even after this tirade, Mrs. McGrath managed to keep her features entirely impassive. It was so unnerving that Julie started to feel properly afraid. She had seen what the old woman could do to a front door, and Julie had no reason to think that she wouldn't be willing to subject her to the same treatment. Just as she had resolved to turn tail and run, Mrs. McGrath strolled past her back to her own house as if they had been discussing the most trivial of matters and not engaged in a public shouting match. Julie was left on the street, still trembling slightly in her fury.

CHAPTER EIGHTEEN

I t was 8.15 when Julie finally arrived for her date with Mike. She hadn't wanted to arrive first and be forced to sit agonising about the evening ahead. It had seemed like such a good idea at the time, a natural extension of their enjoyment of one another's company. Getting ready that evening though, she had felt sick with anxiety. By the time she had made it into town, she was feeling almost lightheaded with unease.

The Italian restaurant was filled with all the normal types. A few married couples on dates identifiable by the token effort they had made for their one night out a week and the absolute lack of conversation passing between them. The obligatory long table of teenagers not quite yet old enough to spend a birthday in a pub or somewhere a bit more exciting. She was happy to find that Mike had taken the initiative to book a table and was shown to her seat by a young, blonde waitress who possessed the artificial cheer necessary to work in a chain restaurant.

'Can I get you something to drink while you wait?' she asked once she had shown Julie to the table.

Julie felt as if the whole restaurant was looking at her. There was an overhead light which she was sure illuminated her drab clothes and every blemish on her face. The wrap that she was wearing across her shoulders now felt silly and something that her grandmother would have chosen.

'Oh, is there a list or something?' She barely had time to finish the sentence before the waitress had passed her the laminated card that had been in the middle of the table. Julie scanned it but couldn't take the words in. She was aware of this young woman's impatience, her irritation that it was, in fact, her job to be polite despite it being the last thing in the world that she wanted to do.

'I'll have one of those please,' Julie said pointing at something that had vodka and some fruit juice in. The waitress's features contorted slightly as she reviewed Julie's choice.

'That one is quite...elaborate. Are you sure?'

Julie wasn't sure what point she was trying to make, but she didn't like her tone. 'Yes, thank you,' she said in a voice that she hoped conveyed that she was just as adventurous as the next person, and if she wanted an exotic drink then she'd bloody well have one.

'Alright then,' the waitress said. 'I'll be back in a moment with your cocktail.'

Julie took out the food menu in an attempt to distract herself. What had she been thinking? She'd only been on a handful of dates since Greg died, and they had all been absolute disasters. Friends of friends with the same dreary dress sense and a personality to match. She reminded herself that she knew Mike, and he wasn't like that. But what if it didn't work out? She finally had someone who made work a little more bearable. It was no longer just her and poor Mr. Peg.

Sitting there waiting for her drink, Julie's thoughts circled around and around. She should just leave, there and then before Mike could see her. She'd phone him when she was in the taxi home and explain that she'd had some sort of emergency. With reassurances that they would definitely reschedule, she'd pretend that she was busy until he lost interest.

But was that what she really wanted? It didn't seem right that going out with a nice man should make her feel this overwhelmed. If Julie was honest with herself, her morning with Mrs. McGrath had affected her more than she would like to admit. Yes, the old woman had been acting like a crazy person, but what else was new? If she wasn't willing to put up with some outlandish behaviour, then why had she gone in the first place? Up until now, she had surprised herself by how well she had been dealing with Jack's death. Maybe she was having a delayed reaction. You would be hard pressed to find anyone who didn't think that Mrs. McGrath deserved a public dressing down, and Julie was sure that anyone would forgive her for being fraught as of late. However, even in the most extreme of circumstances, it was very hard to justify shouting at an old woman in the street.

It didn't matter what the reason was, she just couldn't be here. She couldn't face an evening of polite conversation and the prospect of the painfully awkward situation that it would inevitably result in when this all went wrong.

After a few false starts, she had finally made the decision to leave when the waitress reappeared at the table. There was something mocking about her smile. 'Here we are,' she said. It was only then that Julie's eyes panned down and saw that she was carrying. On a tray that was buckling under the weight of the liquid was a huge container full of a florid substance with a scattering of straws around the edge, interspersed with cocktail umbrellas.

'What's that?'

'The party punch bowl.'

'I didn't ask for the party punch bowl.'

The waitress scowled momentarily before placing the tray on the table. She reached for the drinks menu and passed it to Julie again. 'There you are, see,' she said, pointing at the drink that was listed under their 'cocktails to share' section and began to recite from memory. 'Great for any special occasion. Best shared between two to three friends.'

'Right, okay, if I'd realised that it was served in a fishbowl then obviously I wouldn't have ordered it.' The waitress ignored this comment and began to move the condiments to one side of the table to make space for the immense vessel. To Julie's horror, she reached into her apron and took out a handful of sparklers.

'No, actually, I'm not sure I want this.'

'I'm sorry?' the waitress said with the lighter in her hand.

'I said I don't want this drink.' The couple on the table next to her were staring unashamedly as if Julie was some sort of bizarre after-dinner entertainment.

'But we've mixed it already.'

'I can see that. But I thought it was just a glass of something.'

'I did warn you that it was something usually ordered by a group of people.'

'I think what you actually said was that it was elaborate, which could cover anything from a piña colada to an Agatha Christie novel.'

'Right,' the waitress said with forced politeness. 'So you don't want the drink?'

'No, thank you.'

'I'm going to have to speak to my manager then.' She slapped the unlit sprinklers on the table and walked away from Julie in a huff.

A few minutes later, the waitress reappeared with a slightly older manboy at her heel.

'This is her,' the waitress said. She folded her arms and looked smugly at Julie like a nasty playground informant.

'Emma says that you ordered this drink, but you don't want it anymore,' the manager said and then added, 'madam,' at the end for good measure.

'That's right.'

'All sales are final,' he said but wasn't able to meet her eyes.

'Why would I buy a drink that was obviously designed for an 18th birthday party? Clearly, I'd made a mistake.'

The manager turned to the waitress. 'Did you tell her that it was a party drink?' The waitress nodded, and he turned back to Julie. 'There you go, then. All sales are final.'

Julie thought about debating the definition of the word 'elaborate,' again with this new youth, but it just didn't feel worth it. Even before she'd made this decision, the little boy manager was half way back across the restaurant from the direction he'd come from. 'I'd like to pay then,' Julie said, feeling emboldened by her self-righteousness.

'We can add it to your bill at the end of your meal?' the waitress said, all false smiles once again.

'I'm not staying,' she said, picking up her handbag and securing her wrap around her shoulders. 'If you'll bring me the bill, I'll pay now.'

'But what about your party punch bowl?'

'I don't bloody want the party punch bowl,' Julie said in a voice loud enough that several other diners now turned to watch. The waitress gave her a look as if she couldn't comprehend anything as alien as not drinking a beverage that you were going to have to pay for. Having realised that they couldn't depend on Julie for any further custom, the bill took a maddeningly long time to arrive. 'Service isn't included,' the waitress said, placing the metal dish in front of her. Julie almost let out a little laugh.

She began to rummage around in her handbag for her purse and was irritated to find that she didn't have any cash on her. After a wait of another five minutes, the waitress returned to the table, only to have to leave again to find a card machine. The customers on either side of her were watching her building irritation keenly, clearly hoping for another outburst. Julie had been following the progress of the waitress across the room so intently that a man's voice saying, 'Julie, I'm so sorry,' made her jump violently. She rapped her knees painfully on the bottom side of the table and gave a little cry of pain. The contents of the party punch bowl slopped dangerously from side to side.

Mike was standing before her in a wrinkled shirt, looking almost as unkempt as she felt.

He folded his enormous frame under the table, and his legs collided with Julie's. 'Oh shit, sorry,' he said, moving them to one side.

'I'm so sorry I'm late. I had it in my head that I was supposed to be picking you up from your gaff. But then I realised that I didn't know where you lived, and I didn't have your number. This was about half past seven. I thought Mr. Peg might have it, but he's been missing in action since all that sand business with the Wilkins the other day. So then my next bright idea was to go over to the garden centre and see if I could find your number in the files there. Anyway, I was halfway through a stack of paper as tall as you like when I realised you were probably already at the restaurant, so here I am.'

The waitress had reappeared over his right shoulder carrying the card machine. 'Hello, love, pint of lager please,' he said before noticing the party punch bowl on the table before him. 'Oh sorry, are we sharing that?'

Julie held her card out to the waitress who snatched it from her hand and pressed it against the pay terminal that she was holding. She passed it back to her and stormed away without another word.

'I'm sorry, Mike, but I've got to go.'

'Shit, is this because I was late?'

'No, it's not because of that. It's because, I just have to go. We can rearrange.'

She shuffled across the bench she was sat on. Unfortunately, the gap between their table and the one next to them was impossibly small for even the most petite person to fit through. Her body now felt so bulky, and she was sure that she was perspiring so heavily that she had a mortal dread of Mike feeling her pressed against him. Thinking that she had more space behind her than she did, she took a small step backwards only to bump into the man dining behind her.

'Steady on, love,' he said with a letchy smile on his face.

'Watch where you're going,' Julie replied nonsensically to the seated diner. Then, she rushed out of the restaurant, shooting the waitress one last dirty look as she went.

Once she was outside, she took a few moments just to breathe the fresh air. She also hadn't thought through what she was going to do next. It was too early in the evening for taxis to be in the rank and it had been years since she'd caught a bus home. Thinking about it, it had been an absolute age since she'd spent an evening out anywhere, let alone in the city centre.

'Are you alright?' A voice said from behind her. She turned to find Mike with a concerned look on his face.

'I told you, we can do it another time. I need to get a taxi.'

'Okay, but...'

'I think I have a number somewhere.' She started routing in her bag and then surveyed the square in front of her again looking for a car. 'Or maybe I'll get lucky and find one down by the supermarket.'

'Julie...'

'We'll do it another time, Mike. I've already told you that.'

'Yeah, forget about all that for a minute.' He moved around her so that they were face to face. 'Are you okay?' His question was asked with such sincerity that Julie could feel her eyes beginning to water.

'You're the first person to ask me that throughout all of this.' Julie pressed the root of one of her fingers to the bottom of her eye. She hoped that it would look like she was trying to blot her make up rather than that she was desperately trying to stop herself from gushing.

'Through all what?'

'Oh, it's silly. I wouldn't want to bother you with it.'

'If you don't want to talk about it, that's fine. But I'm always here, you know.' He looked down, suddenly bashful in his earnestness. 'If you want someone to talk to.'

The tears came freely now. Instead of coming up against a further cruel provocation, she was met only with the innate comfort that Mike somehow provided.

'That's really nice of you,' Julie said, her eyes streaming. 'You barely know me.'

'I know you're a good person, and that's good enough for me.'

Julie couldn't take it anymore. Without thinking, she closed the gap between them and embraced Mike so firmly that she could feel the air escaping from him.

'Thank you,' she said once she was stood a sensible distance away from him again. 'For being kind.'

'How about that drink, then?' he said, still looking a bit shy. 'Or we can find you a taxi if you like. No pressure.'

'A drink would be nice.'

'Okay great. We can have some food too if you like. Only, not in there.' He looked at her sheepishly. 'They brought me that lager even after I told them I was going and then tried to make me pay for it. I might have been a bit rude.'

Julie smiled at him. 'Why don't we start with a drink and see where we go from there?'

A few minutes later, they were comfortably cloistered in a quiet pub on the other side of the market square. Despite the pair being decidedly middle aged, the patrons eyed them suspiciously when they entered. The old boys looked at them, certain that the newcomers were going to be standing on tables screaming karaoke within half an hour. It said something about the nature of

Julie's normal Saturday night regime that she felt especially exotic drinking the pint of mango cider in front of her.

'You've been through the ringer a bit, then,' Mike said once Julie had explained about what had happened with Jack. 'It's understandable that you're upset. It's not exactly normal to find a dead body in your spare room. Did you know him well?'

'I'd only met him a few weeks before. Although...,' she said pausing, wondering how much to divulge.

'Yeah?'

She buried her face in her hands. 'I'll tell you, but I can't look at you when I do.'

'Alright,' Mike said, sounding concerned.

'I slept with him.' She let it hang in the air for a moment before continuing. 'It's not something I'm proud of, and it only happened once, but it happened.' After 10 seconds, Mike was still silent, so she risked a look at the expression on his face.

'Is that it?'

She nodded.

'Bloody hell, Julie. I thought you were going to tell me you'd killed him. I was preparing myself for this evening taking a right left turn.'

'You don't think I'm a daft old woman?'

'People do daft things all the time; it's nothing to beat yourself up about.'

'Okay, good.'

'And seeing as I thought you'd murdered him, anything else is going to look pretty tame in comparison.' They both laughed at this. They were met with scowls from some of their fellow drinkers and had to check themselves.

'Did he have a history of drug abuse, then? Do they think he was just a bit out of it and went over the top?'

'That depends on who you talk to.'

'Oh yeah?'

'Well I've got this neighbour who thinks there might be more to it.'

'So, you did murder him? And you're planning to knock off the woman next door, so she doesn't talk?'

'Not me, you prat. But yeah, she thinks that someone else might be involved.'

'Jesus, that's exciting,' Mike said enthusiastically. 'It's like being at one of those dinner parties, isn't it? Where one of the guests gets murdered and the rest of you have to figure out who did it.'

'But in this case, it's happening in my house, and I can't say that I don't want to be part of it.'

'Of course,' Mike said, adopting a solemn look, 'sorry.'

'Anyway, Mrs. McGrath, that's the neighbour, she's been dragging me all over the place to question people with her.' She saw Mike's face light up again. 'Which isn't as fun as it sounds.'

'Do you have any leads? Is that what you'd call them, or is that just something they say on TV?'

'I wouldn't know; we don't have any. We have this jumble of information that doesn't point to anyone else being involved, or anyone we know, at least.'

'What's next then? A return to the crime scene to see if you've overlooked any clues?'

'That's a bit more methodical than the way Mrs. McGrath likes to work. She has this theory…,' Julie said, chuckling to herself. 'Oh, it's so ridiculous. She has this theory that she can just tell. When she looks at someone, she'll be able to tell you if they are the murderer. So, in her eyes, all we have to do is keep talking to people who might have met Jack at some point, and eventually, she'll bump into the guilty party. And then if she lets me, I ask a few questions while we're there.'

'And that works, does it?'

'I can't speak for any of her previous cases, even if she has any previous cases. It hasn't been much of a success this time round. Not yet anyway.'

'It's nice that you have people living near you that you can depend on though. Especially when something like this happens.'

'Well…,' Julie paused. 'I was going to say she's just the mad old lady next door, but she let me stay with her when all of this kicked off, and she came to the station with me when the police were being difficult. I didn't even have to ask her; she was just there.'

'That's a silver lining to all this, then, making a friend.'

'I'm not sure I'd go that far. Especially after this morning. We had a bit of a falling out.'

'You can't be blamed for that, though. You're having a hard time, and she was being difficult.'

'She's just trying to find out who killed Jack. She says it's everyone's duty to see that justice is done.' It felt odd to be defending Mrs. McGrath. 'I mean, she's impossible, and it's a bloody wonder that she hasn't ended up in prison up to this point the way she carries on. But she's just doing what she thinks is right. Even if she is a bit misguided.'

'I'm sure it will all work itself out in the end,' Mike said with a look on his face like a happy labrador, 'except for the dead boy that is.'

CHAPTER NINETEEN

Julie and Mike had spent the rest of the evening in happy conversation. Julie wasn't sure if there was anything more than friendship between them, but there was at least something relaxed and pleasant there that she hadn't experienced in a long time. Maybe that's what love was when you got on a bit. It didn't need to be frolicking and wild outbursts of emotion to make it genuine. Perhaps it was enough to find someone that you wanted to watch TV with on a Saturday night. After all, if her brief dalliance with Jack had taught her anything, it was that torrid affairs weren't all that they were cracked up to be.

Julie hadn't gone to bed late but still decided to sleep in the next day. She had been due to work again that Sunday. However, Mr. Peg had left a very brief voicemail on the answering machine saying that the garden centre was closed. It seemed very odd, given that Sunday was often the only time of the week when they made a sizable profit. In fact, it often saw them afloat through the six barren days that followed.

It was 11 o'clock when there was a knock at the door. Julie was sitting in the living room with a cup of coffee and two pieces of toast. Knowing only one person who was likely to ring her doorbell before noon on a Sunday morning, she was very hesitant to surrender her breakfast for another unpleasant encounter. However, when the ringing persisted, Julie felt that she had no choice but to answer it. She was astonished to see DI Morris and DS Rowntree standing on the doorstep. Behind them, she could see a flurry of police activity around Brian's house. One officer was unrolling police tape along the front fence and two others were approaching the front door.

'Mrs. Giles, hello. May we come in?' said DI Morris. He looked around nervously as if he expected Mrs. McGrath to materialise at any second.

Julie stood to one side and held out her arm, inviting them to enter.

When Julie had provided them both with hot drinks, and they were comfortably seated at the kitchen table, she said, 'I've told you everything I know. I don't think I'm going to be much use to you.'

'It's all part of the process, all very proper and above board, I assure you. I wanted to ask you about your neighbour, Mr. Kent.'

'Who, sorry?'

'Brian Kent, he lives at number 30. I believe the two of you are fairly well acquainted?'

'I don't know him that well if I didn't know his surname.'

DI Morris mused on this for a moment, as if it was of material significance to his investigation. 'We have reason to believe that is culpable in the murder of Mr. Harper.'

Julie's heart stopped. 'You think that Brian killed Jack?'

'We are still looking into a number of lines of enquiry, but there is a strong indication that Mr. Kent was involved.'

She took a moment to think through what she knew of Jack's murder and then came to a realisation. 'It's the fingerprints, isn't it? They're Brian's. He's been on the wrong side of the law before, so you had a copy of his print on file.'

'There is a strong indication that Mr. Kent entered your property, yes.'

'Why, though?'

'It appears that Mr. Kent didn't, in fact, have a legitimate leg injury and that he was fraudulently claiming Universal Credit. From what Mr. Kent tells us, Mr. Harper discovered this and used the information to blackmail the suspect. On the night of his death, the suspect claims that he entered your house in the hopes of recovering the money that he had parted with.'

'But then why was there still some money found in Jack's room?'

'I don't think your Mr. Kent is the sharpest tool in the box. He claims that by only taking the money that he believed to be his, he hadn't committed a crime. Benefit fraud aside.'

Julie tried to take this information in. Brian was a letch and a nuisance, but she had a hard time believing that he was a murderer.

'Wait, what do you mean my Mr. Kent?'

'I'm led to believe that there was something romantic between the two of you.'

Julie's draw dropped open. 'Brian told you that?'

'It doesn't matter where we received the information from. Could you please confirm if it is correct?'

'He asked me out, but I'm sure that's true of most of the women that he met. Nothing ever happened.'

'Forgive me, Mrs. Giles. Is that entirely the truth? You do have a history of fraternisation with the opposite sex.'

'By which you mean, what?' Julie said accusingly. DI Morris realised he was in danger of becoming embarrassed again and changed tact. 'Please, don't shoot the messenger. I'm merely cross checking the facts that have been presented to us.'

'No. There has never been and there never will be anything romantic between me and Brian Kent, which is apparently his surname.'

'I see,' DI Morris said, sounding disappointed.

Julie wondered how many criminals succumbed to this very pedestrian form of questioning. 'I'm sorry,' she said, 'but then why does that mean that Brian would have killed Jack? If he got what he wanted?'

'The criminal mind isn't always straightforward.'

'Yes, but Brian is. Painfully so. What would he have to gain out of Jack being dead?'

'Perhaps out of a misguided sense of pride. Or he may have learned about your affair with the young man and was driven to action through his envy.'

'It doesn't quite add up, does it?'

'Not yet, but in the absence of any other credible suspect, I'm afraid that it doesn't look good for Mr. Kent.'

'What about those two lads from the bar he was fighting with? Or the jilted lover?' The words were out of Julie's mouth before she realised what she had said. DI Morris glared at her.

'Is there something you should have told me, Mrs. Giles?'

Her cheeks flushed. She felt like a schoolgirl being reprimanded. She relayed what had happened at the bar the night that Jack had performed and gave an abridged account of the interviews that she and Mrs. McGrath conducted.

'I'm sorry, but you seem to know better than most what Mrs. McGrath is like. You just kind of get dragged along with whatever mad idea she has on a given day.'

'That may be the case, but there is no excuse for becoming a vigilante.'

'I think that's maybe a bit far.'

He reached into his inside jacket pocket and removed his mobile phone. They sat in an awkward silence for a few seconds before he began to read. 'Vigilante. A member of a self-appointed group of citizens who undertake law enforcement in their community without legal authority.' He let the definition hang in the air. Julie was marvelling at just how insufferable he was when he continued, 'Would you say that is a fair explanation of your recent activities?'

Julie didn't want to answer him, but it appeared as if he wasn't willing to continue the conversation until she did. She mumbled a small, 'Yes,' and he responded with a curt, 'Good.'

'Do you want their names, then? The guy what Jack worked with and the woman they were falling out about.'

'I don't think that will be necessary.'

'You mean, you'll get their details from the bar?'

'If they are needed, but that seems very unlikely at this stage. Whatever the television programmes may tell you, we don't arrest members of the public on a whim. There is usually a very good reason for them to be in custody, and so that's where they tend to stay.'

'So what? You're saying that just because you've arrested Brian, he must be guilty?'

'No, I'm saying that with almost 200 years of institutional learning behind us, the police force very seldom arrest an innocent party. In the very unlikely event that we have made a mistake, I can guarantee you, it won't be because an old woman and a bored housewife have accidentally discovered a hidden talent for detection.'

'You said it yourself though, it doesn't make sense. Why would Brian kill Jack?'

'Hence why we continue to investigate, Mrs. Giles. It is very rare that we are presented with a fully formed solution to how a crime was committed. You have to work at it. Otherwise, there would be no need for police officers. However,' he said moving his chair out to leave, 'I think you have helped us as far as you are able today, so my colleague and I will leave you to enjoy the rest of your day in peace.'

'Actually, before you go, could I ask you something, please?' He'd been so condescending that Julie wanted nothing more in the world than to slap the smarmy detective right across the chops. However, she appreciated that this might be her only opportunity to speak to him without Mrs. McGrath present.

DI Morris looked taken aback, like in all his years in the police force, no witness had ever been audacious enough to put a question to him.

Julie attempted to adopt a more conciliatory tone. 'I wanted to ask you about Mrs. McGrath.' The inspector's face immediately pinkened. 'Obviously, there's a history between you. Between all of you, really,' she glanced at Jimmy who smiled at her. 'But she won't tell me what it is.'

DI Morris stared at her for a second, probably considering whether or to tell her to mind her own business. Finally, he relented and said, 'You probably aren't aware, but Moira's husband was a police officer. A very fine one too, even if he did get the occasional lofty idea in his head. He and I worked very closely together for many years until...,' He paused to find the words. 'Well, there was some unpleasantness towards the end of his career, and Moira still harbours some ill will about it.'

'Can I ask what happened between you?'

'No, I'm sorry,' he said, standing abruptly, 'we must get on.' Jimmy necked as much tea as he could before joining the inspector on his feet.

'Thank you for your continued cooperation, Mrs. Giles. We shall see ourselves out.' The detective constable gave her a friendly wave as he followed DI Morris out of the room. With a slam of the door, they were gone.

Julie spent the next hour pacing. She simply couldn't get her mind off what the inspector had told her. It was a stretch to think that Brian could dress himself in the morning and downright insane to believe that he could murder someone. In an effort to distract herself, she extracted the hoover from the cupboard under the stairs and took it around the house absentmindedly. It didn't help. If anything, the white noise generated by the machine helped her to concentrate on Jack's murder more keenly. It didn't take long for her to give up on the enterprise entirely.

She felt incensed. Brian was a cock, that was no secret. She would be lying if she said she hadn't considered that the world would be a better place without Brian in it, or at least behind bars. But none of that meant that he was a murderer. Even if he was, it didn't mean that it was right to ignore potential evidence that may prove that he was innocent. What if Oli had lied about his nan dying? It wasn't as if they had actually checked his alibi, or anyone else's, come to think of it. It really hadn't been the most thorough of investigations. Stuffing the hoover back in the cupboard and attempting to close the door before it could fall to the floor again, Julie made a decision. She was involved in all of this now, and she had to see it through to the end. If Brian had killed Jack, then fair enough, but she had to be sure, although she was fairly certain that she couldn't do it alone.

Walking up the garden path to Mrs. McGrath's front door, she did momentarily consider whether she had lost her mind. A few weeks ago, wild horses couldn't have dragged her here. At this present moment though, she was literally the only person she had any interest in speaking to. Julie knocked and waited. The scrape and tap of the old woman's cane were audible long before she flung open the front door. Her appearance remained so consistent between their meetings that Julie wondered if she ever changed her clothes. She stared at Julie dumbly, not willing to make the first move.

'Hello,' Julie said brightly, but received no response. Instead the old woman looked at her impassively. 'It's me, Mrs. McGrath, Julie, from next door?'

'I know who you are.'

'Can I come in?'

'What for?'

'DI Morris was just here. They've arrested Brian.' Julie had hoped that when she delivered this news, Mrs. McGrath would have been stricken and immediately bustled her into the house. Instead, she continued to look at her as serenely as a cow chewing the cud. 'I don't think that he's guilty. I can go into the details when we're settled, but they think it has something to do with the money. Jack was blackmailing Brian, you see, because he was only pretending...'

'I know all that,' Mrs. McGrath interrupted.

'Great,' Julie said enthusiastically, 'what's the plan then?' She took a step forward as if to go into the house, but Mrs. McGrath didn't move.

'Nothing to do. Police have got their man, haven't they, so what's left?'

'But what if they haven't? What if Brian is innocent, and he goes to prison for it?'

She gave another one of her infuriating shrugs. 'Not my problem, is it?'

'Look, I'm sorry, okay? It all felt like it was getting out of hand. You know, us knocking on that old man's door like that after it all getting so nasty with Mrs. Stuart. I didn't understand what you were saying, but I get it now. If we don't do anything, then no one will.' Julie felt proud of this little speech until she saw the look on Mrs. McGrath's face. It remained so unchanged that Julie may as well have read her the shipping forecast.

'I've got some things to do in the house if that's it.'

'No, that isn't it,' Julie said, feeling annoyed now. 'You started all of this; you can't just drop out of it again when you're no longer interested.'

'I didn't kill the lad, and it looks to me like they've found their murderer without my help. I think I'm done.'

Julie tried to protest. Unsurprisingly, Mrs. McGrath wasn't interested. She closed the door in her face with a decided thud. Again, she could hear the sound of her cane scraping on the tiles as she retreated back into the house.

Dejected, Julie made her way down the path and returned to her own house. She spent the rest of the day wandering around aimlessly, looking for something that needed doing. It was useless. She couldn't think of anything else.

When the evening arrived, and Julie hadn't managed to do anything of any use, she decided to resign herself to her fate. If she wasn't going to be able to focus on anything else until this mess was resolved, then she may as well steer into the skid. She convinced herself that she had just been out of sorts yesterday, and that's why she'd given it all up. All she needed was a bit of fun to revitalise her, which Mike had given her in spades.

She firmly placed herself at the kitchen table, a glass of pinot within easy reaching distance. On the notepad before her, she began to write everyone's name who they had spoken to.

Julie was the first to admit that her memory wasn't the best. Therefore, the local drug dealer who had chased them off the industrial estate was listed as 'angry thug,' and each of his companions were listed as 'henchmen,' one to four respectively. Not knowing what to call the drug dealer's girlfriend, she googled it and found the term 'moll.' It sounded horrendously dated, even to her ears. She reasoned that if she allowed herself to get bogged down into every little detail, she wasn't going to get anywhere.

Why hadn't they thought to speak to the underlings and ask them where they'd been on the night Jack was killed? Had the police done that, or had they dismissed them just as Julie and Mrs. McGrath had done?

And what about the girl at Nixons? Just because she said Jack left the bar at midnight didn't mean that she had. Surely, that's the kind of thing that the police would look into as a matter of course. Or maybe not, if they weren't willing to consider that anyone but Brian was the murderer. As Julie made her notes, the amount of questions that she didn't know the answers to began to increase exponentially. It started to make her feel overwhelmed, and she began to sip at her wine with increasing regularity. Her attention then waned completely, doodling in the margins of her notebook.

She felt that their investigation was such a mess that it might be better to give up on this one and wait for the next local murder. That way, she could ask all the right questions from the start instead of letting Mrs. McGrath convince her that you could tell if someone was a killer just by the look in their eyes.

Having almost decided to give up and order herself a takeaway, she remembered Brian sitting in custody for a crime he might not have committed. This wasn't, in fact, something she was doing for the enjoyment factor, but to prove that the local letcher was innocent of this crime at least. She did feel like a bit of a hypocrite after giving Mrs. McGrath such a hard time about forcing her to investigate Jack's death. Brian's arrest had brought it home somehow and made the injustice of it feel more real.

"Okay", she said to herself, "you shouldn't give up, but you don't want to cover old ground again. What else can you do?" She decided the best approach would be to walk herself through the last few days again, from when Jack arrived up until the present day. Each of the supporting characters that came into her mind's eye seemed like such an unlikely choice for the part of the murderer. The obvious exception was that group of yobs, although Jack's death was all a bit too cloak and dagger to consider them serious suspects. Surely if they wanted Jack dead, they would have stabbed him with a Stanley knife and then passed around a bottle of white lightning to celebrate. There was something more cold and calculating to all this.

Again, her mind processed all the faces she had seen throughout this drama. All of a sudden, the fat banker popped into her head. The greasy old boy that Jack had punched in the bar. Through some mad reasoning only known to her, Mrs. McGrath had decided that he wasn't worth tracking down because it didn't make sense for him to kill Jack. This, coming from a woman who had thought it necessary to pound on the doors of all her neighbours on the off chance they were capable of homicide.

The idea of exploring a lead that they hadn't previously considered was exciting, invigorating even. So what if it came to nothing? It was somewhere to start, at least. There were no messy thoughts of previous failures to contend with either.

And DI Morris couldn't really object. He'd disregarded the information as inconsequential already. Surely then, it was fair enough that Julie could go and speak to the man. If she thought he said anything important, she could tell the police straight away.

But how was she going to find him? Once again, she tried to remember the details of that evening of high drama through the fog of alcohol. There was something clawing just at the corner of her mind. Yes, he had been carrying an umbrella with something printed on it. What was it? Jerry something? Jerry Something Bloors. With a roaring lion underneath it.

She opened her laptop and typed, 'jerry,' and 'bloors,' into the search engine. There it was, number one on the list. Jerryman Bloors, a distinguished boutique trader based in the city. As luck would have it, there was only one branch. Julie couldn't have felt prouder of herself if she had just caught the Yorkshire Ripper. She was looking for someone and had actually managed to find them on purpose. Unscrewing the cap on the second bottle of wine in the fridge, Julie remarked to herself that the case was definitely looking up.

CHAPTER TWENTY

J ulie's first thought when she walked into the offices of Jerryman Bloors was that it was possibly the least welcoming place on earth. Everything was glass and polished floors with no soul whatsoever to speak of. This extended to the receptionist who was eying her suspiciously as Julie approached the desk. She wore a slim fitting white shirt and a pencil skirt, her hair neatly scraped into a bun.

The best part of two bottles of wine the night before had made the journey into the city a very unpleasant experience. When Julie had woken up that morning feeling like death, it wouldn't take much convincing for her to remain in bed for the rest of the day. But then she had thought of Brian, probably still sitting in a police cell and the power she might have to get him released.

In the end, the guilt trumped the nausea, and she had heaved herself out of bed. She had thought that she couldn't feel any worse than she already did. That was before she realised how she must look to the sprightly young thing behind the desk. She had tried to look the part, selecting her outfit the night before with vigour when she had first cooked up the plan. However, when she had gone to put the clothes on this morning, she was pained to see that both the smart blouse and trousers that she had chosen were ravaged with creases. The thought of dragging the iron and the board from under the stairs and attempting to make the clothes look presentable proved too much for her in her current state. Instead then, she had opted for whatever was clean and not too rumpled in her bottom drawer.

It had really taken her a long time to get going this morning. Then, when she finally got to the station, she realised that she hadn't checked the timetable. Unbeknownst to her, there was a reduced service in place because of some engineering works. When she had finally managed to get on a train, it was the middle of the afternoon. Catching a glimpse of her reflection on the journey into the city, she was horrified to see that she looked like an oversized school girl. The only thing missing was a striped tie worn too short. The whole enterprise felt doomed before it had even started.

'Hello there,' Julie said when it became clear that she wasn't going to ask how she could help. 'I'm here to see Charles Bond.' After a few false starts, Julie had managed to find the picture of the chap who Jack had fought with on the company website. This was no small feat, given that she had been half cut the one time they had not even really met. That coupled with the fact that every man who worked in the financial sector looked almost exactly the same. It helped that Jerryman Bloors was a relatively small firm, and after going through the photos about a dozen times, she was fairly certain that it was Charles Bond who she needed to speak to.

'And do you have an appointment?' the receptionist said. Her nose crinkled as she spoke to Julie, as if she was the source of a fairly unpleasant smell.

Julie nodded her head and instantly regretted it.

'For what time?' The receptionist looked towards her computer screen, her fingers poised above the keys.

Not quite sure of what time it was, Julie tried to surreptitiously look at her watch.

'3.00pm,' Julie said. The receptionist gave her an unimpressed look. 'Or was it 3.30? Sorry, I can't quite remember.'

'Well, that depends. I'm guessing you're not Mr. Lyons?'

Julie did a little laugh, just in case the receptionist was, in fact, buying into this routine but was afflicted by a perpetually sour face.

'If you would like to take a seat then, Mrs. Watanabe, I'll call Mr. Bond's PA and let him know that you've arrived.'

The two women stared at each other for what felt like an impossibly long time.

'Come to think of it,' Julie said, picking her handbag up off the floor, 'it wasn't today that I was seeing old Charlie.' She began to step backwards towards the entrance, feeling ridiculous as she did it. Julie reminded herself that she wasn't, in fact, trying to rob a bank, and she should probably stop acting like she was. 'Sorry about that.'

As Julie struggled backwards through the revolving door, the last thing she saw inside the lobby was the smug look of self-satisfaction plastered across the receptionist's face.

Standing outside with a constant stream of incredibly well dressed professionals passing by, Julie had to fight the overwhelming urge to give up. She was starting to get very fed up with herself, all of this despair every few minutes when something didn't go exactly as expected. No, she told herself, you're here now, you may as well make a go of it. She was currently standing in a courtyard with impossibly high buildings surrounding her on all sides. In the very centre, there was an uncomfortable looking bench. 'There we go, then,' she said, talking to herself again. 'I'll sit there and wait for the bugger to come out.' It wasn't like she had anything else that she needed to do today. She was supposed to be working this afternoon, but Mr. Peg had left another message telling her not to bother coming in. The poor sod had probably bankrupted himself, buying all that sand. Hopefully, he hadn't got himself into too much trouble.

It was a shame really, Julie thought as she walked over to the bench. It hadn't been a bad little job. Mundane, of course. Not much asked of you though, and the customers were always friendly. And then there was Mike, of course, the great oaf. Julie had the very distinct impression that he had wanted to kiss her on their night together, but it didn't feel quite right. At the time, she thought that maybe it was because it had been such a long time since she had kissed anyone, except for Jack, of course, but somehow, she didn't think that counted. Or maybe it was because he felt like more of a friend. Regardless of what their relationship was, she felt a sudden pang at the thought of not seeing him most days at work.

It wasn't a bench that was designed for a prolonged stay. Its granite base was uncomfortable to sit on, and with no back to the seat, it took a fair amount of effort to remain sitting upright. For the first twenty minutes that Julie was sat there, she could at least enjoy the warmth of the afternoon sun making its way down into the space. However, once the light had passed behind the tall buildings, a chill came over her, and she wished that she had brought something to cover her bare arms. A handful of people had exited the buildings of Jerryman Bloor since she had taken up her station, but none of them were Charles Bond as far as she could tell.

'Is anyone sitting here?' A voice said from behind Julie. She turned to see a woman of about Mrs. McGrath's age. Despite the slight chill in the air, the wool cap that she was wearing seemed superfluous to Julie. In each hand, she was carrying at least three plastic bags stuffed full of Lord knows what. Julie held up her open palm to indicate that she should sit. She gave Julie a happy smile and joined her on the bench.

The old woman lowered herself by degrees towards the seat and then dropped herself the final distance. 'Bloody hell,' she said, placing her bags on the floor, 'not very comfortable this, is it?' Julie half turned her head towards her and smiled. She'd just shaken off one unhinged, elderly companion. She wasn't keen to acquire another.

'Of course, they don't actually expect anyone to sit here,' the old woman continued unprompted. 'This lot have all got sticks too far up their arses to sit down anyway.' She began to rummage in one of her carrier bags and pulled out a loaf of bread. 'Murder on my piles though. I usually bring a cushion with me, but I forgot it today.'

Opening the bag that it was in, she took a piece out and ripped it in half. She placed the slightly smaller section down on the bench and then began to eat the larger segment.

'Do you want some?' she said, holding the bag out to Julie. 'Don't worry, I'm not a pedophile or anything.'

'No, thank you,' Julie said. She tried to keep her attention focused on the exit of Jerryman Bloors, although the old woman was incredibly distracting. Not only did she keep shifting her weight every few seconds, but after she had finished her snack, she picked up the other piece of her bread and started to tear it to pieces. When it was entirely shredded, she pulled her hand back behind her head and flung the pieces on the floor. She beat her hands together, and the crumbs that had been stuck to her fingerless gloves fell away.

'For the birds,' she said, when she saw that Julie had been watching her. Julie did a quick survey of their immediate surroundings but couldn't see another living thing in their immediate proximity, winged or otherwise. However, this didn't stop her new companion to continue to take piece after piece of bread from the bag. Each time, she would eat half and then distribute the other on the ground.

At one point, the snotty receptionist from earlier came out of her building to have a cigarette. Now that the lunchtime crowd had all returned to work, it was only Julie and her new companion who were left in the courtyard. Therefore, for the entire time that she was smoking, the receptionist fixed them with the most disapproving of looks. This did little to deter the distributor of the bread, who continued to happily make her way through her loaf. The receptionist dropped the cigarette on the ground and extinguished it with the high heel of her shoe. She then collected it from the ground and placed it in the bin hanging from the wall. With one last look of utter contempt, she went back through the revolving doors and returned to work.

'Sorry, love,' the woman with the bread said, standing up, 'would you mind looking after my things for me?'

Julie looked down at the mass of carrier bags that were heaped around the bench and said, 'I'm sorry?'

'Don't want anyone nicking them. Got to use the ladies, you see.'

'Right,' Julie said, not quite understanding.

'Harder to sneak in, isn't it? When you're holding on to all that gumpf.'

Julie looked at the old eccentric's mad winter garb on this summer day and thought it was very unlikely that she would ever be able to sneak under the radar regardless of what she was carrying. Before Julie could tell this stranger that no, she wasn't willing to act as watchman to her selection of carrier bags, she was a good ten metres away from her and making her way into another one of the grand office blocks surrounding them.

Julie thought about moving to another bench before she realised that there wasn't one. Instead, she had to satisfy herself by moving to the opposite end that the bags were gathered around. About two minutes into the woman's absence, Julie clocked a bloke walking directly towards her. There was no doubt that he was coming to speak to her as there wasn't another soul in sight. It was also clear that the man was a security guard of some kind. He was wearing what was evidently a clip on tie and the kind of cheap wooly jumper that would only be worn by someone who was required to do so by their profession.

'Excuse me, miss,' he said when he finally approached her. 'We've had some reports of fly tipping in the area. Wouldn't know anything about that, would you?' He eyed the shopping bags on the floor as he spoke to her.

'They're not mine,' she said instinctively and a bit too quickly for someone who was, in fact, innocent of this mild infraction. The security guard raised an eyebrow and gave her a knowing smile.

'And what about all this bread?' He kicked at one of the nearest stray pieces. 'I'm guessing you don't know anything about that either, do you?'

'It was this other woman. She asked me to look after her bags while she went to the loo.' Julie attempted to remember which of the buildings the woman who owned the bags had gone into. The problem was that they all looked so similar. She ended up pointing vaguely in the general direction that the woman had walked in a not too convincing manner.

The security guard chuckled to himself. 'If I had a penny for every time that I'd heard that.'

'She'll be back in a minute, I'm sure.'

The security guard looked sceptical. 'I will wait for her with bated breath.'

Julie had thought that this would be the end of the conversation, but the security guard continued to look at her expectantly. 'I'm not doing anything wrong, am I?' She said. 'Shouldn't I be sitting here?'

'Just you now, is it? What happened to this friend of yours?' He said it in such a grandiose manner, as if he had caught her out in some great scheme. Julie wondered whether this little dictator was related to DI Morris.

'Well, obviously, it's just me sitting here now. That other woman will be back along shortly.'

'That other woman?'

'Yes, I told you. The one who the bags belong to.'

'What's her name?'

'I don't know, she didn't say.'

The security guard laughed as if this was the most ridiculous thing he'd ever come across. 'Now I've heard everything,' he said, lifting his hands above his head. 'You mean to tell me some random stranger came up to you, scattered a loaf of bread over the floor and asked you to look after all her worldly possessions stuffed into carrier bags?'

'Pretty much, yeah.'

'Well, I very much look forward to meeting this friend of yours. In the meantime, I'm afraid I'm going to have to issue you with a community disturbance notice.' He reached into his pocket and took out a long, rectangular notepad like the type that traffic wardens carry.

Julie looked at him with disbelief. 'I'm hardly disturbing anyone, am I? It's just a bit of bread. I'm sure the birds will get at it in a minute.'

'The rats, don't you mean? We'll have hundreds of them streaming in with all this lot on the ground. And what about the foxes? Badgers even.'

Julie got the distinct impression that this security guard didn't have much to do. 'Badgers?'

'People think that they're just feeding the pretty birdies. They forget what happens after they've gone home, and the bread stays where it is. What happens then, ey?'

Throughout this bizarre exchange, Julie had attempted to keep an eye on the entrance of Jerryman Bloors, but understandably, her attention had wavered. It was only by chance then that she had once again remembered her overall purpose here and looked up at the exact moment that Charles Bond was walking out of the building. Or at least she thought it was him; it was hard to tell from this distance.

'Could you excuse me for a moment?' Julie said to the security guard. He looked at her incredulously, as if he was some great agent of the state rather than someone who might not even have the authority to tell her to pick up some stray bread.

'We're not finished!' he shouted after her. Julie was already away. Unless she was quick, Charles Bond would be out of the courtyard and into the throng of the capital before she had been able to speak to him, and she definitely wasn't going to repeat this ordeal again. It was now or never.

'Excuse me,' she said as she approached him. To begin with, he wouldn't make eye contact with Julie at all. He increased his speed and continued to look at his shoes, like someone who was attempting to evade an especially persistent beggar. 'Sorry,' Julie said, falling into step next to him, 'can I talk to you for a minute?'

The security guard had pursued her as she had walked towards Mr. Bond. 'I wasn't done talking to you, love,' he said, 'we need to sort out this mess.'

'In a minute,' Julie said, momentarily turning back to him before returning her attention to her mark. 'I need to speak to you,' she repeated, 'I need your help.'

'No, I can't help, sorry,' he said, not looking at her. 'I'm sure you can sort it out between you.'

'If you don't move these bags, I'm going to have to call the police,' the security guard said from behind Julie. She ignored him and continued to follow the banker.

'Mr. Bond,' she said, speeding up to step in front of him, blocking his path. 'I need to talk to you about a crime.' There was half a second when she thought that he wasn't going to stop and just crash into her. Luckily, he paused just before their bodies collided and looked up at her for the first time.

'Journalist, are you? Anything like that should be addressed to the press office,' he said, but didn't move to go. Julie saw that he looked exhausted. He looked like the type who would have a pint for his lunch. His hair was greasy, and there were great, dark rings under his eyes. Julie wouldn't have been surprised if he had been sleeping at the office.

'It's not to do with your company. It's to do with you.'

A glint of panic appeared in his eyes. 'Oh yeah?' he said, attempting to mask his unease with what Julie expected was his accustomed bravado. 'What would that be, then?' The security guard observed the two of them from a few feet away.

'I was there at Nixons. You know, the bar near Kings Cross?' He looked at her blankly, so she continued. 'You got into a fight with a young man called Jack Harper.'

'Doesn't ring any bells, but if I hit him, I'm sure he had it coming.' He looked relieved that Julie's accusation had been so mild and went to walk past her. Julie once again blocked his path and waited for him to return her gaze before delivering the next blow.

'You might not have heard, but Mr. Harper was found dead a few days later. The police suspect foul play.' Julie studied his reaction. The only way she could think to describe it was absolutely bloody dumbstruck. His eyes bulged out of their sockets, and several more beads of sweat formed on his forehead than had already been present when they first began their conversation.

'Can I ask where you were in the early hours of Monday 26th July, please?'

'Jesus, I don't know.' He put one hand on his brow. It was like this was another in a long list of hassles that Mr. Bond didn't want to deal with. 'So what, I have to come to the station with you?'

'Well, no,' Julie said, feeling as if she was treading a very dangerous line. 'Not if you can tell me where you were and give me a good enough reason to believe you.' He ran his hands through his greasy hair.

'What day did you say, the 26th? I think I was here.' He thought quietly to himself for a moment before a light came on behind his eyes. 'No wait, I definitely was. It was the day before those bastards from Japan flew in to break my balls. Had to pull an all-nighter with the troops, try and get ourselves prepared.'

'And what time did you leave?'

'I didn't. The girls in the pool keep the sheets on a few beds in the back clean in case we need to hang about. Much easier than trekking all the way home only to be back again in a few hours.' He sounded more sure of himself now despite a definite look of apprehension still present on his face.

Julie's heart sank. If this greasy old toad had been here for most of the weekend, it didn't bode well for her theory that he might have had something to do with Jack's death. She was sure that he had been up to no good, but he didn't look like he had the slightest clue who she was, let alone Jack. For someone as unpleasant as him, perhaps being clocked in face was such a common occurrence that you didn't feel the need to take note of it.

'Can anyone verify this?' In a reasonable approximation of Mrs. McGrath, Julie reached into her pocket and extracted a small notebook.

'Arkwright was here. Jonathan Arkwright, that is. Oh, and Sampson. Can't remember his first name, the new chap on the Asian desk. The receptionist will be able to point you in his direction.'

'Very good,' Julie said, making a note of the names despite knowing that she would never have any use for them. 'That's all for now, Mr. Bond. I know where to find you if I have any more questions. If you're leaving the area, please first notify your local police station.'

Charles Bond nodded obligingly before racing out of Julie's sight. She continued to look down at her notepad until he was far enough away that she wouldn't risk bumping into him on her way back to the tube station. As she went to leave, a voice called out behind her, 'Sorry, love.' She had forgotten the security guard lurking just out of sight. 'I don't care if you're a copper, you still need to clear that mess up.'

CHAPTER TWENTY-ONE

The journey home had done nothing to improve Julie's mood, even with the two cans of gin and tonic that she had bought from the convenience store in the station. The train had been so crammed that she had, not only been forced to stand the entire way, but worse still, she had only just managed to fit into the carriage before the doors closed. No handrail was available for her use, and she had to wedge herself between the wall and one of her fellow passengers to stay upright.

She had continued to refuse the pushy security guard's calls for her to clean up the rubbish until he had once again threatened to call the police. Knowing her luck, it would have been DI Morris or one of his underlings who arrived to resolve the situation, and she would have found herself in a very precarious situation. It was only when she was picking up handfuls of dirty bread off the ground under the watchful eye of the courtyard comandante that the rightful owner of the bags had returned to claim her belongings. The guard didn't apologise. He just refocused his attention on the old bag lady and seemed to instantly forget that Julie had ever existed.

When Julie arrived at Brumpton, the crush of people making their way home from a day of working in the city quickly took all of the available taxis. Initially, she had waited in the queue for the returning minicabs, but ultimately her impatience and her general feeling of dejection won out. She couldn't bear to be around anyone else for however brief a time. From start to finish, this episode had been a disaster. Arguably, her solo investigations formed the most painful chapter, having been borne out of her own imagination. She decided that she would be better off on the move. It didn't matter that it would take her longer than if she just waited for another car. At least this way, she wouldn't be forced into an awkward conversation with the driver.

Standing at the bus stop, she opened her second can of gin and tonic and necked it warm in several desperate mouthfuls. She then turned and began the long walk home. The whole way there, she couldn't get the voice out her head reminding her what a silly woman she was. It wasn't that long ago that she had chastised Mrs. McGrath for her delusions of any discernible skill in the art of the detection, only to then go and run off on a fool's errand herself. What had she been playing at? Who was she to think that she could do anything useful? She was done. Done with all of it. If Brian was innocent, then the police would work it out in the end. If her recent experience had taught her anything, it might take them a while to get there, but she was sure they'd reach the right conclusion.

Walking across town, it seemed as if at every possible opportunity, some idiotic pedestrian was in her way. On a warm summer evening like the one they were currently experiencing, no one was in any sort of a rush. She frequently found herself stepping into the road to navigate herself around them, huffing as she went. She made a quick detour into Mr. Baker's shop, grabbing a few bottles, some ready meals and a loaf of bread with the view to not coming outside again until the supplies were depleted. Luckily, the little gang of hoodlums wasn't standing guard at the shop's front door, as Julie was fairly sure her patience couldn't stand seeing them again.

By the time she reached her road, Julie was ready to close herself from the world and never open it again. Absentmindedly, she noticed that the police cordon around Brian's house had been removed. She made her way into the house, and once the door was closed, she immediately began to engage the locks. Safely barricaded in her house, Julie went to talk towards the kitchen only to be confronted by the hedge clippers propped up against the wall. They sat there, taunting her. She needed them out of the house. They were a reminder of her own stupidity throughout this whole sorry ordeal. While they were still sitting there, she couldn't start to put it out of her mind. Mrs. Sinclair had said they weren't hers, and she didn't own any garden equipment of her own. Therefore, they must belong to Brian.

A moment later, the door was once again unlocked, and Julie was walking across the street, hedge clippers in hand. She walked up Brian's drive and knocked on the front door. When there was no answer, she tried again. After a third and final attempt, she considered leaving the clippers propped up against the door. Would it bother her if someone stole them? Julie tried to convince herself that it wouldn't, especially in light of her new devil may care attitude, but she couldn't quite bring herself to do it.

Unlike Julie's, the houses on this side of the road were terraced. Because there was the need for communal access across the back gardens, the inhabitants seldom locked their back gates. Julie decided that if she left the clippers at the rear of the property and then someone pilfered them, she could live with it. At least then she had taken reasonable care to stop them from being taken.

Without thinking, she walked down the alleyway at the end of the block of houses. Initially, she was perturbed to find the back gate locked. However, reaching her hand over the top, Julie was able to pull the bolt back and gain access to the path that led across the neighbour's garden through to the rear of Brian's house. It was only when Julie began to walk across the grass that she remembered this was Mrs. Sinclair's garden. That, in itself, was less of a surprise than the general state of the space. The grass was unkempt, and weeds had sprouted up from between most of the paving stones. Only the hedges looked as if a passable effort had been made to keep them tidy.

'Can I help you?' Julie turned to find Mrs. Sinclair standing at the top of the steps leading up to her back door.

'Sorry, I didn't mean to intrude. I wanted to return these hedge clippers that you brought around to Brian.'

'Right.'

Julie began to walk across the garden to the gate leading next door before she stopped herself. 'It doesn't look like Jack did a very good job for you,' she said, turning to face the woman who had been watching her progress. She was holding a tea towel and was drying her hands.

'I'm sorry?'

'Jack said that you had been paying him to keep your garden tidy, but it doesn't look like he did much.'

'You know what most young people are like.'

Julie nodded and said, 'That's true. Only I know that he wasn't working on Brian's garden much, so I wonder what he was spending so much time doing on this side of the street.' She looked into Mrs. Sinclair's eyes, but she gave nothing away.

'Would you like to come in for a cup of tea?' Mrs. Sinclair said, finally breaking the silence. She forced a small smile. 'Criminal really that we've been neighbours for so many years, and I've never invited you in.'

'That's very kind of you, but I really should be getting back.' Forgetting her mission, Julie turned back the way that she had come, intending to return to the street.

'No, no, I insist,' Mrs. Sinclair said, taking a step forward to block her progress. 'I'd like to. To apologise for being so rude to you. Twice.'

Feeling as if she had no other choice, Julie made her way up the steps into the house, with Mrs. Sinclair following closely behind her. Once they were inside, Mrs. Sinclair closed and locked the door behind them.

'It was nice with it open,' Julie said, feeling a bit nervous. 'You know, let a bit of air in.'

'I'll keep it shut if you don't mind. Don't like the insects buzzing around when I'm trying to make dinner.' Julie saw that there was an assortment of chopped vegetables on a chopping board on the counter.

'But you had it open before?'

'I don't have anything posh, I'm afraid,' Mrs. Sinclair said, ignoring the question entirely, 'it's either instant coffee or English breakfast tea.'

'A coffee would be lovely, thank you.' Julie hadn't been told to sit down, so she stood in the corner of the room with her hands crossed over her front.

Whilst the kettle boiled, Mrs. Sinclair returned to chopping vegetables. Not sure of anything else to do, Julie kept her eyes on her host's preparations for dinner.

'Your hands are very red,' Julie said in an idle attempt to make conversation. She had noticed it before when she had bumped into Mrs. Sinclair at the summer fete. 'It's funny, I have these flowers in my front hall. Weeds, really. That's why they lasted so long. I took them from work, you see. Mr. Peg, that's my boss, he's always chucking perfectly good stuff out, so I take it home with me. Only, I didn't realise that the pollen in these flowers stains like nothing else you've seen before. It's still under my nails, and my fingers are still pink with it. There's a great red patch on the front seat in the car.'

Mrs. Sinclair stopped chopping but kept the knife in her hand. With the other, she placed her hand flat on the surface of the counter.

Julie had her hands tucked into her armpits, giving her some small comfort. 'But you know that already, don't you? Because you've been in my house.' Mrs. Sinclair spun around and stared daggers at Julie. The absolute malice in her eyes only lasted a second before her entire posture slumped, and she stood in front of Julie looking absolutely dejected.

'You were having an affair, weren't you?'

'And what if we were?' Mrs. Sinclair spat. 'Does it even count as an affair if you're married to a vegetable?'

'Was it an accident?' Julie asked, trying to keep her voice kind. 'He was experimenting, and it all went wrong maybe. So you ran, scared of what the police might say.'

Mrs. Sinclair said nothing.

'Or maybe not.'

'It was flattering, you know,' Mrs. Sinclair started. 'It made me feel young again. Such a disgusting cliché, but it's true. Back before I married Paul, I had an endless line of them trying to take me out. All that falls away though, doesn't it? When you find the right one. Then, of course, there was the accident, and I was trapped. No partner to speak of but no way of starting up with someone else.'

'Who wants to be involved with someone when their permanently disabled husband comes as part of the package? I'm not saying I ever seriously considered leaving, but you know, it was nice to fantasise every once in a while.' Her features softened as she talked, although Julie was very aware that she had still kept hold of the knife.

'I probably would have said yes to anyone, truth be told. I mean, of course, he was handsome. It wasn't about that though. It had been so long since someone had taken notice of me as anything but a carer that his attention was just, well overwhelming.' Julie thought about that first night with Jack when they had got drunk together, and he'd first turned on the charms. The thought that only a few small circumstances separated her from the woman standing before her, who had started to cry gently, made her feel overwhelmed, like she was perched on the edge, and the smallest pressure would tip her over.

'I'd come over on that Sunday with those clippers he'd left behind on the pretext of seeing him again. If you were there, I could just say I was dropping them off and then go home. If not, then maybe we could spend the afternoon together in bed. There was something that always felt a bit wrong about us being in my bed, you know. Our bed, I should say, mine and Paul's.'

Her eyes had shifted to the floor as she had been talking, but then they flicked back towards Julie when she said, 'But of course, you know what happened next. You were there.' Julie's face immediately flushed with the shame of it.

'I may have been out of the game for a while, but even I know that the only people who fight like the way you two were are lovers. Can you even comprehend how that felt? Not only to have fallen for that silly little Lothario's charms, but then to realise that I was just one of a harem of middle aged concubines.'

Mrs. Sinclair seemed to become more aware of how she was slumped all of a sudden and snapped back up to attention. Her eyes passed up and down Julie's entire body. 'It was only when I found out about the two of you that I realised how low his standards were. If he was attracted to you, then what the hell did that say about me? The little shit.' There was real venom in her voice now. She had started chopping again, the knife hitting the board hard with each word she spoke. 'Who did he think he was? Treating me like that.'

Something occurred to Julie. 'It didn't take you long to make a decision, did it? There was what? 12 hours between when you decided to kill him and actually doing the deed?'

'He made me look ridiculous,' Mrs. Sinclair said, her voice becoming suddenly shrill. 'I was willing to throw away everything I had in the world for him, and it turns out I was only one of many.'

Julie's mind started racing. Why hadn't she and Mrs. McGrath considered Mrs. Sinclair a suspect before. 'But I heard that 24 hour plumber arrive at your house the night that Jack was killed. He'd come into my room just before that.'

'Did he?' Mrs. Sinclair said with a wicked grin on her face. 'Are you sure about that?'

The day had been overcast, and as the sun moved from behind a cloud, it lit Mrs. Sinclair from behind through the kitchen window. The light made Julie feel dizzy, and for a moment, she could only see the woman's outline. All of a sudden, it seemed ridiculous to her that someone with such beautiful hair would decide to inflict that boyish crop on herself. It was then that the realisation came crashing down on Julie.

'It was you in my bedroom that night. I'm so stupid, how did I not see it before? No wonder he didn't say anything. I thought it was because he was too drunk, but you couldn't do anything more than mumble, otherwise, I would have realised it wasn't Jack.'

'Very good,' she said in a patronising tone. 'Astonishing really for someone with your obvious lack of intellect.'

Julie ignored the slight and pressed on. 'And so Jack was...'

'Already dead, yes,' Mrs. Sinclair said, jumping in. It was the indifference with which she made the statement that made Julie feel the most uneasy. 'It wouldn't take a great stretch of the imagination for anyone to believe that the young Romeo had died of an overdose, but it's better to be safe than sorry, isn't it? Of course you see all these clever plots of the television. You just don't know how they're going to stand up to scrutiny though. For all I knew, there was some sort of test to tell what angle the needle went in at, or who pushed the plunger. That's why I had to come up with all that nonsense of dressing up like him and coming into your room. From what I gather, you've usually drunken yourself into a stupor by that time of the night. I thought you could at least be depended upon to make out basic shapes.'

Julie wanted to make a real show of indignation at this fairly accurate yet entirely unnecessary statement. However, as Mrs. Sinclair still had a firm grip on the vegetable knife, it didn't feel like the best time to kick off. 'How did you even get in? Through the window like Brian?'

Mrs. Sinclair gave Julie such a look that you would have thought she had been dribbling into her hands for the past thirty minutes. 'You weren't the only one to spend the night in that bed, dear. I'm surprised you didn't hear us coming in. He could barely stand up.'

'Through the front door, then,' Julie said, coming to another small point of realisation. 'That's why Jack's shoes were in the rack, not scattered across the floor of the kitchen.'

Mrs. Sinclair ignored the reference to her error and pressed on with her own version of events. 'It's easier than you think, with a bit of foresight that is. I loosened some of the joints under the sink. Gave it a bit of a whack with the hammer, you know? Then I sent the boy a text asking him to meet. He let me into the house, and it was one more trip around the maypole to get him off to sleep. Then the needle went in as easy as you like. I deleted the text and called the plumber. After I'd popped in to say hello to you, I was on my way.' She explained it all so rationally that it was hard to remember that she was talking about murdering someone.

'Then when those daft plods came knocking, it was easy enough to tell them about your lovers' spat with Jack and drop a few more hints to throw them off the scent.'

'But how did you know that Jack would have the heroin? Wasn't it a bit risky to just assume that he'd have some in his room?'

Mrs. Sinclair laughed. 'Oh bless you, so naive. No, I came thoroughly prepared. It's not hard to find someone who can sell you the right equipment. I'm not exactly the kind of customer that they're used to. That didn't seem to bother them though when they saw that I could pay for it.'

Julie suddenly remembered the yobs that had chased them off the industrial park. One of them had mentioned that she and Mrs. McGrath weren't the first respectable clients he had catered for recently. How had they missed that? It all felt so simple now.

'Where did Brian fit into all of this?'

'Brian?' she said, looking at her quizzically, 'From next door?'

Julie nodded. When Mrs. Sinclair said nothing and continued to look perplexed, she said 'Jack was blackmailing him. He broke in to steal the money back.'

'Nothing to do with me,' she said. 'It's a shame really; he would have made a much better scapegoat than you. He just sort of looks the part, doesn't he?' As Mrs. Sinclair's attention waned, the tension returned to her arm, and she seemed to remember the knife in her hand again. Julie began to feel herself becoming panicked and desperately sought for another question to distract her would-be assailant. 'Was it worth it then? Getting your revenge.' She tried to maneuver herself closer to the doorway without making it too obvious.

'I'd say so.' She still looked very pleased with herself.

'It doesn't change anything though, does it? He still made you look a fool.'

Mrs. Sinclair's expression instantly soured. 'Well, he won't be doing it again, will he?'

'But you're going to go to prison. Your husband will have to go into a home. Just so you could get your revenge.'

'I'm not going anywhere.' She closed the gap between them, and Julie flinched. It was then that there was an almighty banging at the door. Without realising what she was doing, Julie spun around and flung herself out into the hall. 'Help!' she screamed. 'She's a murderer; she's going to kill me!' She only managed to make it a few steps before she felt a slash across the length of her back and then a sharp pain in one of the fleshy deposits towards the top of her legs. The blow instantly floored her, and as she hit the ground, her face collided painfully with the wooden floor.

From where she lay, dazed and confused, Julie heard footsteps running away from her. A few seconds later, she could just about make out the sound of the back door opening over the continued banging at the front of the house. A moment later, the thudding stopped and was replaced by the unmistakable sound of two people shouting. She tried to raise herself up onto her elbows and instantly started to feel faint. As the light of the world began to dim, Julie was sure she heard an almighty smack that she couldn't quite identify, but it didn't seem important anymore. She fell flat and everything went dark.

CHAPTER TWENTY-TWO

I t took Julie a few moments to realise that she was in a hospital bed. Once she remembered that her last memory involved being stabbed in the back and then crashing to the floor face first, it wasn't much of a surprise. She touched her face and instantly recoiled at the pain. Returning her hand more gently now, she felt that her nose had a great deal of padding surrounding it, with some adhesive tape keeping it in place.

'Shouldn't mess with it too much,' a voice said from the other side of the room. 'Took them ages to get it to stop bleeding.' Julie turned her head too quickly and saw stars in front of her eyes. There was a horrible moment when she was sure that she was going to be sick before the nausea receded, and she saw Mrs. McGrath sitting in one of the chairs next to her bed. Julie's head was sore, and her back was stinging a bit, but apart from that, she felt pretty much okay.

'The doctor said they're superficial,' Mrs. McGrath said as she saw Julie reach to touch the bandages on her back. 'Conk on the head, that was the real worry. Ran you through the machines though, and there's no real damage. Probably keep you in overnight, and then you're good to go.'

Julie took a moment to take the information in and then said, 'You've been in the wars too,' pointing at Mrs. McGrath's leg, which was covered in a long, plaster cast. Julie could only see the woman's foot, as she was wearing a baggy pair of hospital scrubs over her injured appendage.

'Look who's talking.'

'What happened to you? Did you get in another fight? Who was it this time? An orphan child begging for some scraps?'

'If I was, then they deserved it,' she said grumpily.

'How did you even know I was here?'

'Called the ambulance,' she mumbled, 'after I found you.'

Julie looked at her, incredulous. 'How did you even know where I was?'

'Just because you had a wobble didn't mean I wasn't keeping tracks on you. You're a liability. I had to make sure that you didn't get yourself killed.'

'So you were following me?'

'I've got better things to do than follow you around. I saw you marching over the road with that pair of clippers like a mad woman. Then I clocked you going into her majesty's garden. When you hadn't come home after 30 minutes, I thought something must have gone wrong, so I came to have a look.'

'I was only there for about ten minutes.'

'You're alive, aren't you? What are you complaining about?'

'It was you then, banging on the door.'

'Yeah, well, never liked the look of her. Always something a bit nasty about her.'

'I'm guessing she got away then, if you've ended up with a broken leg.'

'Did she buggery. She's done at the station now, the bobbies turned up just before the ambulance. The silly bitch. She came running down the side of the house, obviously up to no good. So I clocked her with my stick. Right in the nose. No place better for dropping someone, except maybe the balls.'

'And then what? You just fell over?'

'Took me down with her, didn't she? I fell at a funny angle. Doesn't take much at my age to break a bone. Jimmy's been in once already after a statement. He'll be back again this afternoon.'

'What would have happened if she had been running away for a legitimate reason?'

'I still would have hit her. Might have helped her up afterwards though.'

They sat there for a few moments in silence before Julie said, 'You called the ambulance, then.'

Mrs. McGrath shrugged.

'And you came with me to the hospital?'

'Made sense. Had to get my own leg sorted out.'

'Only I think I can remember someone holding my hand on the way here.'

'You should report that paramedic to the medical board. Indecent to be grabbing patients like that, especially when they're unconscious.'

'Mmm, I'm sure.'

Again, the conversation ceased, although Mrs. McGrath seemed to be fairly content sitting quietly. Julie was surprised she hadn't taken the time to cook up some new conspiracy theory about MRSA.

'Don't you have any questions about how she did it?' Julie asked. 'Even though we knew she was with the plumber and the paramedics when the police thought it happened.'

'Not really,' Mrs. McGrath said. 'None of my business, really.'

'You don't want to know why she did it?'

'Weren't they sleeping together?'

'Yes...'

'Then I know it all already.'

'What was all this about if you weren't bothered with how it was done? Why spend all this time and energy on it if you're not interested.'

'I told you, it's about doing the right thing, and DI Wanker Morris wouldn't have got there on his own. If we hadn't done anything, then she would still be running around knocking off her toyboys.'

'I'm guessing they've released Brian?'

'Dunno, I guess so. Although how they could have thought that wassock could do anything more complicated than peel a potato is beyond me.'

'Funny that it's all over,' Julie said, rearranging herself in the bed. 'Hopefully, I can get a bit of normality back in my life now.'

'Normality is overrated. Wouldn't be able to go back to the way you were even if you wanted to now. You've had a taste of something better.'

Julie said nothing, although inwardly reflected that Mrs. McGrath had a point. 'What's the plan, then? You and I setting up our own detective agency, are we?'

'I've heard worse ideas.' If Julie didn't know better, she could have sworn that the corners of Mrs. McGrath's lips turned up a fraction into something resembling a smile.

'Not a bad way to make a living. Following my geriatric neighbour around as she stares people down to decide if they're capable of murder.'

'Be as snotty as you like; it worked, didn't it?'

'No, as it goes, I'd say it didn't. The only reason we caught Mrs. Sinclair is because I returned those hedge clippers and questioned her.'

'That's because you told me we didn't need to talk to her. You said she had an alibi.'

'She did have an alibi!' Julie said indignantly, 'Just for a different time, that's all.'

'And I can't be blamed if I got told that someone wasn't a suspect when they were. I was right about everyone else.'

'You were right in saying that all of the people you forced me to chase down with you weren't murderers?'

'I was, yeah,' Mrs. McGrath said as if it wasn't surprising in the slightest.

'How are we ever going to know for sure if we don't ask them any questions or look for any evidence? They might have killed someone else for all you know.'

She picked up a magazine from the table next to her and opened it at a random page. 'Not my problem. We got our killer.'

'I'LL BE round tomorrow at eight then,' Mrs. McGrath said, climbing out of the taxi with even less ceremony than usual.

'Why do we have to go at eight? Do you think that there's going to be a massive rush for food shopping on a Wednesday morning?'

Mrs. McGrath made no move to pay, so Julie gave the driver a £20 and told him to keep the change. The old woman had appeared that morning when Julie was about to be discharged. God knows how she actually got there with her leg in plaster, and she hadn't invited her to accompany her home. Whatever the reason for her presence, Julie supposed that while she didn't have much to offer in the way of reassurance or sympathies, it was a nice gesture. Of course, she'd spent the whole journey explaining what an imposition it was and how much Julie owed her as a result. It was because of this that she had been forced to agree to take her neighbour to the supermarket the following day.

'Want to get there before all the biddies. Can't be doing with them shuffling around like they haven't got anywhere to be.'

'They probably don't. Besides, shouldn't you be a bit more understanding? It won't be long before you're one of them.'

She raised her stick and pointed it between Julie's eyes. 'I've got some fight left in me yet, girl,' she said, placing her foot firmly on the floor despite strict instruction not to do so when she was outside.

Mrs. McGrath had refused the hospital's offer of a pair of crutches. Her argument was that she hadn't lost the leg, and she'd been getting on fine with her stick for years. The nurse had then offered a wheelchair, although the offer was instantly rescinded when she saw the look of homicidal rage on Mrs. McGrath's face.

'I'm well aware. I'll see you tomorrow at eight then.' With no words to mark her departure, Mrs. McGrath stormed up her front garden like the hordes of Genghis Khan were pursuing her and went immediately inside.

Mrs. McGrath hadn't thought to bring Julie a change of clothes. Her blouse from the day before was still covered in blood and had been handed to her in a plain plastic bag shortly before being discharged. The only other clothing made available to her was the top half of a pair of hospital scrubs, which she wore with the smart skirt that she had been admitted in. As she made her way up to her own front door, she couldn't think of anything better in the world than getting into a hot bath with a glass of wine. Unfortunately, the doctor had told her that she wasn't allowed to get her stitches wet and that with the drugs she was taking, it was probably best to steer clear of alcohol for the next few days. She would have to settle for a wipe down with a flannel and a strongly brewed cup of tea.

She had only been inside for a few moments when there was a furious knock on the door. It was quite impressive really, she thought to herself. Mrs. McGrath had only been home for a few minutes; how could she have already whipped herself up into a frenzy and about what? Again, she went through the inner turmoil of deciding whether she could get away with pretending she wasn't in when a man's voice called, 'Julie, are you there?'

She opened the door and was amazed to see Mike standing there.

'Jesus, are you alright?' His eyes fell to the bloody top in the bag that she was holding by her side.

'Mike, I'm fine. What's wrong?'

'When you didn't show up for work this morning, I got worried. The old boy hadn't told me not to come in like he has been doing for the last week, so I thought I better. Only it was all locked up when I got there.' He was short of breath, like he had run part of the way to the house. 'Fair enough, I thought, he's probably remembered to call Julie but forgot me, not the end of the world. Only then I got it into my head that he might not have done, and you could be lying dead on the kitchen floor for all I know. What, with your son being away and your... well, you living by yourself, I thought bloody hell, I better give her a call.'

'Mike,' Julie said, trying to interrupt to no avail.

'Only then you weren't answering the phone,' he continued. 'First time I tried, it didn't faze me, thought you were probably at the shops or something. Only then when I couldn't get you after the third attempt, I really started to worry.'

'Mike...'

'So I thought I'd come and check; didn't think there was any harm in that. Besides, with us being, you know, spending time together, I didn't think you'd mind, even if there wasn't anything wrong. And then I find you with a bag of bloody clothes, wearing whatever that is that you're wearing, and I think, Christ, what's been going on here?'

'Why don't you come in for a cup of tea,' Julie said. 'And I can tell you all about it?'

His eyes returned to her bag of bloody clothes. 'Are you sure you don't need to go to a hospital or anything?'

'I just came from the hospital.' Mike's eyes bulged in alarm, so Julie interjected 'I'm fine, I promise.'

'Should you be drinking tea? If you're injured, I mean.'

'It's not crack cocaine, Mike. I think I can survive one cup.'

He still didn't look sure, but said, 'Alright then, as long as you feel up to it.'

Julie wasn't sure that she did, but she let him in anyway.

Printed in Great Britain
by Amazon